BLOOD WEALTH

MIKE MCNEFF

WHIDBEY WRITERS GROUP PRESS

Whidbey
Writers
Group Press

Cover Design: Derrick at www.greatbookcover.com

Edited by Audrey Mackaman

PRINT ISBN 978-1-944215-08-8

EPUB ISBN 978-1-944215-09-5

Library of Congress Control Number: 2020930082

This book is dedicated to those in the clandestine services of the free world who risk their lives everyday gathering the intelligence and doing the direct actions necessary to protect our freedom.

CHAPTER ONE

June 7, 1977

Jonas Carrington held the group of agents in a friendly spell as he spun another tale about the bureau "in the good old days" as only Jonas could. Jonas was a legend because he had done it all. Every assignment an FBI agent could catch, from the plum assignments to the garbage ones, because Jonas *could do* them all.

They were in an historic saloon-turned-restaurant in the Valley of the Sun foothills near Scottsdale, Arizona, with its roughhewn walls adorned with six-guns and pictures of Wyatt Earp, Bass Reeves, Bat Masterson—and John Wayne. Harry Meridan thought it a fitting setting for the retirement of what was a true legend of the FBI, akin to the last western gunfighters.

A wave of sadness flooded over Harry as he watched his partner weave his magic over the younger agents crowded around him, all leaning in so they wouldn't miss a word. There was also a mild sense of insecurity as Jonas's unofficial retirement party wound down. Harry and other fellow agents from the Phoenix FBI office had kidnapped Jonas and had taken him out on the town. They had treated him to a fine dinner and good drink while they royally roasted him. After ten years as partners, Harry was troubled about facing the job without Jonas.

An older agent, Randy Coloso, plopped down beside Harry. "So, how you gonna do your job without Carrington holding your hand?"

"Not as well."

"Oh c'mon, don't give that old fart so much credit. I bet he bored you half to death with recounts of his career while you guys were on surveillance."

"Only what I needed to know to do a better job."

"You seriously expect me to believe he didn't give you every detail about his days investigating the Nazis at Nuremberg after the war?"

"He has never spoken of Nuremberg to me, but then, Coloso, Jonas doesn't need to brag because he actually did investigations."

A deep shade of purple crawled up Coloso's face. "Fuck you, Harry." He abruptly stood and walked away.

The conversation did nothing to quell the uneasiness in Harry.

The laughter was dying down after the last tale when Jonas leaned over to Harry. "I think it's time you drove me home."

Harry put his arm around Jonas's shoulders. "Runnin' out of steam, old man?"

"I have a belly full of good food and good booze. It's been a great time, partner, but we have some unfinished work to do."

"What work? You're officially retired now."

"Some business never ends. C'mon, we gotta go while I can stay awake."

T he two men walked into Jonas's house, where he lived alone. Harry always felt comfortable in the orderly and simple home. His favorite place was Jonas's office, the one place the older agent splurged. It was furnished with an oak roll topped desk and oak chairs, lined with rosewood paneling and a hardwood floor decorated with a beautiful Navajo rug. A fireplace added to the comfortable feel, although in Phoenix it didn't get much use.

"Pour us a drink while I get some stuff out of the safe."

Harry walked over to the bar cart and poured two whiskeys.

Jonas emerged from the closet, where he kept a walk-in gun safe, carrying a large file box. He did this three more times until the boxes were stacked on his desk.

"I've always wondered about those boxes. What's in them?" Harry asked.

"A curse I'm about to bestow upon you."

Harry was about to make a wisecrack until the look in Jonas's eyes shot a shiver of disquiet through him. They sat down at an oval table in front of Jonas's desk.

Jonas took a deep breath. "We've been partners for ten years now. Even though you were a pain in the ass, fucking new guy when we started, I've come to love and trust you like a brother. I've also come to respect you as an agent. You do damn good work."

"Thanks, Jonas...."

Jonas held up his hand. "I'm telling you this because I want you to know why I'm passing this curse on to you. The information contained in these boxes will shake you to your very core. The mere possession of this stuff could be a death sentence."

Jonas opened one of the boxes and handed Harry an envelope. "Here's a letter that explains how I came to possess the original documents. The rest of the information is work I've done as follow up. No one knows I've done this until now. The letter is just as relevant today as when I received it. Let it be your guide."

Harry looked at the envelope.

"Go ahead and read it," Jonas said.

Harry opened the envelope and unfolded the letter.

July 12, 1946
Nuremberg, Germany

Dear Jonas,

We are a group of people involved in the investigation of the crimes of the Third Reich. You know many of us, but there are many you haven't met. In a way, you have been a member of our group, but we kept you out of our secret operations because we knew the time would come to lay a heavy responsibility on you.

You have been chosen to be the bearer of the truth. The documents now in your possession are excerpts from many investigations. Each excerpt can stand on its own, but each excerpt also tells you the location of related reports and how they can be recovered. We have all gone through what you have endured here at Nuremberg, some worse than others. Evil people have been released. Investigations have been stopped or diverted with the evidence and records confiscated. There are forces at work here that make the military power of the allied nations look like a wooden sword against an armored division.

There is nothing any of us or you can do about this at the present time, or in the foreseeable future. The distant future is a different matter. You were chosen to carry the torch because you are a fair, honest and honorable man—and fearless. You were also chosen because the FBI seems to be the least corruptible of all the agencies at work here. Take this package and expand it when you can. When you've reached the end of your career, pass it on to a man like you with the instructions to do the same. It is our hope that someday the person holding these documents will realize the time to act has come and use the information to take the power from the few and give it back to the people.

If you begin to believe this mission is impossible, do not despair. You are the tip of the spear.

Harry put the letter down, sipped his whiskey and searched his partner's face. Jonas's brown eyes were sad and tired. His wispy, white hair was thinning. There were no laugh lines around his mouth, just lines of worry carved into this face. He seemed to have aged ten years in ten seconds.

"Harry, these boxes contain information about crimes committed by the most powerful people in the world. They are so powerful that even when some of their most horrendous crimes became publicly known, nothing could be done about it. When the time is right, they and their organizations need to be destroyed. I've done a lot of work on them. Now it's your turn."

"We can do this together, even if you're retired."

"I can't, partner. I'm not going to be around much longer."

"What? What are you talking about?"

"The big 'C' has got me. I'm dying of cancer."

Harry jumped to his feet. "Jesus, Jonas, I'm your partner, your best friend, and you couldn't tell me this?"

"Calm down, I just found out myself."

Harry fell back in his chair, trying to hold back the tears. "Hell, I'm not even sure I want to continue on in the bureau without you. Why would I want to take this on?"

"Okay, number one, you *are* going to stay with the bureau. You're an outstanding agent. You'll do fine without me. Number two, you need to continue my work. It's more important than you can imagine."

"Aren't you going to give me a choice?"

Jonas looked off into the past. "I wasn't given a choice. I'm passing this on to you for the same reason others passed it to me. You're the only one I know I can trust to do what's necessary."

"What *is* necessary?" Harry stood and walked over to the boxes. "Can you give me an idea of what's in here?"

"The original information detailed the crimes of the military and industrial leaders of Nazi Germany and how the United States, Britain, Russia, and the Catholic Church worked to get many of the suspects free."

Harry met Jonas's eyes. "If you weren't the one telling me this, I'd smack you in the face."

Jonas smiled. "Thank you for that."

"What did you find out?"

"For starters, how about the fact that the Nazi party is alive and well- financed thanks to Hjalmar Schacht and Martin Boorman? Schacht was the Nazis' banker and economist. Boorman was Hitler's right-hand man."

"But the official position of the United States is the remaining Nazis are just a cult...oh fuck, Jonas. Is it that bad?"

"No, it's much worse. We now know that about a year before the war ended, Schacht and Boorman worked with bankers and industrialists around the world to form as many as seven hundred and fifty corporations all over the world. They moved Nazi assets worth hundreds of millions of dollars—billions in today's dollars—into these corporations and hid the ownership through a maze of bearer bonds and stock transfers. American intelligence knew all this."

"And they did nothing?"

"That's right. They didn't because we imported thousands of Nazis into the country to work on our space program, aeronautics, pharmaceuticals…and my personal favorite, our intelligence services."

"Why the hell did we put them in our intelligence services?"

Jonas gave Harry a cynical smile. "To fight communism, of course."

"Jesus, you're right. I need to read this stuff." Harry pulled out a folder from the first box and opened it. A photograph of a SS officer was on the top. "Who is this?"

"Hermann Schinner. He's one sick, vicious piece of work. A member of Hitler's inner circle. He's still alive, living near Vienna. I would be forever grateful to you if you could find a way to make him die a slow and agonizing death."

"Jonas!"

"Don't worry. It's just wishful thinking." Jonas winced as he forced his trashed knees to get him to a standing position with a long groan. "There's another reason why I need you to do this."

"What's that?"

"I'm not dying from natural causes. I've been murdered."

Harry jumped to his feet. "Who? How?"

"Someone got me to ingest a radioactive isotope that started the cancer, according to my doctor. He says the concentration indicates food or drink. So, in addition to working on Nazis and terrorists, I'd like you to try and find out who did this."

"We need to report this, so a bureau investigation can be started."

Jonas shook his head. "No, my doctor wanted to do that, but that would lead investigators to these boxes and that wouldn't be good. All my work would disappear. Plus, whoever did this is in the FBI."

"Goddamn, you're piling a load on me."

"I know, but you're the only one I can trust."

Harry looked at his partner and the anger that was growing inside of him subsided. They had been through too much together. He reached out and put his hand on Jonas's shoulder. "I'll do my best to live up to your trust, Jonas."

The older man pulled his friend to him in a bear hug. "I know you will. Just one more thing."

"What's that?"

"This curse is why I don't have a family. I can't tell you what to do, but anyone close to you will be in danger. Once you read all of this, you'll understand."

"Is this also the reason why you always took vacations alone?"

A sly smile crossed Jonas's lips.

"I'll keep all of that in mind."

"Okay, enough of this serious shit," Jonas grinned. "We have to go on one last weekend deep-sea fishing trip."

"Are you crazy? You could get sick and die out there before you tell me everything you need to."

Jonas broke into a larger grin. "Well if that happens, you can throw me overboard for chum."

CHAPTER TWO

September 15, 1991

Concern nibbled at FBI Special Agent Chris Fleming as he walked through the Beirut International Airport. His plane had landed thirty minutes ago. Steve Burns, the Special Agent in Charge of the FBI detachment at the US Embassy, had failed to meet him as planned. *The embassy just reopened and maybe things aren't quite organized yet.* Chris headed down the main concourse where cracked lime green walls, dirty windows, and grungy floors traveled by unsmiling faces greeted him. The unpleasant odor of burnt tires lingered in the air. Chris just wanted to get out of the place. He started for a phone booth.

"Agent Fleming?" a clean-cut Lebanese man in a suit asked.

"Yes."

"I'm Isa Itani, assistant to Agent Burns." Itani produced FBI civilian credentials.

Chris recognized the credentials as authentic. Still, a little voice in his head murmured an insistent warning. He carried secret reports and the last-minute change in plans heightened his situational awareness. This Itani guy checked out so far.

"Agent Burns is in an extended meeting with the ambassador. I will take you to the embassy. I have a car waiting."

Itani led Chris to a black sedan waiting at the curb. The sedan bore diplomatic license plates.

"I'll take your bag and put it in the trunk," Itani offered.

Chris handed Itani his bag while holding onto the diplomatic pouch and climbed into the right rear passenger seat. The driver of the car nodded to Chris and he smiled back. Itani seemed to be struggling with the bag, but he managed to close the trunk. He got in the left rear passenger seat.

They left the airport and entered a major thoroughfare. The late morning sun showed Chris they were headed north, the right direction. The air-conditioned car warded off the rising temperature. "I understand the embassy is north of Beirut proper in the municipality of Awkar," he noted.

"Yes," Itani replied, "Awkar is an upper-class area and somewhat removed from the unrest."

"I hope things have calmed down since the cease-fire agreements."

"There is less shooting, but tensions are still high."

"I imagine they are. It's hard to erase fifteen years of civil war."

The sedan exited the thoroughfare and turned west.

Alarm bells went off in Chris's head. "Why are we headed west? West Beirut is reported to still be dangerous."

Itani shifted and extended his arm. His hand held a revolver pointed at Chris. Years ago, Chris had vowed to himself that if anyone pulled a gun on him, he would act, not talk. He grabbed the gun with his right hand, closing his fist around the hammer. Pulling the gun hand past him and Itani along with it, he gripped Itani by the back of the neck and slammed the man's head into the right rear passenger door jam. Chris wrapped his hand around Itani's chin and twisted the head with a jerk until the neck snapped with a loud *crack*. The driver started yelling and reached inside his coat. Chris brought the revolver up and shot the driver in the head. The .357 caliber round exploded brain, bone and blood all over the windshield. The driver slumped over the wheel. The car slowed to a creep.

Chris pushed Itani off his legs and jumped out of the car. He dragged the dead man out and threw him onto the street. People turned to look. Training and experience took over now. Running to the driver's door, Chris pulled the driver out and took his pistol. He jumped in the car. One man started coming at him. Gunning the engine, Chris spun the sedan around and headed back to the main thoroughfare. He didn't know his location. He didn't know how to get to the embassy. Never mind he could just barely see through the gore on the windshield. He just wanted to get the hell out of West Beirut. The information he carried directly applied to Hezbollah, the terrorist group controlling the area.

Chris heard knocking sounds on the car. He looked in his rearview mirror and saw a small pickup truck with a man in the bed shooting an AK-47 automatic rifle at him over the cab. His foot slammed on the accelerator and the sedan surged ahead. A small car tried to cut him off at an intersection, but Chris fishtailed by him, the sedan's tires screaming and smoking. The pickup went broadside, trying to avoid the small car, and rolled in a cloud of dust, flying debris and bodies. Chris turned onto a small street.

He raced through narrow streets, feet and hands constantly moving on the gas pedal, brakes, clutch and gear shift. He made turns within seconds of each other until he realized he was attracting attention. He slowed down for a few more turns and then turned into an alley. He stopped the car, jumped out and ran to the trunk. As the trunk lid rose, Chris recoiled. Open, empty eyes and a slit throat proved Steve Burns was dead. Chris swallowed hard before he pulled out his suitcase and searched Steve. *Sorry I can't treat you with more respect, brother.* He retrieved Steve's FBI identification, wallet and twelve extra rounds of ammunition. The empty holster on Steve's belt told Chris the revolver Itani used had to be Steve's issued FBI weapon.

Chris walked quickly away from the car for a few blocks and then slowed down. He looked up at the sky to get his bearings from the sun. Then he ducked into another alley and changed out of his suit into jeans, polo shirt and his running shoes. He dumped the suitcase after removing all identifying articles.

Chris took stock. He still had the diplomatic pouch and all of his and Steve's IDs. He had a Smith & Wesson Model 10 .357 magnum revolver and seventeen rounds, plus a Walther PPK 9mm with a full magazine. He ejected the empty cartridge from the revolver and loaded another round to fill the cylinder. His hands shook from the adrenalin rush. He put both pistols in his waistband under his shirt, leaned against the wall and took several deep breaths, trying to slow down his heart. *This is not good. I'm in enemy territory and they're no doubt looking for me. If they catch me....* Apprehension twisted Chris's gut.

He surveyed the immediate area. No one took notice of him. *Time to move.*

Chris walked casually in a westerly direction. His tactical plan had boiled down to the utter basics. He would head to the coast and then start working his way north. He couldn't get lost that way. The beach would require him to only cover himself for 180° and if he ran into trouble, he could always go into the sea. He thought about hiring a car or a boat...or even stealing one.

He heard a roaring engine coming down the street and stepped into a doorway alcove. It was another pickup with a machine gun mounted in the bed. Chris tried to melt into the corner of the alcove when the door gave way and a woman with a sad but determined face gently tugged him into the home and closed the door behind him. They looked at each other for a moment. A young boy stepped out from behind his mother.

The woman was small with olive skin and long, flowing, dark hair that fell on her shoulders framing her oval face with a classic Greek nose and a full mouth. Her eyes were large hazel almonds.

"You are the American they are looking for?" she asked in English.

Chris didn't answer right away, but then said, "Yes."

"You cannot be out in the daylight. They will find you."

"Who's looking for me?"

"Hezbollah. You can stay here until it is dark."

"No, I don't want to put you in danger."

"This is West Beirut. Everyone is in danger every day."

"How do you know Hezbollah is looking for me?"

"It is on the radio. They control most stations."

"Damn. That's not good."

"You will have a better chance when it is dark. They lose interest in the night, when they smoke their marijuana and look for women."

"Why are you helping me?"

The woman looked at pictures on the fireplace mantle. "They came one day for my father and my husband. My mother pleaded with them not to take her husband, so they shot her right here in this room in front of all of us. Then they dragged my husband out the door. My father collapsed on my mother's body, so they shot him too."

"What happened to your husband?"

"Hezbollah threw his body in front of our door two days later. His body was badly mutilated from their torture. My husband was a gentle man...the principal of the high school. There was no reason to torture him."

"Why did they do it?"

"He defied Hezbollah's orders several times. They wanted the school to teach only the Qur'an, but he refused. He wanted his students to have a full education. Then they told him he had to join their army, but he was not a fighter and would not join. They said if he would not fight, he was an apostate. So, they made him an example."

"I'm sorry that happened to your family. There's no sense to it, but from what you've told me it sounds like your husband was a fighter after all."

Tears brimmed the woman's eyes and she briefly turned away. "You are an American soldier?"

"No, ma'am, I'm a policeman."

"DEA?"

"No, FBI."

The woman nodded. "Are you hungry?"

The question made Chris realize his hunger and thirst. "Yes, ma'am and I could use some water."

The woman reached into a small refrigerator and handed Chris a bottle of water.

"Thank you...I'm sorry. I don't know your name."

"My name is Dialya."

"I'm Chris. And who's this young man?" Chris nodded to the young boy.

"My son's name is Karam."

"Hello, Karam."

"He will not answer you. He has not spoken since the day he saw his grandparents murdered."

Chris knelt down and held out his hand in an offer of a handshake. Karam looked at him for a moment and then firmly grasped Chris'ss hand. The boy smiled.

CHAPTER THREE

R obin Marlette was deep in thought as he read sales reports from Tim Echoles, the chief operating officer for Blue Marble Connections, the front for the covert direct-action team Robin led called the Guardians. His office was in the company's three story warehouse in Seattle. His office phone rang.

"Rob, you need to get down here right away." Jamie Slater's voice was tense.

"I'll be right there." Robin went down from the office level to the main order processing area of the building. Here goods came in from all over the world and were in turn either sold in the United States or exported to other sales reps all over the world. Everyone who worked in the business end of the company was either prior military or law enforcement who became disabled during their service. They also supplemented the covert team, if necessary.

Robin made his way to a small alcove with an elevator door. He leaned into the retina scan. The door opened and the elevator took him down to the communications center. "What's going on, Jamie?"

"Grassley's on the phone."

Robin wondered what the CIA deputy director and head of the directorate for operations wanted. He picked up the headset and put it on. "Hello, Bill."

"Rob, we're working a situation I thought you might want to know about."

"Shoot."

"Chris Fleming is missing in Beirut."

"What? What the hell is Chris doing in Beirut? He's retiring soon."

"He was investigating...."

"Just a minute, Bill." Robin muted his microphone. "Jamie, put out a pager alert for every available man to be at the hangar ASAP."

Jamie nodded.

"I'm sorry, go ahead, Bill."

"Chris was investigating the flow of money from different organizations to several Nazi groups and the terrorist group Hezbollah. From search warrants he did on American banks, he identified some of the banks in Beirut who are secretly facilitating the money transfers. He went to Beirut to brief the FBI detachment at the new embassy and pass the case on to them."

"Nazis and Hezbollah is a strange combination to be investigating."

"You would think so, but apparently Chris had discovered several connections between the two groups."

"Interesting. When did he disappear?"

"About six hours ago. They found the bodies of two embassy employees in a street. They found the vehicle of the FBI special agent in charge of the detachment in the Beirut embassy in another section of West Beirut with the body of the SAC, Steve Burns, in the trunk. Chris has just disappeared."

"Sounds like someone set up Burns and his men."

"It did until the embassy realized the two employees weren't supposed to be in the area in the first place. One of them, the SAC's assistant, met Chris at the airport instead of Burns. It looks like they were agents for Hezbollah. The embassy figures they killed Burns and tried to kidnap Chris."

"So, Chris is on the run."

"That's what it looks like."

"What are you doing to find Chris?"

"There's not much we can do. The Secretary of State has made a formal request to the Lebanese government to find Chris, but they don't have the firepower or the will to deal with Hezbollah at this point. We're working with Mossad to see what their agents can come up with, but nothing so far. It would be suicide to just walk into West Beirut and we don't have any real military assets there right now. The Syrians have a presence, but we can't trust them. The whole thing is further complicated by the peace talks over the civil war there."

"So what you're telling me is this country is doing nothing for Chris right now."

Bill didn't answer.

"Isn't the FBI doing anything?"

"They want to, but they're being held back."

"Okay, Bill, you called me."

"Tag, you're it."

"Can you give us support?"

"Any support that can be kept quiet. I'll put five million in your account."

"All right, we've been here before."

"You know we don't negotiate with terrorists," Bill cautioned.

"I wasn't thinking of negotiating."

"What I'm trying to say is...."

"Bill, you don't have to keep reminding us we're expendable. We get it. Can you put me in contact with Mossad?"

"I...I don't know, Rob. I'll have to get back to you on that."

Robin's voice turned terse. "Make it happen, Bill. We'll be on Fatboy."

F ive members of the team and the flight crew made it to Fatboy, the team's custom Boeing 747-400, before Robin ordered the pilot, Jack Moore, to takeoff and head for Israel. An hour after they were in the air, Ernie Jackson, Robin's second-in-command, called.

"Rob, the rest of the team is really pissed off...including me."

"It can't be helped. Time is of the essence here, Ernie. Just do what it takes to get the rest of the team to Israel."

"Goddammit, Rob, how? You have all our pilots."

"Call Bill and ask for a crew."

Ernie let out a long breath. "Damn, you make things hard sometimes." He hung up.

Robin came out of his Fatboy office and almost bumped into Gary Perkins, a team operator who specialized in transportation, escape and evasion assets. "Gary, why did you come?"

"Chris is our good friend. I can't just sit home while he's in trouble."

Robin sat down. "You've been asking to be relieved of operator status for months. I finally got Grassley convinced to allow it and you do a flip-flop on me. The reasons you gave me haven't changed and they won't, Gary. You're right, you are too old for the front line. You need to be back at the company manning the com center and going home to Ellie at night." Robin took a deep breath. "I don't want you leaving this plane. You stay here with Jamie for this op."

"Rob, I promise this will be the last op for me. Look, you don't have enough people as it is. You really don't have anyone to arrange evasion and escape assets but me. Let me finish operator status with this op, then I promise to lay low at HQ.

Robin considered Gary's words for a moment. "Okay, you're right about not having enough men. You can work on E&E assets, but that's it. You don't leave Israel under any circumstances."

"I won't."

Robin went forward to the cockpit. He greeted his flight crew. "Gentlemen, I'm glad to see you all made it."

"We are too, now that we know what this is all about. We can't leave a friend hangin'," said Jack Moore, the team's chief pilot.

"The only drawback is that Jack didn't get all of his beauty rest so he's uglier than ever," Oscar Leighton, the team's assistant chief pilot chided.

"Yeah, but I'll never be as ugly as you," Jack retorted.

"Rob, can you see why I should be paid more than these two clowns?" Eric Newman, the team's third pilot asked. "I'm always caught in the middle of these guys and their bickering."

"Sure, Eric, just as soon as you go to marriage mediation training, so you can keep marital peace between these two. "

Robin left the cockpit to the sound of laughter.

Hans Boorman's feet kicked up dust as he paced back and forth in a dilapidated office in Hezbollah's Verdun headquarters. The importance of capturing this FBI agent Fleming seemed to be lost on his Arab allies. How the man could escape from two armed operatives and disappear into thin air defied logic. The extent of the agent's knowledge of money laundering and transfer operations must be determined. If the operatives in the banking world were discovered, especially those in the Bank for International Settlements, the Fourth Reich's operations would be jeopardized.

He wished he was back in his group's peaceful compound in the Argentine mountains, where he loved to listen to the wind winding its way through the pines. The chaos of Beirut frayed his nerves. His presence here was necessary to keep relations with Hezbollah and Iran on an even keel. They were valuable for training Fourth Reich operatives, like the Greek Golden Dawn and other Nazi terror cells. They gave the operatives an opportunity to get combat experience and conduct terror operations.

"Stop pacing, Hans." Helmut Fuhrmann leaned back in his chair and let cigarette smoke drift into the air from his mouth and nostrils, forming a wispy cloud around his sharp-featured face and white hair. Fuhrmann was an original Nazi who had served on Heinrich Himmler's staff. "You need to just let things run their course."

"That's easy for you to say, Helmut. You're not responsible for the success of this operation."

"Oh, come now, you must know this assignment is for you to get experience."

"Is that why you're here? To take care of me?"

Fuhrmann's cold, gray eyes drilled into Hans. "I'm here

for the good of the Reich. Please do not forget that. And do not forget your last name is a Nazi legacy to be protected."

Colonel Adar Khoroushi of the Iranian Revolutionary Guard came into the room. He was younger than Boorman, much younger than Fuhrmann, and much more arrogant. He was accompanied by Farrok Mokri, a member of VEVAK, the Iranian national intelligence agency.

"You should not look so worried, Hans. We will find Agent Fleming. He could not have gone far."

"Your confidence is somewhat reassuring, Adar, but neither your soldiers nor mine are involved in the search and Hezbollah seems a little disorganized today."

"They were definitely caught by surprise. Agent Fleming is more aggressive and savvy than they realized, but they are closing the circle. He will not escape."

Hans did not reply as he stared out the office window, trying to will Fleming's capture.

Adar came up and stood by his side. "Your organization has been using the BIS to launder money for half a century. I would not worry about a breach of security at this juncture. Switzerland's secrecy laws concerning the BIS are too strict to be breached."

"I take nothing for granted, Adar. My great-uncle and father did not believe the Third Reich would fail, but it certainly did."

"I'm not really sure it was a failure. The Fuhrer is still revered around the world. You and your friends have kept the fire of the Fourth Reich alive as Martin Boorman and his comrades planned."

"We try, but I fear I will not live to see the Reich reach its former glory."

"You will, if we all work together. We have been allies with Germany and the Reich for one hundred years. We want the same things. The destruction of the Jews and other undesirable races, our world order supreme across the globe as we march to a society filled with the wealth of pure blood."

"That is true and that makes our bond unbreakable," Mokri chimed in.

Boorman turned to them. "It is the only way to save the world, gentlemen. The only way."

CHAPTER FOUR

*D*ialya looked at the clock. "This is a good time for you to go."

Chris rose from the kitchen chair. "Dialya, can you get to Awkar without much trouble?"

Dialya thought for a moment. "I take the bus to work in the hotel district, but I don't know the routes to Awkar."

"Can you take a taxi?"

"I don't have the money for a taxi."

"How much do you think it will take?"

"Maybe fifteen US dollars."

"Is there a taxi driver you can trust?"

"There is Johann. He has been trying to get me to have tea with him. I think he likes me. I know he is a good Catholic man."

Chris took out his wallet and handed Dialya two twenties and a ten-dollar bill. "Here, take this and keep it no matter what you say next. I have some documents that need to get to the American embassy. I'm afraid my chances of getting there are not good since they're talking about me on the radio. I'm asking you to take the documents for me."

Dialya started to say something, but Chris held up his hand.

"Dialya, if Hezbollah catches you with these documents, they'll kill you."

"What do the documents say?"

"The documents give the FBI at the embassy information that will help the American and new Lebanese government stop the flow of money to Hezbollah."

Dialya looked at Chris with intense, investigating eyes. "I will do it."

Chris reached into his briefcase and handed Dialya the thick, diplomatic pouch. Then he took out one of his business cards and wrote something on the back. "The folder has the documents. When you get to the embassy, give them this card. I've written on the back for them to give you sanctuary and to get you and Kamar into the United States."

"Will they do that?"

"I don't know, but at least we'll try." He reached into his coat and handed Dialya both his and Steve Burns's FBI credentials. "Please give them these also."

Dialya nodded.

Chris reached out and put his arms around Dialya. "Thank you for everything, Dialya. I'd probably be dead by now if it wasn't for your help."

She put her hand on his cheek. "You must go now. Stay on the narrow streets and in the shadows. Go to the water and then go north. You should make it to the hotel district before morning. Things are not as bad there. You can find a phone and call the embassy. The Green Line is only two miles from the district." Dialya turned to Kamar. "Son, make sure no one is out there."

Kamar hurried to the door and went out. He came back a minute later, pointed to Chris and motioned for him to leave. Chris nodded to Dialya and went to the door. He stopped and held out his hand to Kamar. He smiled and took Chris's hand in both of his. Chris knelt down and gave Kamar a hug and then went out the door.

Stepping into the night, Chris stopped and listened to his surroundings. The air seemed heavy and was laced with a mixture of woodsmoke and the acrid smell of burning coal. He didn't hear any engines. The immediate area seemed quiet. He looked up and down the street...nobody. He started west at a normal pace. After he walked two blocks he turned north for one block and then west again. He wanted to distance himself from Dialya and her son.

The damage from the civil war had largely escaped him in the excitement of trying to get away. The moonlight cast a pale glow on destroyed buildings and walls pockmarked with bullet holes. Chunks of concrete knocked down by exploding artillery or rockets lay scattered all around. The glow of campfires in bombed out buildings flickered against shattered walls, creating jagged shadows that danced a wicked jig in the night.

Chris came to the main thoroughfare he remembered from the ride from the airport. He crossed it without difficulty. He was on the street where the two embassy employees had tried to kidnap him. Moving to the west, he started walking in a neighborhood he figured was loyal to Hezbollah because it was in the same area.

The narrow streets were empty and Chris continued to move west in the shadows. Soon, he saw a raised highway. He approached it cautiously and peeked over the concrete edge. A roadblock was set up one hundred yards north of him. He could see armed men in the area. There was a median separating the lanes and large barriers on the other edge of the highway. He ducked down and moved back onto the narrow street and started south.

Out of the corner of his left eye, Chris saw a moving light

and realized it was a flashlight. Suddenly, the light focused on him and a man yelled. Chris broke into a sprint. A long burst from an automatic rifle shattered the quiet. Green tracers came at him. He could hear the crack of bullets flying past him, impacting behind him. More men were yelling. More guns shot at him. He turned toward the raised highway. Sprinting up the incline, Chris vaulted the wall, ran across two lanes, jumped the median and made it to the other side of the road and the barriers. Chris saw spaces in between them and ran through one of them. A path led to the right, down into a field of brush. His heaving chest and gasping breath didn't stop him. He ran through the brush until he tripped and tumbled onto a field of grass.

He heard vehicles on the raised highway. *It must be the men from the roadblock.* He hoped the median prevented them from driving closer to him. Chris got back on his feet and started running again. The grass confused him until he made out a green and pin flag of a golf course. Men were on the edge of the highway shouting. Automatic weapons began to rake the golf course. Green tracers arched over Chris's head and bounced around the area. Bullets hit the trees and the grass, spraying debris in every direction, some so close he could hear them crack by. His heart was pounding in his ears. Chris made it to a stand of trees and stopped for a moment to catch his breath and assess his tactical position. He saw flashlights on the highway, but none down on his level. The men on the highway were shooting blindly, so they didn't see him. To the west, he made out more trees. He started toward them at a trot, staying in the cover of the tree line. He came to a fairway and crossed it into another stand of trees.

Looking back, Chris saw headlights making their way down to the golf course from the highway. He picked up his pace and crossed another fairway at the end of the course.

Moving into a field of brush, he could hear traffic and see headlights moving two hundred yards away on another street. Behind him more vehicles were on the golf course. The rattle of automatic weapons continued.

Chris neared the street and his heart jumped into his parched throat. Two armed men wearing the yellow and green bandanna of Hezbollah stood next to a Toyota truck with the engine running and lights on. They were twenty yards away. One of the men was talking to someone on a portable radio. The vehicles on the golf course were getting closer. Chris knew he had to move. He pulled out his revolver and put the sights on the chest of the man with the radio. The man spoke into the radio and then lowered it. Chris squeezed the trigger. The .357 boomed and the man crumpled to the ground. Chris moved the sights to the second man and shot him. The terrorist fell backwards in a sprawl before he could react to the first shot.

Sprinting to the truck, Chris took the first man's AK-47 and the portable radio. He jumped in the driver's seat and headed north. He drove fast but had to dodge potholes and craters caused by old artillery strikes. A pickup with a Russian DShk 12.7 mm machine gun in the bed sped past him going the other direction. He watched in the rearview mirror, but the truck didn't turn around. The chatter on the radio was constant. He could tell by their voices the speakers were angry.

He approached a section of the highway where a statue appeared to be in the middle of road. Even with the moonlight he couldn't figure out what was happening. He took an exit ramp. Chris looked to the left and realized the highway went into a tunnel under the statue. He slowed down to figure out what he should do. He saw a roundabout with an exit going west toward the sea, so he decided to take it.

As he moved into the roundabout, a pickup roared in front of him from the street to the right. Chris blurted, "Shit!" and jerked the wheel to the left. The vehicles collided sending his pickup into a spin. It hit the short wall around the statue and rolled, tossing Chris's body in every direction against hard surfaces in the truck. His head slammed against some metal object.

He lay on his side inside the truck as his mind fought for understanding. His body wouldn't respond to his attempts to move. Rough hands grabbed at him and men were yelling. Something kept hitting his head again and again. The world slipped away.

CHAPTER FIVE

Robin sat across from Ben in the conference room on Fatboy. The Mossad agent was about Robin's height, but he was much heavier, not with fat, with muscle. His face bore a scar down his left cheek and his deep-set eyes were dark and offered no insight into Ben's words.

"I am authorized to give you logistical support and what intelligence we have on the FBI agent's situation."

Robin nodded. "We appreciate any help you give us. Just letting us stage from this airbase is a great help. What do you have on Chris?"

"I'm afraid it is not good." Ben spread a map of Beirut on the table and pointed with his finger. "Hezbollah radio traffic indicates he was spotted on the Hafez El Assad Highway and chased into the Beirut Golf Club. He made it across the golf course, killed two Hezbollah men and stole their pick up. He then went north on the Chiekh Sabal El Salem Sabah Highway. A Hezbollah vehicle rammed him near the Verdun District, a very bad place. We believe he has been captured."

"When did this happen?"

"About four hours ago."

"Do you have a contact for us in Beirut?"

Ben sat back in his chair and gave Robin a hard look. "We are willing to do what I said in the beginning of our conversation. Our interests in Beirut are long term. Yours are not—we cannot risk losing an agent."

Robin felt his jaws tighten but checked himself. "I understand, Ben. Just thought I'd ask."

Ben just nodded.

"What's your best guess as to where they have taken Chris?"

"I do not have to guess. They have two headquarters." Ben pointed with his finger. "Here in this bombed out office building in the Verdun District and here at the Holiday Inn on the Green Line. It is logical that they took him to the closest one."

"I assume it's heavily guarded."

"It is and I don't think you understand what you're getting into. This is a very dangerous area for anyone, let alone Americans. You'll have to accomplish your mission before dawn or you will surely be captured or killed."

Robin let the comment hang. "What's your recommended method of infiltration?"

"We can get you there by submarine from Haifa. I understand you are qualified for submarine lock-out operations, is this correct?"

Robin nodded.

"Good. We are ready to fly your team to Haifa. The submarine will take you to Beirut and wait off shore until dark. Then you can conduct your operation. The submarine will not wait for you. You will have to make your own way back."

"Fair enough. We'll be ready in an hour. If you'll excuse me for a few moments, I have to check on a few things."

"Certainly."

Robin went down and found the men in the team room.

"We're heading for Haifa in an hour. The Israelis are going to infil us into Beirut by submarine. Burke, are we packed?"

Burke Jamison, was a six-foot-two muscular man with black hair and blue eyes. The result of a union between his Irish father and his Native American mother. Among his many skills, he was the team's expert on hand-to-hand combat. "Roger, boss," replied the former state trooper and Special Forces Vietnam veteran.

"How about the rest of you guys?" Robin was talking to Rocky Barnett and Rick Santos. Blond haired Rocky, a former Phoenix police officer and Recon Marine Vietnam veteran gave Robin a thumbs up and said, "I was born ready." Rick, a Mexican-American former Arizona State Trooper and Army sniper, flashed his infectious grin and said, "Si, hefe."

Robin nodded to the two men and turned to Gary. "Gary, when we get to Haifa, I need you to find an extraction asset that provides us flexibility and can be armed. You have an unlimited budget. I'll keep you posted by sat phone, so you'll know when to get us out."

"Do you really think you'll find him, Rob?" Gary asked.

"I don't know, but we're sure as hell going to try."

Dialya finished her morning work at the hotel, went down to the lobby and out to the taxi stand. She looked to the right and spotted Johann. She went to his window. "Hello, Johann."

"Dialya! How are you?" Johann's eyes softened and his mouth spread in a wide smile.

"I am well. I would like to hire your taxi."

"Where do you want to go?"

"Awkar."

"Dialya, I would have to charge you three hundred pounds."

"How many dollars?"

Johann's widened. "You have dollars?"

"I do."

"Normally it would be twenty dollars, but for you, it is only ten."

Dialya handed Johann a ten-dollar bill. "Meet me at the back door. I have to get Karam."

She hurried to the atrium garden where Karam was reading. "Come, Karam, we must go."

They went to the rear doors and got into Johann's taxi. He drove to the corner and started to turn.

"Stop, Johann." Dialya could feel her heart pounding.

Johann stopped and turned to look at Dialya.

"Before we go any further I must tell you I'm carrying something that Hezbollah would kill me for if they found it. I'll give you forty dollars more to get me to the US embassy."

Johann gave Dialya a hard look. "What is it, Dialya? If I'm going to risk my life, I need to know what for."

"I have documents given to me by an American policeman that would stop money coming to Hezbollah."

"The missing FBI agent?"

Dialya nodded.

Johann looked down and shook his head. After a few seconds he lifted his eyes, meeting Dialya's. "I should tell you to get out of my taxi. I should drive away like this conversation never happened."

Dialya looked down. "I know."

Johann crossed himself and said, "Jesus, Mary and Joseph, I must be going crazy. All right, Dialya, we will go. You must do exactly what I tell you to do if we are stopped at a check point."

"I will."

Johann put the car in gear and made the turn.

G ary's sat phone rang. "Gary here."
"This is Ernie, Gary. Where the hell is Robin? Why isn't he answering the phone?"

"He's traveling low."

"What?"

"Underwater, Ernie."

"Oh. What are you doing, looking for exfil transport?"

"Roger that."

"Where are you?"

"Haifa."

"Don't do anything yet. Things have changed. We'll be there in about six hours."

"What's changed?"

"I'm bringing a tour group who want to see an old friend. We are also going to need infil transport."

Gary knew Ernie meant reinforcements, but he didn't know who. "Roger. I'll get to work on different options for both infil and exfil."

"That'll work. See you soon."

CHAPTER SIX

Consciousness gradually returned to Chris's senses. A bolt of pain shot through his head and vomit surged into his throat. His mouth opened, but the vomit didn't clear. Chris realized his face was covered. He couldn't move his arms and hands. He aspirated some of the vomit and started choking. Panic grabbed him. Someone jerked the cover off his head. Chris's body twisted in violent spasms as he struggled for air. Water was thrown on his face. He vomited again and retched until his mouth started to clear. Tears and mucus streamed down his face. His chest heaved as he gulped lungs full of air until the panic subsided. Chris's mind worked to understand his condition and surroundings. He knew he was weak, injured, sick and naked. Someone was moving around near him. A door opened. It slammed and a man began yelling. He spoke English with a thick German accent. He warned the others to get Chris conscious and alert. The door opened and closed again.

A warm cloth started cleaning Chris's face. As he became

more alert, putrid smells bombarded his senses. He vomited again.

"You seem to have a weak stomach, Agent Fleming."

Chris managed to get his eyes to open a little. An Arab man stood in front of him. He looked young to Chris, with an arrogant, but handsome face. An older Arab man was cleaning him. The room had a bare concrete floor and walls. Chris was bound to a rough-hewn wooden chair in the middle of the room. Three men stood at the front door. One was Middle Eastern, the other two were white.

"The doctor is going to clean you and attend to your injuries. You should not consider this a kindness. You see, I need you alert and thinking. You are no good to me in a stupor.

"Your stay here will not be pleasant and you will not leave alive. It will be up to you how much pain you will endure before you die. If you cooperate, you will not suffer much and you will die quickly. If you resist questioning, you will suffer greatly and we will make sure your death is slow and agonizing—and make no mistake, you will talk."

"I don't know what I can tell you. I'm just a policeman."

"Ah, see! You start off by being foolish. The man who met you at the airport told us all about you. We know how long you have been an FBI agent and we know the different assignments you have worked. We know you are highly regarded. You've worked important assignments including counterespionage and so-called counterterrorism. We are interested in these things and we have friends who will be here soon who are also interested. You are going to tell us everything we want to know, including your investigation of our money sources and where your report is hidden."

"Look, I'm supposed to retire in one week. I don't give a rat's ass about all this shit anymore. You ask me the questions, I'll give you the answers."

"Oh, I'm sure you will give us answers, Agent Fleming, just as I'm sure it will take some time to get the *real* answers from you. Collect your thoughts. We will begin in a few hours."

J ohann drove slowly through the back streets of West Beirut, working his taxi closer to some of the smuggling routes along the Green Line. He kept wiping his hands on his trousers to dry off the sweat. Inside, he cursed himself. Dialya's beauty and kindness had captured his heart long ago. That's why he gave in to her request. He had asked her several times to have tea with him, but she politely declined. He knew Hezbollah had killed her husband and Johann thought that helping her might give him a chance for her affections. Of course, he had no love for Hezbollah. They had killed several of his family and friends.

Johann's actions confused him. He did not consider himself a brave man. *Is Dialya worth dying for?* He looked in the rearview mirror and his heart leaped as Dialya's eyes met his, and she smiled. *Yes, she is worth dying for.*

Johann stopped the taxi at a junction of streets. A turn to the left would take them to the Green Line. He rolled down the window and listened. Isolated gunshots rang out from different directions, like drunks trying to start a fight. He didn't hear any vehicles. *Things are as good as they can get for a run across the Line.* He put the car in gear and turned left.

The street was strewn with rubble and the taxi bounced and jerked along. The smell of death and smoke hung in the air. Low shafts of light from the late afternoon sun cast jagged, eerie shadows around the bombed-out buildings. The taxi came to the edge of the Green Line and Johann's heart leapt into his throat. A Hezbollah fighter stepped out and blocked the car. The fighter came to the window.

"Where do you think you are going?"

"I am taking this lady to see her sister."

"You should be going through the checkpoint."

"I know, but it was backed up and I thought I could save some time. I do not make money waiting in line."

The fighter stepped to the rear window and looked at Dialya and Kamar. His face turned into a leering sneer. He pointed his rifle at her. "Well, lovely lady, step out so we can get a better look at you." Dialya froze looking straight ahead. "You, get out of the taxi, NOW!"

Dialya's eyes met Johann's in the rearview mirror again, but this time they were full of fear. He jerked the gear shift down and stomped on the gas pedal. The taxi shot forward and Johann fought to avoid chunks of concrete and rock. Bullets hit around the car and ricocheted into the air. Johann jerked the wheel left to aim for a clear spot when he felt a sharp pain in his right side. Still he pushed his taxi through the rubble until he reached the other side of the Line. He made a series of turns until they were behind several buildings in from Green Line. He stopped and looked at his side. He saw a bullet exit wound and blood flowing onto his lap.

"Dialya, you are going to have to drive. I am wounded."

No answer.

Johann looked in his mirror but couldn't see Dialya. He fought the pain as he turned to look in the back seat. His heart dropped. Dialya was laying on her side on the seat, her eyes open, but unseeing. A bloody hole was just below her chest. Johann realized the bullet that hit him had gone through Dialya first. He raised himself a little higher. Kamar sat on the floorboard hugging his mother's bag and shaking.

Johann heard engines and settled himself behind the

wheel. He put the car in gear and started driving. He had an idea of the location of the US Embassy, but he had never been there. He fought the searing pain and the realization that death loomed as he drove. Then he saw it. The American flag. He turned a corner just as bullets started to disintegrate the inside of the cab into flying metal and glass shards. Kamar screamed in pain.

"What the fuck is that, Master Guns?" Lance Corporal Waxman asked.

"Gunfire, Waxman." The master gunnery sergeant keyed his portable radio and called the sniper team on the roof. "Sawtooth to Overwatch."

"Go, Master Guns."

"Whaddya see?"

"A Hezbollah technical chasing a taxicab and shooting the hell out of it."

"Roger."

"This is Sawtooth, all stations—Code Alamo. I repeat, Code Alamo." Code Alamo put the entire embassy on defensive lockdown and scrambled a security team to the front gate.

"Waxman, open the pedestrian gate. When I go out, close it and don't open it until I tell you to."

"But, Master Guns..."

"Godammit, Waxman, just do as I tell you!"

"Aye, Master Guns."

Master Gunnery Sergeant Bobby Joe Harris, a thirty-one-year veteran of the United States Marine Corps, strode out the embassy gate and into the street standing erect and unafraid. A combat veteran of many battles, it was said that magnets were dangerous for him if he got too close in full dress uniform, because of his chest full of medals and awards. He carried an M-14 rifle instead of the standard issue, but less powerful M-16 rifle. A concession the new ambassador made to get Harris on this staff. He referred to the M16 as a Mattel plastic piece of shit.

A taxi careened around the corner and chugged to a stop twenty-five yards from the gate of the embassy. Steam vented from under its hood. In the waning light, Harris could see the shattered windshield and the bullet holes that riddled the vehicle. The driver weakly tried to wave to him.

⌐ ⌐

J ohann could not raise his hand all the way to get the American soldier's attention. He summoned his remaining strength and leaned over the seat and looked at Kamar. "Kamar, put your mother's hand in mine."

Tears flowed down Karmar's face and his lips quivered. He kissed his mother's hand and raised it to Johann's.

Johann smiled. "Now, Kamar, take your mother's bag and run to the soldier in front of us." Dialya was still warm to the touch. Johann died satisfied he had finally won her hand.

⌐ ⌐

A pickup came around the corner and a young boy, bleeding from different parts of his body, bolted from the taxi running towards Harris. The men in the pickup jumped out and ran after the boy. They were all carrying AK-47s.

"Overwatch, fire!" Harris yelled into his portable radio.

The driver of the pickup raised his AK-47, but only got it halfway up before his head exploded in a red mist. Harris snapped his rifle to his cheek and fired two rounds, dropping the two men coming from the right side of the pickup. The sniper also took out the other man on the left.

Harris barked again into his portable. "Security and corpsman up!" He scooped the boy up with his left arm and jogged back to the gate as the security team ran up to him. "Check out the cab!" he ordered. The boy shook like he had a vibrating motor inside of him. Harris spoke to him in a soft voice and tried to wipe some of the blood from the boy's head. The boy sobbed and put his arms around Harris's neck and clung to him. Harris knelt down and pried the boy from him with great care.

"You're safe now, little guy. What's going on?"

Kamar's chest heaved in sobs as his shaky hand retrieved a thin wallet from his mother's bag. Harris opened the wallet and a card fell out. Harris recognized it as the business card of FBI Special Agent Christopher Fleming. The wallet contained Fleming's credentials. He pulled the trembling youngster to his chest and held him.

The ambassador's voice interrupted his thoughts. "What do we have, Master Guns?"

"This boy has been in contact with Agent Fleming, sir." He handed Chris's credentials to the ambassador. Harris noticed Waxman staring at him. "What the hell are you looking at, Waxman?"

"Well, Master Guns, I never knew you had a heart."

The team was checking their gear when Ben stuck his head in the lock-out compartment.

"Robin, you are wanted on the bridge."

Robin followed Ben through the narrow passageways and ladders of the Gal-class submarine to the captain on the bridge. The captain handed Robin a headset.

"You have an encrypted call."

Robin adjusted the headset and microphone. "Robin here."

"Rob, it's Bill. I have some good news."

"I could use some. Let's hear it."

"We have a contact in Beirut. He knows where Chris is and will lead you there."

Robin let out a long breath. "That's great news, Bill."

"The captain has already given me your infil coordinates. The challenge word is Fred. Answer is Ginger."

"Got it. Thanks, Bill."

"Good luck."

Robin took off the headset.

"You look much relieved, Robin."

"Our chances of success just took a giant leap forward."

The captain's face broke out with a genuine smile. "That is good news. You better get back to your men. We'll be starting the operation in ten minutes."

Robin saluted the captain and headed for the lock-out compartment.

CHAPTER SEVEN

C hris began to feel a little better as the fog in his brain lifted. The nausea subsided, though his stomach still felt a little queasy. Pain pounded his head, despite the medicine the doctor had given him. He realized he probably had a concussion. He could see better because the doctor had put and ice pack on his eyes and reduced the swelling. Chris smiled grimly to himself. *They're preparing the lamb for slaughter.*

He wondered if anyone was looking for him. He knew the FBI would be doing what they could, but the policy stated no negotiations with terrorists. Especially for the release of an expendable FBI agent. He thought of his wife and the rest of his family...sons, daughters–in–law, and grandchildren. He loved them all and the thought that he would never see them again tore at his heart with despair. *Even if the FBI wanted to come for me, the State Department is probably telling the bureau to stand down, just like they did with Cathy Marlette.*

Chris's head rose sharply. *Marlette! Robin Marlette! If he knows I'm in trouble, the team will come for me no matter what.* A muted joy surged through Chris. He had hope. He knew it was a long shot Robin would know, but damn, if he did know, he would come. *I do have a chance! I've got to do what I can to get ready. I've got to think.*

Just the idea he had hope gave Chris strength and energy. He surveyed the dank, dirty room in the dim light from one naked bulb. There were no windows. Everything was concrete and cinder block except for the crude wooden chair to which he was bound, a small table, and a couple of other chairs. His wrists were tied to the arms of the chair, and the edges of those arms were not sanded. Chris thought they were sharp and rough enough to wear through the rope if he could position his wrists to put maximum pressure between the rope and the edges. He took a deep breath and began his work. In his mind, Chris knew chances were slim Robin even knew he'd disappeared, but in his heart, he believed.

T he Zodiac boat nudged the beach in the darkness.

Robin and his men jumped out and pulled it farther on shore to a small hill covered in trees and bushes. They covered the boat with foliage, formed a defensive perimeter, waited and listened. The minutes rolled by and with each minute the four men made small movements checking and rechecking their gear, and searching all around their location for possible hostiles. Robin's hands were gripping the pistol grip of this rifle tighter and tighter.

Then her heard a rustle to his right and then a hoarse whisper said, "Fred."

"Ginger," Robin replied. He stood up and stepped to the edge of the trees.

A man wearing an olive drab military shirt, blue jeans and a checkered wool head scarf walked up to him. "Hello, Robin. I'm Jason." Jason was shorter than Robin with a wiry frame.

"Good to meet you, Jason. We're really glad you're here."

"The feeling's mutual. You guys are my ticket outta here?"

"We are?"

"Yeah. I'm an Arab-American and a master sergeant with the Army Intelligence Support Activity, the ISA. I've been undercover as a member of Hezbollah for three years. They're starting to ask too many questions and I think they may be getting on to me, so the brass wants to pull me out. When the CIA said you guys were coming in, they decided to hook us up."

"Works for us. You going to lead us to where they're holding Chris Fleming?"

"Better than that. Follow me."

Jason led the men up the embankment to the road where his extended cab pickup was parked. He pulled a duffel bag out of the back seat. "Here, put these arm bands on." He looked at Rick. "You need to change your scarf. It's the wrong color." Jason handed Rick a yellow-and-green-checkered scarf.

"Shit, I feel like a gang banger now," Rick commented.

After everyone had put the items on, Jason looked them over. "Okay, gents, you're now members of Hezbollah. We should be able to penetrate pretty far into the building before they figure us out."

"So you're going with us?" Robin asked.

"Hell, yeah. I know what these animals do to prisoners. We need to get your man out."

"Good, but first things first. We need to do a recon of the area and the building."

"Roger that. I've got just the place that will give you good view. Get in."

The men got into the truck and headed into West Beirut. Jason stuck to back streets as he worked his way northeast. Robin noticed the destruction all around and occasionally tracers would arc into the sky. He turned to Jason. "I thought a cease fire was in effect."

Jason laughed. "A cease fire to these people means going from a thousand rounds a minute to a hundred rounds a minute."

He drove for another ten minutes and then said, "Hang on, I gotta make sure we don't have a tail." For the next two minutes, Jason drove like a crazy man, making turns every few seconds. Then, suddenly, he turned into a partially collapsed parking garage under an office building.

"We're here. The hard part is now we have to climb a lot of stairs."

The team started up the stairs and climbed at a good pace until they finally reached the fifteenth floor. Jason led them to a door that opened into a large abandoned flat. There were holes in the walls where explosive rounds had hit. Jason walked to one of the larger holes and Robin stood next to him.

"The building at the T-intersection directly in front of us is our target."

Robin turned to the team. "Rick, come over here."

Rick looked out the hole as Robin pointed.

"That's the target. Pose any problems for you?"

"Not really. Looks like about two hundred yards. I'll have to use the suppressor to minimize sound and muzzle flash, but I'll hit anybody I shoot at that distance."

"Good. Once we enter the target, you pack up and get out of here. The stairs are your only way down, and if they know you're here, they can easily trap you."

"Don't worry, Rob. I'll scoot. I'll start setting up."

"Jason, can you draw us a diagram of the building?"

"Yes, sir. Let's go out into the hallway so we can use some light."

The team except for Rick moved back into the hallway. Jason used a flashlight with a red lens and drew a rough diagram of the lower floor and basement of the building.

"The front of the building is what you see when you look at it from the hole in the flat. When you go inside, there are stairwells at either end of the building that go all the way to the roof. Then there are stairs directly across from the front door that go to the lower floor where Chris is. At the end of the stairs we go left. The only door in that direction will be the room I last knew your man to be located."

"That stairwell is the only way in and out of the basement I take it?"

"Roger that, sir. There are no other stairs, doors or windows down there."

"That means you and Rocky here are going to have to stay at the top of the stairs and keep people from coming down. It will also help if you whittle down the odds for our escape. Burke and I will get Chris and bring him up. You got enough ammo for that 47 of yours?"

"As long as we don't make this World War III. When we get back outside, keep a look out for a van. Before I met you, I was helping set up a vehicle bomb not far from where we're going. It was a blue van with a load of Qassam rocket warheads. If we start making a lot of noise, it may show up."

Robin nodded. "Let's get back into the flat for a minute."

In the flat, Robin went close to the hole, pulled out his sat phone and called Gary.

"Hello, Rob. Ernie's here and he wants to talk to you."

"Good, put him on."

Ernie came on the phone. "What's your situation, Rob?"

"We're getting ready to make entry into the building. It's

the Verdun Headquarters. We should hit it in about forty-five minutes."

"We're about thirty-five minutes out. I've got the rest of the team and eight FBI HRT guys. Can you wait for us?"

"Have you landed on shore yet?"

"We're not on a boat. We have two Hueys. We've covered over the numbers and just waiting to take off."

Robin thought for a minute. "Are the Huey's armed?"

"Mini-guns and rocket launchers."

Robin pulled out his GPS receiver. "Here's what I need you to do. Launch in twenty minutes. Head for these coordinates." He read off the coordinates. "Contact me on Tac 1 scrambled when you get here."

"Rob, why don't you wait for us to get there before you go in?"

"When the alarm sounds, the cockroaches will be flooding the area. If my timing is right, you should be able to do considerable damage before they take cover. That will whittle down the odds more in our favor for extraction."

"What do we do then?"

"You'll probably be pulling our asses out of hell and making a shit load of tactical decisions."

Ernie gave a nervous laugh. "Thanks a lot."

"See ya when you get here, brother."

Robin looked out towards the target building and Rick came up beside him.

"I've been watching with the infrared scope, Rob. You've got three bandits on the roof. I've seen between three and four of them in and around the entrance and there's a pickup that keeps patrolling the area."

"Well, we're going to drive up like we own the place. As we approach, take out the guys on the roof. We'll take out the guys at the entrance."

Rick bit his lip. "You got it, boss."

Rob put his hand on Rick's shoulder. "I know it's a shit sandwich, but we just can't leave Chris in there."

Rick nodded, but in the shadows, Robin could see the concern didn't leave his face.

C hris stared at the men as they set up the table with what appeared to be surgical instruments. There was also a car battery with wire leads attached. *Not a good sign.*

The young Arab and the doctor were back. Two other men stood in the shadows so Chris couldn't make out their facial features. They were talking to each other in low voices.

Chris had been able to make progress on the ropes and was able to move the frayed parts under the arms of the chair when he heard the men coming. If he could summon his strength, he felt he could break the ropes and at least free his hands.

"Well, Agent Fleming, you're looking a little better," the Arab man said.

"I'm cold. Can I have a blanket or something?"

"No."

"Your hospitality leaves a lot to be desired."

The Arab frowned and nodded to the doctor who reached over and attached the wire leads from the battery to Chris's testicles. The Arab flipped a switch.

A strangled, guttural sound came out of Chris's throat as his legs slammed together. Urine shot from his penis. The Arab flipped the switch again and Chris's body sagged in the chair as he drew desperate, rasping breaths. After a few moments, he raised his head. "I get the point."

"Excellent. I knew you were a reasonable man. We are going to begin your questioning with one of our friends."

One of the other men stepped forward.

Chris laughed. "Nikolai Prokonzky, is that really you?"

"Hello, Chris. It has been a long time since we followed each other around D.C. and Virginia."

"Yes, a very long time, Nikolai. Why the hell did the FSB or whoever send you to this hell hole?"

"Ah, Chris, we are not here to answer your questions, and for old time's sake, I wish you will answer the questions truthfully. I really do not wish to see you suffer."

"That's very kind of you, Nikolai, but you can go fuck yourself."

The Arab flipped the switch again.

CHAPTER EIGHT

Rick settled behind the scope on his M14 rifle. He'd set it on a table about five feet back from the hole in the wall. The previous wounds in his leg and side he'd received in the Taiwan op were throbbing from the exertion of climbing the stairs, but he pushed the pain to the back of his mind.

Three guards on the roof of the target building roamed from the front to the back and it appeared they had their respective areas of responsibility. Besides the two stairwell structures on either end, there were two large structures in the middle of the roof that appeared to be old air conditioning units. The middle man would walk in between them. Rick picked areas he would shoot each man to use the structures to block the view of the others.

"Rick, we're rolling," Robin's voice came over the radio.

"Roger." Rick sucked saliva into his mouth and put the cross hairs on the man on the left. He breathed in and as he let his breath out his finger started to squeeze the trigger. His breath stopped and the rifle kicked into his shoulder and the man crumpled down. The suppressor did its job, reducing the sound of the shot so that it was masked by the ambient noise in the area. He moved the rifle to the center man, who was in between the two structures and shot him in the head, causing him to fall flat on his back in a spread eagle position. The man on the right had disappeared.

"Shit," Rick cursed softly to himself. A few seconds later, the third man came to the front of the roof and then walked toward the middle. Rick tracked him in the scope and saw the man look in between the structures. He seemed to jump as Rick figured he saw the body of the middle guy. The man's hand rose to his face with a radio just as Rick's shot went off —three down.

Rick keyed his mic. "Roof is clear."

"Roger," Robin replied. "We're going in. Get out of the building."

Rick moved closer to the hole and surveyed the area below. *No, Rob. I got the feeling you're going to need me right here.* He topped off his magazine.

W hen Jason stopped in front of the target building, the four members of the team casually got out the truck. Robin could see four men at or near the front door as he fell in next to Jason.

The closest man spoke Arabic to Jason. "Ali, what are you doing here?"

"Jamal sent us here to reinforce security."

The guard gave Jason a hard look. "I was not told about this."

The other three men started moving closer.

Jason chuckled, "When have we ever been told what we need to know?"

Burke walked behind Jason and he and Robin held their

suppressed pistols down along and slightly behind their legs. As the guards drew closer, both men raised their guns and dropped the guards with two rounds in each head in two seconds. The last guard died with the look of surprise on his face punctuated with two holes between his eyes.

"Go, go, go," Robin urged in a whisper.

The team flowed into the main lobby and Robin and Burke immediately engaged another terrorist, quickly killing him. They got to the stairs to the basement and Rocky and Jason took up positions at the top. Robin and Burke went down the stairs and turned left. They stopped at the only door in the hallway. As Robin tried the door handle, he heard a noise that sounded like a hard slap.

"Chris, Chris...you are making this so hard on yourself."

Robin nodded to Burke and turned the door handle.

C hris had reached the point where he didn't care anymore. He knew in his soul he wouldn't tell them anything, so he was resigned to pain and death. He found it strangely liberating. He had just thought of another smartass remark and raised his head. Through the blood and perspiration in his eyes, he thought he saw Robin and Burke come through the door.

He started to laugh at the hallucination but stopped when the men started shooting the terrorists. With all his might, Chris pulled his arms up, breaking the ropes he'd cut through. He saw Robin in hand-to-hand combat with the Arab and Burke's back turned to the doctor standing in front of Chris. The doctor was drawing a gun from under his coat.

Chris couldn't move his feet, but he stood and reached out, grabbing the doctor around the neck with his left arm and knocking the gun out of his hand with his right. Then he pulled him in and squeezed the headlock with all the fury he could. Remembering what this monster did to him allowed Chris to ignore the pain shooting through his body. He squeezed...and squeezed...and squeezed and felt the man's windpipe collapsing. And squeezed some more.

W hen Robin went through the door, he was surprised to see six men in the room with Chris. Adrenalin surged through him and everything seemed to go into slow motion, with the room and the terrorists in sharp focus. The terrorists were caught by surprise, which gave Robin and Burke precious seconds' advantage. Two men in the corner to the left were drawing pistols and posed the most immediate threat. He put the front site on the closest man and pulled the trigger so fast the two shots sounded like one as they tore into the man's upper chest. Robin was moving toward the targets as he did this. The second man had his gun almost up when he saw Robin less than two feet away. The eyes of the two men locked as Robin put two rounds into the man's forehead.

An older white man fired a shot at Robin, the bullet going by his ear with an angry buzz. Robin double tapped his trigger. The man's head snapped back and he fell flat on his back with a heavy thud. Turning, Robin saw Burke had one suspect down and was in hand-to-hand combat with another. An Arab man was going toward Burke, but Robin couldn't shoot without risking hitting Burke. He started to sprint, grabbing a chair as he approached the terrorist. The man turned just as Robin smashed him in the face with the chair. The Arab went to his knees for an instant and then was back up. Robin threw a hard fist to the man's throat and kicked the attacker in the groin. As he started to fall, Robin grabbed his head with his left hand pulling it down, slamming the Arab's face with his knee. Robin could feel the man's facial bones giving away with a *crunch*. He finished the terrorist off with a shot to the back of head.

Burke had taken care of his last man and Robin looked over to see Chris choking a man who was obviously dead.

"Chris, you can stop now. The man's dead."

Chris let the doctor's body drop. "Rob? Is that you?"

"Damn straight, brother. We're getting you outta here."

"It's really you? I'm not hallucinating?"

"Well, you're an FBI agent, so I really can't say you're not hallucinating," Robin cracked as he untied Chris's feet.

A combination of a sob and chuckle came up Chris's throat. "It really is you."

"C'mon, Chris. I need you to get yourself together. We're in a world of shit here."

Chris took a deep breath, shuddering with pain. "Okay, Rob. I'm good now that you guys are here."

Robin tried to sound tough, but his heart ached. The pupils in Chris's eyes were uneven, his face and head were covered with lacerations and bruises and his testicles were swollen to the size of grapefruits. Robin wasn't sure his friend could move on his own power, which made an already perilous situation much worse.

Burke had stripped one of the dead men of his clothes and he helped Chris get dressed. Chris's face contorted with pain when Burke helped pull the trousers up. Robin changed magazines in his Glock and handed it to Chris along with another magazine.

"You'll probably need this."

He then unslung his AK-47, checked to make sure a round was in the chamber and hit the bottom of the magazine.

Burke steadied Chris, who stumbled. "Easy, Chris."

"I'll be all right, guys. Just get me outta here."

Robin nodded. Then he searched each dead terrorist and collected all the identification and papers he could find.

A thundering roll of gunfire erupted above them. "We gotta go, Rob!" Rocky's voice blasted over the radio.

Rob looked at the other two men. "Ready?"

"Ready as we'll ever be, I guess," Burke answered.

Chris nodded.

As they stepped through the door, Robin knew in his gut they were walking into hell.

The three men ascended the stairs to the sound of continuing gunfire. Rocky and Jason were shooting in two different directions, a very bad sign. Robin waived Burke forward, but pushed Chris back.

"Rocky! Jason! Get ready to sprint for the front door." Robin keyed his mic. "Rick, how does the front look?"

"Get movin'! Bad guys are closing in."

"We'll cover your run to the door, Rocky. Then you cover us. On the three count," Robin ordered. "Three, two, one, GO!"

Rob and Burke laid down cover fire as Rocky and Jason raced for the door. Both men used short aimed bursts to keep the terrorists' heads down. Robin's shots got at least one man.

"Rob! Come on," Rocky yelled.

Rob and Burke each took one of Chris's arms and literally carried the man across the lobby. On the way across, Rob heard Burke growl with pain. A searing hot line burned across his own shoulders. The three men tumbled onto Rocky and Jason.

Robin got to his feet and looked outside. "Fuck!" More terrorists were closing in. Then one dropped. Then another under Rick's accurate fire. The others took cover.

Robin turned back to the other men to get them moving and saw everyone was bleeding. Jason was bleeding badly.

"Who can move under their own power?"

"We all can," Burke answered. "We don't have a choice." He struggled to his feet...and fell back down.

R ick saw the rest of the team at the front door of the target building, fighting for their lives. Then more terrorists appeared and headed for the building. Rick hunched at the corner of the window picking off terrorists as fast as he could.

His sat phone rang. "Rick here."

"Ernie here, Rick. Tell me who's who down there."

"Where are you?"

"Twenty-five hundred feet above the target location."

"Roger. Rob and the rest of the team are pinned down at the front door. The bad guys are both inside and positioned around the front of the building. I'm afraid more are coming."

"Roger. Where are you?"

"On the top floor of the high building two hundred yards to the west of the target building."

"Roger. Go to radio."

"Roger."

E rnie's brain launched into high gear. He was in the chopper designated Spider One, being flown by Jack. Spider Two was the call sign chopper being flown by Oscar. Ernie started giving orders.

"Spider Two, descend for rocket runs on the area just west of the front of the target building. Spider One, our team is pinned down at the front door of the target building. We'll make some gun runs and then pick them up. Make the runs on the east-to-west axis. If you're hit, make for the sea. Copy?"

"One, roger."

"Two, roger."

Ernie then called Robin. "SpearTip, this is Spider One."

"Go, Spider One," Robin answered.

"We're here and commencing pickup. Stay put. Say status."

"We're all shot to shit, with one critical."

Ernie's gut tightened. "Do you have the package?"

"Roger."

Ernie tensed with fear for his comrades as he heard the smack and ricochet of bullets over the radio. "Hang tough. We're working on getting you out."

"Better make it quick, brother, or we're gonna die right here.

CHAPTER NINE

Rocky, Jason and Chris were fighting it out with the Hezbollah men in the building while Robin and Burke battled the terrorist around the front of the building. Robin watched with some satisfaction as the Hezbollah men across from the headquarters vaporized in rocket explosions. His satisfaction turned to fear as he ducked shrapnel peppering the building. Then a helicopter came in firing machine guns at terrorists around the front of the building.

"Fuck! I'm out of ammo," Rocky yelled.

Robin felt his vest, realizing he was down to two magazines. He gave one to Rocky.

After each chopper made another gun run, Ernie's voice crackled over Robin's radio. "We're coming in for pickup. We'll have to land at the intersection across from you. It's the only area that looks like it has room."

Robin looked at the men around him. "We all can't make it that far."

E rnie looked at the men in the chopper and keyed in the intercom. "Everyone get ready to fast rope down to the trapped team. We'll have to carry them to an extraction point."

"Don't you fucking leave me, Ernie," Jack yelled into the intercom. "You need to run this shindig from here."

Ernie realized Jack was right. "Emmett, you're ground commander."

Emmett, a six-foot-six black man, was a senior member of the team and medic. He gave Ernie a thumbs up.

***

R obin took stock of his men. Everyone was wounded to the point of being disabled. Jason's wounds were serious enough that he was no longer an effective combatant. Bullets smacked the concrete all around them, filling their cramped space with shrapnel. Robin knew he had to do something. He reached down and took two of Jason's remaining magazines.

"Everyone give me one of your grenades."

Burke's face showed alarm. "What the hell are you planning to do, Rob?"

"Don't argue with me, Burke. Just do it."

Burke looked at Robin for a moment, then handed him a grenade.

"Concentrate all fire on the left stairwell. I'm going to assault the right stairwell...on the three count."

The team adjusted their fire to the left stairwell.

"Three, two, one, FIRE!" On the word "fire," Robin jumped up and charged the terrorists in left stairwell, firing his AK-47 with his right hand. At the same time, he released the spoon on the grenade he was holding in his left hand.

Some of the men in the stairwell started moving to get out of the way. He ran two more steps and lobbed the grenade at the top of the entrance to the stairwell and veered to the left like he was sliding into home plate. He watched the grenade fly through the top of the entrance. A loud bang and flash, followed by smoke and debris, indicated he'd achieved his goal—an air burst in the entrance space where the terrorists were congregated.

He jumped to his feet and charged into the stairwell, firing short bursts from his rifle, stepping on top of the carnage created by the grenade. He shot two men trying to get up the stairs. One dropped onto the landing while the other pitched forward and flopped down the stairs, hitting Robin's legs, causing him to trip. He struggled to his feet as two men came around the corner at the next flight up. The first one fired a burst that went high because of the angle. Robin fired his rifle with one hand, the third round causing a crimson hole in the man's chest. He seemed to collapse into himself.

In slow motion, Robin saw the muzzle of the second terrorist's pistol moving towards him. He fought the fear surging inside him and concentrated on the phrase that had saved his life many times...*slow is smooth, smooth is fast.* But hours upon hours of training and experience made Robin's "slow" lightening quick. His rifle snapped into firing position and he put the front site on the man's center mass and fired. An instant later he saw the muzzle flash of the terrorist pistol and was slammed in the left shoulder, which spun him off the stairs onto the pile of bloody bodies at the bottom of the stairwell.

He lay in the stairwell for a few seconds before struggling back to his feet. He put his hand on his left shoulder and felt wetness. His hand was covered in blood. He lifted his arm. It hurt like hell, but there was no grinding of bone. He reached down and grabbed extra magazines off the dead bodies around him and put a fresh mag in his AK-47. He started back up the stairs.

Robin hoped each floor was connected to both stairwells. He slowly opened the door to the next floor and felt a rush of elation to see the hallway went all the way to the other end. Gunfire reverberated from the other stairwell. Pain shot through his left shoulder as he raised his rifle and moved down the hallway clearing each door as best he could. He reached the entrance to the stairwell, set his rifle down and prepared two grenades. He opened the door using his foot as a stop and tossed the grenades down the stairwell. He backed up and the slam of the closing door merged with the loud bang of the explosions. Robin picked up his rifle and reached for the doorknob.

"Allah will send you to hell!" he heard a man scream in Arabic.

Robin turned to see a terrorist starting to fire wildly in his direction with an AK-47 on full auto. Flying concrete and plaster engulfed him as he brought his rifle to bear on the man trying to kill him. As Robin fired, he was knocked back in a half-twist, slamming against the door to the stairwell. The world became distorted in time and space, his surroundings morphed in shape; appearing to be liquid. Reality shot back when he started dry heaving. Tears and mucus streamed down his face as he fought for control of his body.

He tried to get up but couldn't get his feet underneath him. He stretched for the door handle, but his hands were covered in blood and he couldn't turn the lever. Searing pain knifed through his body, but Robin wiped his hand and tried again but failed. Then he thought, *Karen is going to be so pissed.*

When Ernie gave the order to fast rope down, Gary was the first one on the rope despite the misgiving gnawing at the depths of his soul. He hit the ground and immediately sprinted to the men in the entrance of the Hezbollah headquarters. As he ran, he was relieved that the gun and rocket runs by the helicopters had greatly reduced the enemy's rate of fire. When he got to the stranded team, he had to suppress his shock. Rocky and Chris were conscious. Burke was in and out, and a man Gary didn't know was out cold, maybe even dead.

Within seconds, Emmett, another team member, Mike and two FBI HRT agents were with him.

Rocky turned to Gary. "The keys to that truck out there should be on Jason." Rocky nodded towards the unconscious man.

"Who is this guy?" Gary asked as he retrieved a set of keys.

"An undercover agent for Army Intelligence."

"Okay, let's get him, Burke and Chris into the truck. I'll need at least one shooter to go with us. Have the others ready to move when I get back."

"Where's Rob?" Mike's voice was filled with anxiety.

Rocky pointed to the stairwell to the left. "Grenades went off over there a few minutes ago. I'm hoping that was Rob. He should be somewhere in or around that stairwell."

"Hang tough, Rock. I'll be right back."

"Gary, watch out for a blue-colored van. The Army guy said they were building a truck bomb around here."

Gary's whole body tensed. "Will do, Rock."

The team loaded the three wounded men in the bed of the pickup. One of the HRT agents stayed with Gary and they headed for the landing zone.

Emmett and Mike started for the stairwell, leaving the other HRT agent with Rocky.

"Rob! Where are you?"

Robin recognized Mike Collins's voice. He tried to yell but his throat was dry, raw and sore. He reached for his rifle and banged on the door. Footsteps hurried to him. Looking down the hall, he saw the man who'd shot him sprawled face up on the floor. Some measure of satisfaction eased his torture.

The door pushed against him and he rolled away.

"Oh, fuck!"

This time he recognized Emmett Frank's voice just as Emmett appeared in front of him.

"Rob, do you know who I am?"

"Yeah, you're the Jolly Green Giant," Robin croaked weakly.

Emmett grinned. "You got the jolly and giant right, but you're off on the color."

"Two out of three ain't bad." It wasn't lost on Robin that Emmett was putting a tourniquet on his left leg. "How bad am I, Emmett?"

"You're fucked up pretty bad, boss, but I'll take good care of you." Emmett gave Robin some injections while Mike bandaged some of his other wounds.

Emmett keyed his radio. "We found SpearTip and will have him ready for transport at the door."

Gary got the truck to the landing zone just as the first chopper landed. Several Guardians and HRT members set up a perimeter. Gunfire roared around him from the terrorists, HRT and the chopper overhead. He fought to control the fear surging through him.

He and two HRT agents pulled the wounded men out of the pickup bed and got them into the chopper. Gary jumped into the truck, cranked the wheel and brodied to face the headquarters building. In an instant, he was at the front doors and saw Emmett and Mike helping Robin and the HRT agent holding on to Rocky. His breath caught as he began to comprehend how badly his friends were hurt.

When they reached the truck, Robin and Rocky were put in the pickup bed with the HRT agent and Mike providing cover fire. Emmett jumped into the front seat with Gary and pointed his rifle out the window, firing in controlled bursts. "Go, Gary," he urged

Gary swallowed his pounding heart in his throat and slammed the truck into gear. The clatter of bullets hitting the truck fueled the adrenalin coursing through him. He slid to a stop next to the chopper. Robin and Rocky were pulled out of the truck and Gary moved it a short distance so that it wouldn't interfere with the chopper's take off. He was reaching for the door handle when he saw a blue van lurch to a stop at the far corner of the headquarters building.

Robin struggled to maintain focus. He knew he had lost a lot of blood from at least two bullet wounds, but concern for his men pushed him. He saw everyone but Gary and Rick were on board the helicopter. Gary still sat in the pickup. Robin painfully inhaled a deep breath. "Gary, get in here!" Then Robin saw the van and he looked back at Gary.

Gary's eyes met Robin's. Horror started building in Robin as he realized what the blue van was and what Gary was going to do. Gary raised his hand and saluted Robin.

"No, Gary...no!" Robin screamed.

The pickup's tires squealed as Gary gunned the engine and turned toward the van. The van lurched forward. Robin could hear the pickup's engine roar as Gary ran through the gears, heading directly toward the van. Robin was yelling, "No, No," as he watched Gary's truck and the van merge into a brilliant flash. The helicopter shuddered and rocked from the following blast wave and shrapnel. Men cried out in pain and confusion. Robin's only emotion was anguish weaving through numbness. The world was moving in slow motion, and as his head moved back into the helicopter, his ears were filled with Jack's cursing and Ernie's urgent voice. He saw an HRT medic giving CPR to Burke.

Suddenly his shoulders were jerked and Ernie was yelling at him.

"Shake it off, Rob! Where the fuck is Rick?"

Understanding struggled for priority in Robin's mind. When it won its battle, Robin jerked back to the world.

🔫 🔫

Rick heard thumping in the stairwell leading to his position and a curse in Arabic. He thumbed the selector switch of his M14 to full automatic fire and pulled a grenade from his vest. He pulled the pin and tossed it through the door into the hallway.

"Ahiiiiii," a voice yelled.

The grenade went off with a sharp bang. Rick charged the doorway firing short bursts, and moved to the stairwell.

Automatic weapon fire erupted from the stairwell, and shrapnel peppered his body. He forced himself to fight the fear and panic of being wounded again. He pulled another grenade and held it for a couple of seconds after pulling the pin before lobbing it down the stairwell. The resulting explosion was much louder. He could hear men moaning and screaming.

Rick opted to head upstairs instead of down. He hoped the stairs led to a roof exit. A whoosh, followed by a loud bang told, him someone had fired a rocket-propelled grenade at his last position. He was immensely thankful he had moved. Still, the explosion hurt his ears and left them ringing. He turned on the last flight of stairs to see it was partially blocked by debris. There was a hole near the top of the pile Rick thought he could get through, but it had to be fast. A rush of angry voices and footsteps came from below. Rick scrambled up the pile and pushed his M14 through the hole. He started through when a man yelled and a burst from a gun hit the shattered concrete around him. Fear and adrenalin propelled Rick through the hole.

He landed on chunks of concrete with a grunt of pain. Jumping up, he stuck his rifle through the hole and fired an entire magazine on full auto, while moving the muzzle back and forth. He primed another grenade and again waited two seconds before he threw it through the hole. The bang and more screams brought him some feeling of success.

Rick could see the night sky and hear helicopters and gunfire. Scrambling up the rest of the broken stairwell, he made it to the remaining intact portion of the roof. His breath came in gasps and his leg was on fire.

"SpearTip Four to Spider One."

"Go, Four."

"I'm on the roof of the building across from the target with bandits crawling up my ass."

Oscar's voice crackled over the radio. "Spider Two to SpearTip Four, hang tight. We're comin' to get you."

"Roger." Rick hunkered down behind a short concrete wall, loaded a fresh magazine and jacked a round into the chamber. He aimed the rifle at the hole in the roof and waited for the terrorists to come up. *Jesus, Mary and Joseph, please get me out of this.*

CHAPTER TEN

The blast from the van almost knocked the helicopter over enough to ram the rotor blades into the ground. Jack struggled to keep the helicopter under control. The vibration of the aircraft had increased considerably, telling Jack that the blades were probably damaged. He scanned the instruments to see if they indicated any damage to the engine and didn't see anything...yet. He also tried to ignore the gunfire and concentrate on flying.

"Ernie, we've taken damage to the rotor blades. We gotta get outta here!" he yelled into the intercom.

"I'm getting everyone in...standby."

The calmness in Ernie's voice impressed Jack. "Roger."

Ten seconds later, Ernie's voice came over the intercom. "Get us home, Jack."

Jack pulled on the collective and the Huey started to lift off the ground and immediately he knew the controls were going to be difficult. The Huey vibrated and shook. He got the chopper as steady as he could and pulled harder on the collective. Jack's immediate concern was the buildings around him. The helicopter was drifting all over and Jack's right hand and feet were in constant motion trying to counteract the drift. He scanned the instruments again and his sphincter tightened. The engine temperature gauge was rising, indicating the engine had been damaged in the blast, probably by ingesting debris. He got the chopper to just under five hundred feet of altitude and headed for the water, fighting the controls. He was also thankful this was a newer model Huey with extra power. Otherwise, it probably wouldn't be flying at all.

E rnie was greatly relieved when the chopper was airborne, even though he knew they were in trouble because of the damage. He knew Robin was reeling from Gary's death, but still something else was wrong. He looked around and saw the HRT medic working on Burke and a team medic, Willie working on the other man the team brought out with them. Chris was bent over the man, who was trying to tell Chris something. Rocky was slumped over

in his seat, with men trying to stop his bleeding.

Emmett had strapped Robin into the seat next to Ernie and hung a bag of plasma to a hook on the ceiling. An IV ran from the bag to Robin's arm.

"Ernie, shine a light on Rob's leg," Emmett urged.

Ernie pulled his flashlight out and shined it on Robin's body. He inhaled a sharp breath. He could see Robin was covered in blood and the bone was showing in his lower left leg. Emmett had applied a tourniquet. Full realization of how badly the team had been shot up went through him like a searing flame.

Jack's tense voice broke through on the intercom. "Ernie, we're not going to make it back to Israel and we can't ditch with these wounded guys on board. We need to start Eric this way in the backup chopper."

"Go ahead and vector him to us."

"Roger…Spider One to Spider Three."

"Spider Three, go ahead Spider One," Eric Neuman, the Guardians' third pilot replied.

"Start your ingress and head up the coast. We've been heavily damaged and won't make it back in this bird."

"I heard your traffic. I'm already in and will be near Sidon in five mikes.

"We'll be there in eight mikes, if we get that far."

"Roger."

Rick peered into the night, looking for any movement. The reassuring wop- wop sound of a Huey helicopter was coming closer. Suddenly two shadows popped up twenty yards in front of him, flame leaping from the muzzles of their AKs. He started to pull the trigger when both men vaporized in a stream of bright red tracers and the roar of a mini gun from the chopper.

The Huey kicked up dust and debris as it came down to a hover. Men frantically waved to Rick. The sound of the helicopter and the roar of a mini gun were deafening. He jumped up and sprinted, grabbing the first outstretched hand he could reach. That hand and then others pulled him into the chopper. He flopped on his back, looking up at men with big white grins emphasized by faces darkened by camouflage paint. He let out a long-held breath and grinned back.

J ack was losing altitude and airspeed at the same time. In addition, his arms and legs were feeling like lead from constantly moving the heavy controls to maintain flight. Still he fought to get every last mile out of the dying bird. A few minutes later, he knew it was over.

"Prepare for crash landing," he said over the intercom.

He could hear Ernie and the others repeating his call in the back. As it had happened in past flight emergencies Jack had experienced, a calmness settled over him. His eyes searched for a landing area while he mentally went through the checklist for emergency landing, confirming readings and hitting switches. He lined up on a cultivated square of land and immediately felt remorse for the farmer's crops he was about to destroy.

"I may have to come in hot, so brace yourselves," he warned. His plan was indeed to come in hot, but to flare at the last minute and hopefully settle the chopper down. The ground loomed in his windscreen until, at the last moment, he pulled back on the stick. The Huey shuddered hard and Jack immediately knew it was going to be a hard landing. His hands flying, he almost reached the rotor brake when the tail boom contacted the ground and then the cabin. The sound of crunching, twisting metal filled the air as the chopper flopped onto the earth with a bang.

Jack sat stunned for a moment, then his hands started flying around the cockpit, shutting down systems. The acrid smell of chemical- laden smoke began to filter into the cabin. Jack hit his harness release and started to climb out of his seat when sharp pain shot through his right leg. He involuntarily screamed, "Fuck!"

Ernie appeared at his door window. "Jack? Are you all right?"

"I think my leg's broken and it's stuck."

"Hang on."

Jack could hear Ernie barking orders and seconds later several men were prying the door open. Another man came in from the other door and together they worked on the crumpled metal around Jack's leg. Each movement shot pain through the leg and up his spine, but he said nothing. Rivulets of sweat ran down his forehead into his eyes, causing them to sting. He wiped them with his sleeve.

The smoke was getting thicker now and the men were working faster. Then, the glow of flames lit up the cabin.

"You guys get out while you can," Jack ordered.

"Shut up, Jack," Ernie shot back.

Jack could feel heat and he started to squirm.

"Now," a voice said. Men grunted with strain and a loud crack announced the relief of pressure around Jack's leg and he was pulled out of the helicopter, carried a short distance and put in another helicopter. He could hear Ernie yelling, "GO, GO, GO."

Emmett's face appeared with a, "Night, night, Jack." Jack felt a pin prick and shortly faded out.

CHAPTER ELEVEN

E rnie sat in the waiting room of the Ramat David Airbase Hospital. The Mossad agent, Ben, came into the room and sat down next to him.

"I understand you lost a man in Beirut."

Ernie nodded. "Another man just died in surgery a few minutes ago."

"May I ask who?"

"The contact the first team met when they inserted." Ernie noticed a barely perceptible reaction in Ben's usually deadpan eyes.

"I am sorry to hear this. How are the others?"

"We have three seriously wounded. Two critical, mainly due to loss of blood. We have others that were injured in the helicopter crash."

"Robin?"

"He's one of the critical cases."

"I was told you did rescue the FBI agent."

"Yes, we did. He is in fairly good shape." Ernie picked up a file that was next to him and handed it to Ben. "We got these identifications and papers off of some of the men who were there. Do you recognize any of them?"

Ben looked at the documents. He held one of them up. "This one is a deputy commander for Iranian Revolutionary Guard intelligence."

"You mean was."

"You killed him?"

"All of those people are dead."

"I must congratulate you. We've been trying to kill him for two years." Ben held up another document. "This man…this one is from East Germany. He was a Nazi. A real one. He was with the SS during the war."

"A Nazi? Are you kidding me? What the hell was he doing with an Islamic terrorist group?"

"They have a lot in common. They hate us, the Jews, and they want to rule the world. The Nazis give financial support to different terrorists groups as well as manpower in certain circumstances."

"And I thought the Nazis were history. The things I learn in this job aren't very encouraging."

Ben held up the last document. "This poor soul was a washed-up KGB agent. They sent him to Beirut to get him out of the way. His death was long overdue." He handed the documents back to Ernie and stood to leave.

"Do want copies of these, Ben?"

"Thank you, no. There is nothing new to us. But I would like to talk to Agent Fleming."

"It's okay with me, if he's willing."

"Thank you."

"Ben, I noticed a reaction when I mentioned the contact died. Did you know him?"

"Jason?" Ben thought for a moment and then shrugged his shoulders. "He was a good Jewish boy." He turned to go and hesitated. "Ernie…"

"What?"

"Was it worth it?"

Ernie met Ben's eyes with a steady gaze. "Yes."

Ben nodded and walked down the hall.

C hris sat in a hospital bed feeling unsettled. The ice bag on his testicles didn't help, but the cause of this feeling was finding out Gary and the man named Jason had died during his rescue. He didn't believe he was worth it.

He heard a knock at his door. "Chris?"

"Tom Jergenson, how are you?" Tom Jergenson was the Special Agent-in-Charge of the embassy FBI detachment in Tel Aviv.

"Doing good, old timer. Just making a quick stop to check up on you. How are you feeling?"

"Getting better. They send you to check on me?"

"I would've come anyway, but I also have news from the Beirut office."

"Dialya made it?"

"She made it to the embassy, but she and a taxi driver were killed before the Marines could stop it."

Chris fell back on his pillow. "Goddammit, I shouldn't have asked her to take the stuff."

Tom didn't say anything.

"What about Karam?"

"He's safe at the embassy under Marine guard."

"Please get word to them that I intend to adopt Karam and get him to the states."

Tom laughed. "You'll have to take that up with Master Gunnery Sergeant Bobby Joe Harris, who is undoubtedly the toughest goddamn Marine I've ever had the pleasure to meet."

"Why? What's he doing with Karam?"

"The master gunnery sergeant has made it perfectly clear that he intends to adopt Karam and that no one is going to stop him. Considering the ambassador thinks the sun rises and sets on the good sergeant, I'd say you have an uphill battle, Chris. Maybe you can work out visitation."

Chris sat silent for a moment and then just shook his head. "Did they get my paperwork?"

"Yeah, they got it all, including the two credentials and your reports. Sorry to hear about Steve."

"It's always a bad thing to be murdered by someone you trust."

Jergenson nodded. "I got to get going. Anything I can do for you?"

"No, I'm good, Tom. Thanks for coming and letting me know what happened in Beirut."

"No problem. See you later."

Chris looked up at the ceiling. *Five good people killed because of me. Dear God, forgive me.* He rolled and buried his face in a pillow to hide the tears from the torture in his soul.

There was a knock at the door. Chris wiped his eyes and saw a tough- looking man.

"Agent Fleming, I'm Ben from the Mossad. I'm sorry to disturb you at this difficult time, but I have some urgent questions for you."

Chris adjusted himself in the bed. He gasped at the pain in his groin. "Come in, Ben."

Ben approached the bed and held out his hand, which Chris shook. "You've had a rough time, but I need to know if there were other men besides the ones who were killed in the room who took an interest in you while you were captive."

"Yeah, there were two others who came into the room at first, but they left and never came back."

"Can I show you some photographs?"

"Sure."

Ben handed a photograph to Chris.

"Sorry, didn't see this guy."

Ben showed him another picture.

Chris shook his head. "No."

Ben handed Chris a third photo.

"Yes, that guy was there. He spoke English with a German accent."

Ben showed Chris one last picture.

"He was there, too. He spoke English with what I believe was a Farsi accent."

"Thank you, Agent Fleming. I appreciate your cooperation at this difficult time."

"No problem. Can you tell me who they are and can I get copies of those photos?"

"I will give the information to Ernie."

Ben went back to the waiting room and sat down next to Ernie. He handed him two photographs. Pointing to the first one his said, "This is Hans Boorman. He claims to be a nephew of Martin Boorman, but we have never been able to verify that claim. However, the powers of the Fourth Reich hold him up as an heir to the Reich leadership.

"The second man is Farrok Mokri. He is a colonel in the Iranian VEVAK, and a very effective intelligence agent. We believe he is the commander of VEVAK's field operations. Agent Fleming recognized both these men as being present early in his imprisonment. I thought you might like this information."

"Thank you, Ben. This is very useful."

Ben rose to go. "One more thing, Ernie. When your team comes back, we would be honored to support you in your endeavors."

"What endeavors would that be?"

"Vengeance."

Ernie nodded his head. "We'll be in touch."

Heinrich Hessel settled at a table in the Chez Donati restaurant located in the Grand Hotel in Basel, Switzerland. An older man sat across from him.

Heinrich knew him as Joachim Felsa, but he was not entirely convinced that was the man's real name. A waiter came by the table. "Your cognac, Mr. Hessel. Will you be dining tonight?" "No, Joseph, this will be fine, thank you."

Joachim did not look happy. Heinrich suspected the news from Beirut was not good. The FBI agent probably did not talk.

The older man drew a deep breath. "The FBI agent escaped."

Hessel almost choked on his cognac. "How can that be? I thought Hans had everything under control."

"Sometimes Hans likes to talk more success than he achieves. The last name and all that. In this case, it cost Helmut Fuhrmann's life."

"The agent killed Helmut?"

Felsa shook his head. "No, a very skilled team of men rescued Fleming. They killed many more people than just Helmut."

"Americans?"

"We don't know. The American government says they were not aware of any rescue operation. It may have been mercenaries hired by the agent's family."

Hessel rubbed his glass with his finger. "Helmut has been a loyal party member for decades."

"Yes, I think it somewhat unfortunate Hans was in charge of Beirut instead of Helmut, but that is the fact."

"I assume Hans is all right?"

"Oh, yes, he's just fine. He would never allow himself to get too close to danger."

Hessel leaned forward. "Sometimes I wish I could be on the front lines fighting for the Reich instead of being a banker."

Felsa sipped his drink. "An admirable thought, but you are an officer in the Schutzstaffel of the Fourth Reich and you have an assignment…a very important one, indeed."

Heinrich straightened his back. "You are quite right, Joachim."

"You are aware of the service and sacrifices of your predecessors, especially Paul Hechler. You must live up to their legacy."

"Yes, I never forget. They were great men."

"You need to honor their memory by improving on their heroic achievements. They kept the Third Reich financially alive for almost the entire war and helped finance the secret transition to the Fourth Reich. I know it is asking much of you, but we all know you can do it."

"I appreciate the Reich's faith in me. I will not let you down." Heinrich felt like he had pulled off a great coup. He would never leave his employ at the Bank for International Settlements to "fight on the front lines." His current position allowed him to live very well and work in a country club environment. He facilitated money transfers from banks secretly controlled by the Reich to other banks that were not adverse to using "laundering methods" to hide the trail of the money and get the money to the Reich and its allied operatives all over the world. As in the days of World War Two, the Reich could not financially survive without his services, a fact that swelled him with pride.

"What are we going to do about the FBI agent? Do we know if his investigation connected BIS to the American or Beirut banks?" he asked Felsa.

"No, we do not. Of all American government agencies, the FBI is probably the hardest to penetrate. We have assets who can get access to FBI files, but apparently not Agent Fleming's last reports. Plus, we don't know if he reported everything he learned during his investigation.

"Agent Fleming has reached mandatory retirement age, but we cannot take any chances. The Raven has ordered for Fleming to have an unfortunate accident. Hopefully, other agents will not be so enthusiastic about continuing the investigation."

"I will continue to make discreet inquiries about any known investigations through my closest associates."

"Yes, do so. They have proved to be very valuable in the past."

The men smiled and raised their drinks in salute.

CHAPTER TWELVE

April 4, 1992

Alarm bells went off in Jamie Slater's head. As the team's chief intelligence officer, he was also responsible for the company's computer system, which was now showing definite evidence of someone hacking into it. He reached over and took a thick three-ring binder off his bookcase. He opened it and removed a disk from a sleeve and loaded the software. His fingers started flying over the keyboard as he watched the software analyzing the communication hardware and software. An intrusion was identified almost immediately.

The intruder impressed him. He didn't disconnect. In fact, the intruder parried each probe by the detection software and Jamie's manipulation of it. The battle went on for eleven minutes and then Jamie saw an opening. He got two keystrokes in when the intruder disconnected.

"Damn," Jamie muttered. "This guy is definitely a pro."

Although disappointed, Jamie knew one thing for certain. The hacker would be back...and Jamie would be prepared.

He reached for the phone to call Robin, but remembered Rob, Burke and Rocky would be doing their daily bike ride about now. Jamie shook his head. As bad as Robin, Burke and Rocky were wounded, they had fought back to operational status faster than any of the doctors thought they would—physically that is. Mentally, Jamie wasn't so sure.

B urke Jameson sat looking out the window of the waterfront room at the Shiloh Inn in Ocean Shores on the Washington coast. He winced with pain from his healing wounds. The night sky was lit up with the Milky Way that hung like a blanket of crystals. He sipped his wine, not sure if he should be drinking wine because of his nervous stomach. Two people swirled around his mind. He tried to connect them, but there was a wall.

There was Robin. A man Burke had come to admire and love as a brother, but now the thought of him brought bitterness. Burke struggled with the way Robin had led the mission to rescue Chris. Though Chris was a good friend, Burke couldn't bring himself to believe he was worth losing Gary and Jason and suffering the wounds he, Rocky...and Robin suffered. There was heavy guilt about feeling this way, but there it was.

Then there was Kathleen. He didn't understand why he could go into combat feeling no fear. Apprehension, maybe, but no fear. But a woman, a good woman, when you stepped off that terrifying cliff, you either landed on the magical bridge to happiness or dropped into the abyss of dismal rejection. He had dropped before. He didn't want to drop again. But Kathleen, he just couldn't get her off his mind, out of his heart.

So there were the two, swirling around. He knew they were connected, but he just couldn't get over that wall between them.

"Why are you up?" Kathleen's sleepy voice drifted to him.

"I'm sorry. I didn't mean to wake you."

"I woke up because I didn't feel you next to me." She got up, put on a robe, walked over to Burke and sat on his lap. "Is something wrong?"

"Nothing is wrong."

Kathleen lifted Burke's chin and looked him in the eye. "Burke, I'm a psychiatrist and a damn good one at that."

An uncomfortable moment passed. Burke took a deep breath and turned back to the ocean. "I can't shake this bad feeling I have towards Rob. In my mind, he failed Gary and he put us in an untenable situation in Beirut. Chris is a good friend and I'm a believer in no man left behind, but two men died and others were seriously wounded. I'm not sure it was worth it."

"Did you ever stop to think that Rob was handed a difficult choice?"

"I know the choice wasn't easy, but we went in there with no plan other than to find Chris and figure it out from there."

"Have you talked to Rob about it?"

Burke didn't answer.

Kathleen gently put her hand on his cheek and turned his face to hers. "You have to talk to Rob. I'm sure he's been agonizing over whether he did the right thing. You know losing Gary and Jason hit him hard, as well you and Rocky being hurt."

"Sometimes I think he considers the mission more important than us."

Kathleen's head snapped back and she looked Burke in

the eye. "I think you're way off base, Burke. I counsel soldiers for a living. The officers I talk to all struggle with the balance of mission and safety of their men, but in combat there are no guarantees. You know that. I know damn good and well Robin is the same way."

Burke lifted her off his lap and began pacing. He stopped at the window and ran his hand through his hair. He searched the ocean waves and the stars in the sky for an answer.

"Talk to me, Burke. Seeing you this way tears me apart. I can help."

Burke reached out and touched the window, tracing an incoming wave. "Maybe I'm the problem."

She came up behind him. "Why do you think that?"

"I think life has become more precious to me."

"I'm not following you."

"Two times in my life I thought I was in love. Both times I got married and both times things went to hell pretty fast."

"Go on, keep talking."

"I know now I wasn't really in love. I had no idea what true love was." He turned to Kathleen and swallowed hard. "I know now because I truly love you."

Tears welled up in Kathleen's eyes and she laid her head on his shoulder.

"I'm sorry if this is not what you wanted to hear. I just had to say it. I didn't mean to make you cry."

She looked up and he could see a sparkle through the tears "I *am* crying, but only because no one has ever said that to me before."

Burke went over to his suitcase. He returned and held out a small box showing a diamond ring. "Kathleen, life has become precious to me because of you. I'm not the greatest catch in the world, but I want to be your husband and love you for the rest of my life. Will you marry me?"

Kathleen took the ring. "How long have you had this?"

"Months. Hell, I bought it after our second date."

She smiled and put the ring on her finger. "I'm glad I haven't given myself just for the sex." She opened her robe letting it drop to the floor, put her arms around Burke's neck and kissed him. "Yes, I will marry you, Burke Jameson, and you are the only catch in the world for me." She took his hand and led him to the bed.

Joy surged through Burke. He'd stepped off and landed on the bridge. For the first time in many years, he felt complete.

A natoli Maravonovitch, commander of KGB Special Projects Group Two, knocked on the chairman's open office door. Anatoli noticed how much the Chairman had aged in the last year. Even he had to come to realize the Soviet Union was nearing its end.

"Come." The chairman waved him in.

"You sent for me, sir?"

"Yes." The chairman handed him a target package.

He opened it and saw a picture of a man. The name at the bottom of the picture identified the man as Robin Marlette. "I'll assign an agent immediately."

"Assign Lana."

"She is currently on a mission, sir. It may be up to two months before she returns."

"Call her back."

"Sir, she has penetrated a French espionage cell in the Caucasus. Her target is the leader of the ring. She has to initiate contact with us because we do not want to compromise her cover."

"Have someone find her and bring her back and replace her with another agent."

"Mr. Chairman, with respect, the Caucasus are as much of a powder keg as other satellite members. We have to proceed carefully with our clandestine agents for the sake of the mission and for their sake."

The chairman's face flushed around dark eyes that drilled into Anatoli. Then he let out a long breath and leaned back in his chair. "When Lana returns then."

"Sir, we have other…"

"No! It must be Lana. There are lessons to be taught here."

"Yes, sir."

Robin's lungs ached for oxygen and his leg throbbed with pain, but he pedaled his bike up the steep incline. Burke's and Rocky's heavy breath was close behind him. Robin fixed on the summit of the hill as it came closer. His body screamed for the torture to stop and the faint thought of quitting tried to push its way to decision, but Robin erased it with a burst of speed. His bike hit the summit and he slowed his pace, drawing ragged breaths. Burke and Rocky came up on either side, in the same condition. The three men did an easy ride for two more miles and then dismounted and walked for another mile.

They moved in silence, which between the three men was deafening. Robin knew there was unsaid tension between them. He just didn't know how to address it, and it tore him up. These were his brothers, yet they were emotionally detached as well. Gary's death was a driving wedge. Robin understood that. But the rescue of Chris had taken a toll on the overall spirit of the team, which Robin couldn't, or maybe wouldn't, talk about.

They wound their way to Robin's back yard and collapsed on the grass. Emmett's booming voice greeted the men.

"What a bunch of pussies. If you can't do a measly twenty-five-mile ride with a couple of little hills without breathing hard, you should be ashamed to call yourselves operators."

"Shove it up your ass, you ugly wookie," Rocky shot back.

"Is that an offer or a threat?"

The men laughed.

"I'll be back," Emmett said as he walked off.

B urke looked out over the Strait of Juan de Fuca and tried to find calmness in the view. He decided that now was the time to confront Robin about the rescue mission as Kathleen suggested.

Rocky rubbed his hip. "Rob, does your wounded leg hurt a little when we run?"

"Naw."

"It doesn't?"

"Nope, it hurts a lot."

The three men laughed, then quiet settled upon them.

Finally, Burke spoke, knowing he was going to open a hurtful wound, but also knowing he had to. "Rob, I need to clear the air about a couple of things."

"I know."

"Whaddya mean you know?"

Robin's eyes met Burke's and the calm sadness in them cut into Burke's heart. "I've felt it from you since we got out of the hospital. I know the three of us and probably Rick are in emotional turmoil about the rescue. I assume that's what you need to talk about."

"It is."

"Well, let's get it out, brother."

Burke looked down at the grass. "I don't think the way you pushed Gary was right. We all know he was getting scared toward the last couple of missions. You should've put him out to pasture."

"Whoa, Burke," Rocky interjected. "You don't know the whole story."

Robin raised his hand. "It's okay, Rock."

"No, it isn't, Rob. You both need to hear this and you need to hear it from me, because Gary talked to me about things more than he did anyone else on the team." Rocky took a deep breath. "Gary was an enigma. He was a worrier. He fretted over things a lot. Yeah, he was scared…right up to when the mission started and then he was always good to go. "I know he always talked to you before a mission, Rob. I know he always asked you to let him sit it out and you always told him no, until this last mission. He knew why you said no, and he appreciated it."

Burke looked at Robin. "You told him he could sit this last mission out?"

Robin nodded.

"Rob also told Gary not to leave Israel this last time."

"You did?"

Robin nodded. "I expected him to follow that order, but I should've known better."

"So why did Gary appreciate Rob telling him no on his requests to stand down, Rock?"

Rocky looked down at the green grass as if he were thinking about what to say. "Gary loved the team. He told me he never felt more alive than when working missions with us. But he was getting older and it kinda scared him because he just wasn't as fast and as strong as he used to be. He worried about letting the team down. So when Rob would tell him he couldn't stand down, he felt needed and useful. It was like Rob was certifying he has the skills to do the job."

"But you told him to stand down this last mission, Rob."

"I told him he was done operating and was going to work with Jamie."

"Why?"

"Because his eyes had changed. I could see real fear and hesitation."

Burke took that in. "But he came anyway. Like he knew what was going to happen." He looked over at Robin and could see he was fighting back tears. "I'm sorry, Rob."

"You've got nothing to apologize for," Robin answered, wiping his eyes with his arm. "What were the other things you wanted to talk about?"

"Ah, hell—nothing."

"C'mon, Burke, out with it."

Burke took a deep breath. "Well, I don't like rushing into a nest of bad guys without a plan. I feel like the plan last time was when we find Chris, we'll make a plan. To me, that's a crazy way to do business, and in the end, we lost two men and saved one. Shit, Rob, we almost got killed. I wouldn't call that a success."

"I can't really disagree with you on the numbers. And I can't really disagree with you about the plan, if I were just looking at it from your point of view. But as the commander of this team, I know what our strengths and weaknesses are, and our three main strengths are stealth, speed and force of action. So, when we have to move fast, as long as I can maximize those strengths and count on some luck, I don't have a problem how we handled it. Keep in mind we were in contact with Ernie and the rest of the team before we assaulted the building. We knew they would be there when we needed them the most."

"But the numbers don't lie."

"Depends on the numbers you're talking about. If you look at bodies lost versus bodies saved, you're right. But if you consider we proved to everyone on our team, and some

HRT guys, that we won't leave anyone behind, what's that worth?"

Burke didn't answer.

Rob put his arm around Burke's shoulders. "Every time we're up against it, I'll ask if you think we need to plan more."

"And we won't go if I say yes?"

"Now, if I said yes to that question, what kind of leader would I be? I promise you I'll listen to what you have to say and seriously consider it."

Burke shook his head with a chuckle. "That's what you always do."

"That's the best I can do and still effectively command this team."

"What would you say about discussing this with the whole team?"

"I think it's a good idea. I should've done it when we got out of the hospital."

The men fell silent for a while. Then Burke simply said, "Thanks, Rob."

Rocky got a mischievous look on his face. "Should we have a group kiss now?"

Rob looked at Burke. They grabbed Rocky and pulled him to the grass. While Robin held Rocky down, Burke grabbed the pitcher of ice water and poured it on Rocky's head. "There now, that should cool your ardor, young man." The three men laughed together.

An hour later, Dr. Maria Ariel, the wife of team member Doug Ariel, came into the yard and knelt down in front of the men. Maria met the team in the Philippines where Doug was seriously wounded. She treated Doug and they fell in love. Jack Moore and Karen were with her, as well as Rada Rogov, the team nurse and wife of team member Lev Rogov. The Rogovs were brought to the US by Robin after it became untenable for them to stay in Russia, because they had helped Robin get Mark medical treatment for serious wounds.

"How's everyone doing?" Maria greeted the group.

"Just fine, Maria. How are you today?" Robin asked.

Maria exhaled in exasperation. "C'mon, Rob, you know what I mean. How does your leg feel?"

Robin looked at the doctor for a moment, considering his answer. He decided she needed to know the truth. "It hurts."

"What kind of pain?"

"It's a dull ache."

Maria carefully felt around the leg, probing muscle. Then she probed the part of Robin's leg that was now metal.

Robin shuddered. "Damn, Maria! That hurt."

"It's going to for a while longer. You're damn lucky you were able to get this far."

"I figured that."

"Robin, I can give you pain medicine."

"No thanks."

Maria shook her head. "Anything else hurt?"

"No, the rest is good except for occasional aching."

"Where?"

Robin rubbed his left shoulder. "The shoulder wound mostly?"

"Any discomfort in the chest?"

"No."

She turned to Burke and started probing his wound areas. "Are you having any discomfort in your chest?"

"Nope. I watch for it like you told me, but I don't feel any."

She turned to Rocky.

"Do you hurt anywhere?"

"I get side stitches when I run, right in the area where I was hit the worst. Other than that, I'm good."

Maria took the vitals on each man and listened with her stethoscope. When she finished, she stood and looked at the men with almost a glare. "You three have pushed yourselves beyond my recommendations. I can't say the results are bad. Actually, they're amazing. I didn't think two of you would ever be able to operate again, but you proved me wrong."

"So, we're good to go?" Robin asked.

"Yes, you're cleared for missions."

"What about flyboy here?"

"He's been good for a while."

Robin turned to Jack. "How come you don't ride with us anymore?"

Jack laughed. "I'm not a fitness nut like you guys. I'm just fine with my mediocre physical condition."

Robin looked over at Karen. Her face was like stone.

L ater that night, Robin confronted his wife. "Karen, you need to talk to me."

"What's there to talk about? I've resigned myself to the realization that you're going to be killed on one of these missions and there's nothing I can do about it."

"Whoa, do I have a say in this?"

"What can you say? Each mission you come back with more injuries to your body. You have more scars than I can count. I'm watching you physically deteriorate before my eyes."

"Oh c'mon, it's not that bad."

"Robin, I'm not Maria. I've lived with you for twenty-seven years. I see the pain in your face. I see the limp when you're not concentrating. I witness your nightmares, and through your eyes, I see the pain in your soul."

Robin climbed out of bed and went to the picture window looking out over the nighttime ocean. It was a full moon and the water was agitated by a coming storm, the foam-topped waves glowing in the moonlight. Karen came softly behind him and put her arms around his waist and he clasped his arms over hers.

"I'm frightened, Rob. I don't know what I would do without you. I have to worry about Casey in the Rangers and Eddie wanting to go to West Point...." A quiet sob ended the sentence.

Robin turned and took her into his arms. "I've dragged you through hell and for that I'm truly sorry. When I was in police work, I always thought that if it got too bad for us, I'd just quit and open a law practice. But now, we're trapped. As long as we can do the job, they're going to make us do it."

"Do you really think they'd prosecute after all you and the guys have done?"

"I don't *think* they will, I *know* they will do something to force us to keep at it. The only thing we can do is hope we come across something that we can use against them that won't endanger the country. Then maybe we can bargain our way to an end before we all end up dead."

"But you don't know that will ever happen."

"No, I don't."

Karen tightened her arms around him.

Robin gently pushed her back so he could look into her eyes. "Honey, for all we know, we'll grow old together and live happily ever after. The best thing we can do is accept the things we can't change, at least for now, and enjoy the fact that we have each other."

Karen laid her head on his chest and they stood that way for a time. Then Robin scooped her up in his arms and carried her to their bed.

CHAPTER THIRTEEN

The next morning, Robin held a full team meeting in Fatboy. He'd decided on the plane for maximum privacy. He stood in front of his team.

"We're meeting today to discuss two issues. Number one, we need to discuss the Beirut mission. Number two, we need to work out a plan for investigating the scope of cooperation between Islamic terrorists and the Nazis. Burke and I will present some of the issues on the Beirut mission...."

"Oh, no I won't, Rob." Burke squirmed in his seat.

"Yes, you will. Your concerns are reasonable and the team needs to hear them."

Burke frowned and just nodded.

"Ernie will brief us on what we know about Islamic terrorists and the Nazis. Much of the information comes from Mossad and Chris Fleming. He, Rocky and Burke have been working on a plan."

Burke slowly rose and faced the group. "First I wanna say I'm not trying to cause trouble or challenge the boss."

"Jeez, get on with it, Burke. We know you're not trying to cause trouble," Emmett's voice boomed.

"Okay, okay, just makin' sure." Burke took a deep breath. "I know we all are hurt by the loss of Gary and Jason. We didn't know Jason, but he was a soldier and he volunteered to help us when he didn't have to. It just seems to me that if we had a better plan, they might be alive today. I mean, we just went into Beirut with the idea to find Chris and if we found him, then we'd figure out how to rescue him. To me, that's seems a little crazy. That's what I think." Burke looked at Robin.

"All right, you heard the man. Comments?"

Mike Collins raised his hand.

"Go ahead, Mike."

"Burke may have a point because of one reason. I think it was wrong to leave most of the team behind in the beginning. If we all had arrived together, the assault team could've had enough men to suppress the fire that killed Jason and wounded you and the other guys. We also may have gotten Chris out of there before the van showed up. I'll tell you, boss, we were all mad as hell you did that."

A murmur of agreement went through the group.

"How long did it take to get the rest of the team assembled after we left?"

"About three and a half hours. Then it took us another three hours to get another crew to fly the 737. Then we had to make a stop in D.C. to pick up the HRT guys, and that meant flying the long way around."

Ernie stood up. "Those are good points, Mike. As you all know, I was just as pissed about being left behind as you were." Ernie turned to Robin. "And I let the boss know it. It may have turned out better if we had all left together. We'll never know. The team that was there did a hell of a job gathering intelligence for the op in such a short time, which sped up the timetable even more. They were also on their way to Beirut before we were organized to head out. That's not a bad thing because they were eyes on the target before the shindig started. Our luck held and we pulled it off. About an hour ago, I called Delta HQ and talked to our friend Major John...."

"Major?" asked Doug.

"Yep, John got promoted."

Doug nodded. "Good for him. He's a great guy."

"For those who weren't with us in the beginning of our little adventure, Major John is the one who cleared us for operating on our own. He also coordinates our training evolutions. He's aware of what kind of missions we've done and I asked him what he thought of our casualty rate. His answer was that our casualty rate was pretty much along the line of Delta's experience, but our death rate is lower. This is partly because their operations include full blown combat missions, partly because of our skills, partly because of our leader, and partly because of luck. That doesn't mean we're perfect. It doesn't mean Rob is perfect. It seems to me the main problem with this last operation is the fact that we started with half the team. Does anyone disagree with that?"

"I think you hit the nail on the head," Emmett said.

"So, I have a proposal. I suggest we hire two new pilots and buy another Bell 230. Keep two pilots on call 24/7. Using two choppers, we can have everyone here in two hours, tops."

"Whoa, there big guy," Jack said in loud voice. Under your proposal, five pilots would mean each guy would have to be on call for around 144 hours a month. That's a huge strain on the pilots and our families."

Robin stood up. "Thanks, Ernie. I'll take it from here." Ernie sat down and Robin turned to face the group.

"It's clear we need a better call out system that gets the team at Paine Field within two hours. The helicopters are a good idea, but as Jack pointed out, it puts the pilots behind

101

the eight ball. So Jack, Emmett, Marv, and Ernie will get together and work it out."

Robin paused and looked at his men. "I've given the Beirut op a lot of thought over the last couple of months and I've come to the conclusion that I owe all of you an apology."

The room became very quiet.

"I should have waited for the whole team to assemble. There could have been a lot more accomplished in gathering and analyzing intelligence around the Hezbollah headquarters while we were enroute to Israel. I'm sure every man here has heard me say that I count on three things about our team in operations: stealth, speed, force of action. I also count on a little luck. It's a damn good thing we have luck, because while we were trapped in that front door area, I realized I had committed us to a dumb plan. In my mistaken belief we had to get on the ground in Beirut as quickly as possible, I skipped planning steps that we had been trained to do. I put the entire team at serious risk. Gentlemen, I screwed up and I apologize. Because I violated the trust you had in me, I am going to leave the room and you are going to decide whether or not you want a new commander..."

A couple of men started to object, but Robin simply said, "Stop. This needs to be discussed among yourselves. Only you as a group can make this decision." Robin let a moment of silence go by.

With that, Robin left the room.

Burke put his head in his hands. "Oh God, what have I done?"

Ernie got up in front of the men. "You haven't done anything wrong, Burke. Look, guys, I know Robin has been hit hard by Gary's death. He also feels responsible for Jason's death. He hasn't talked to me about this, but I know he doesn't want to lead us unless we have complete faith in him."

"What do you think, Ernie?" Willie asked.

"Sorry, guys, I'm not impartial. Robin and I have been close friends for many years and our families are intertwined. I'll moderate the discussion, but my opinion here is worthless."

"Would you consider being our commander?" asked Marv.

"No, I don't have the strategic vision for the team that Robin has. I also couldn't handle Grassley like he does. There are members of this team that are born leaders...Emmett, Burke, Rocky...hell any one of you."

"Okay, let's cut the bullshit." Emmett's deep voice rumbled like it was Zeus speaking as he rose to his full height of six feet, six inches. "Who here could have handled *anything* Robin has better than him?"

No one responded to Emmett's question.

"My next question is who here, if it were one of us captured, wouldn't want to be secure in the knowledge that the *full force* of Robin Marlette was coming to get you out?"

"You have such a way with words, Auntie Em," Rocky cracked.

"Most of us have known Robin for years. We know we don't work *for* Robin, we work *with* him, because he's that kind of leader. We've survived dangerous times with him, laughed with him, gotten drunk with him, and now cry with him over our loss. We know he's not perfect, because none of us are, but I can tell you after five years in the Army and fifteen years as a cop, I never had as fine a leader as Robin. I vote we keep him as our leader. That's my speech."

"Damn, Emmett, you've said more in the last couple of minutes than you've said all year long," Doug said. "And, you're absolutely right. I propose a motion. I move that Robin stay our commander, because he is the best, and that the next time we get a couple of days off together, we go on a good ol', rip roarin' Guardian retreat."

Rocky raised his hand. "I second that motion."

"All right, cut it out," Ernie ordered. "Robin wanted us to have a serious discussion about this."

"We did, Ernie," Burke said. "There's just one more thing to say. Robin stood in front of us and said he made mistakes. He listened to us. He seriously considered what we told him and stood in front of us and told us we were right. He is the only commander I ever had in the military or the police that ever did that." Burke turned to Ernie. "It's time to vote, Ernie."

Ernie took a deep breath. "Does anyone object to taking a vote on Robin's leadership of this unit at this time?" There was no objection. Ernie picked up a hat and walked among the men. "There are blank strips of paper in this hat. Take one out and write either 'yes' for Robin to remain our commander or 'no' for him to step down." After everyone had a piece of paper, Ernie set the hat down on the table. "Put your ballot in the hat when you're done."

"Don't forget the yes vote is also for the Guardian retreat," Doug reminded Ernie.

"That's bribery, Doug," Rick commented.

"So? That's politics."

Laughter filled the room.

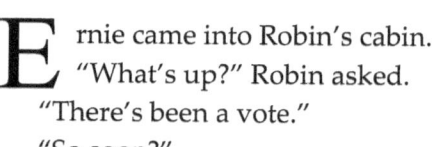

Ernie came into Robin's cabin.

"What's up?" Robin asked.

"There's been a vote."

"So soon?"

"Yep. It was unanimous…go address your men, boss."

"Were there any shenanigans, like pressure put on people?"

"Well, I guess you could call Emmett standing up for you as pressure…I mean who is going to argue with Auntie Em?"

"Auntie Em?"

"Yeah, that's Rocky's new nickname for the big guy."

Robin suppressed a chuckle as he stood up. Then the thought of Gary deflated him.

Ernie put his arm around his friend. "Robin, it's time to let Gary go. You need to and the men need you to."

Robin nodded. "Thanks, brother. Let's go finish this meeting."

Robin and Ernie went back into the team room. Robin stood in front of his team. "Thank you for your vote of confidence. It's important to me that I have your trust and faith in my ability to lead. For sure I'm not perfect, but I think you all know that I do my level best to do the right thing. I will continue to work to deserve your confidence. Ernie, you're up." Robin sat down.

Ernie stood before the group. "We're going to start an operation to investigate our new adversaries. Our objectives are not going to be easy to accomplish," Ernie started off. "Since we don't have any people who can pass as Middle Eastern, getting around unnoticed will be difficult. We can recruit informants, but covering the informants will still be iffy.

"Remember, our goal for this op is to identify and locate Nazi and Hezbollah operatives, not take them out. We've been talking to Ben, and through our conversations, we decided to take a strategic approach to our plan. Ben pegs this Farrok Mokri as a major player in terrorism. Couple him with Hans Boorman and you have the terror-Nazi connection together. Ben believes those two are operating together. He thinks there is a plan in place for a terror attack according to several pieces of intelligence from different sources. Between Mossad and the CIA, they can be located. When we find them, we surveil them, find out where they go and who they're seeing...hopefully they'll take us up the chain."

Mike raised his hand. "Yes, Mike," Ernie said.

"That's a long-term project, Ernie. Are you sure Ben isn't getting us to do his work? It's not like Mossad hasn't done that to other agencies before."

"Do you want to find out who really is behind Hezbollah and the Fourth Reich? I can tell you this...Ben is impressed with our team. What we did in Beirut, the sacrifices we made to get Chris out...well, let's just say in Ben's eyes, we rank right up there with the best. I don't think he is toying with us."

Mike nodded. "I trust your judgement, Ernie."

"We are currently working out the details of the plan, but we will rotate folks back home as often as we can. Does anyone object to the basic idea of the plan?"

No one spoke up.

"Okay, that's all we have. Let's get back to work."

CHAPTER FOURTEEN

J amie was startled out of his catnap by the system intrusion alarm and the CIA direct line ringing at the same time. He put on his headset and hit the open line button. After spending two days and nights waiting for this, he was excited.

"Jamie here."

"Yeah, Jamie, it's Norm." The CIA's top expert on hackers, Norm had realized early on what kind of threat they posed. He developed the top-secret software they were using to catch this hacker.

"Hi, Norm. Give me a second...okay, I'm ready."

"Me, too. Let's see if we can't track this guy."

Jamie started the intrusion detection suite. The hacker immediately started counter moves.

"It looks like you were right. He's taking me down the same path."

"Get ready. We literally have to be two steps ahead of him."

"I see it. Entering trap code...now."

"Code entered on this end. Ambush accomplished.

Standby." After a minute, Norm come back on the line. "He's routing through a remote site in Germany. I've got a response team rolling. I'll let you know what they find."

"I hope they find something. He was gone in a flash."

"If they get there in time, they'll grab all the hard drives in the building. From there we should be able to find him."

"Thanks, Norm."

"Glad we could help."

J amie sat on a bench a block away from an apartment building on Capitol Hill in Seattle. It had taken a few days, but the CIA found a hard drive that had the hacker's IP address on it. Norm tracked that address to this apartment building but could not identify in which apartment the computer and the hacker resided. Using a profile that Norm provided, Jamie had been patiently waiting for a match to emerge from the building since six in the morning. So far, none of the residents coming out fit the profile.

At twenty minutes to noon, a disheveled young man came out. He had long uncombed hair over a bearded face and a pear-shaped body. A Hawaiian shirt clashed with wrinkled sweatpants and bedroom slippers.

"Bingo," Jamie said softly. He followed the suspected hacker as he went down one block and over two blocks to a McDonald's. A few minutes later, the man came out carrying a large sack and went back to the apartment building. Jamie waited for five seconds after the man entered and went in after him. He could hear the suspect plodding up the stairs and Jamie followed quietly. He heard the jingle of keys and sped up just in time to see the door to apartment six closing.

He took a quick look around and left, resuming his surveillance.

At six-thirty in the evening, the hacker left the building carrying a laptop computer. This time the man went to a small pizza shop and sat at a table with four men and a young woman, who all had laptops and appeared to be of the same lifestyle as the suspect. Jamie parked a block down and waited. A half hour later, Mark knocked on his passenger window and Jamie unlocked the door.

"So you got a hit, eh?" Mark asked.

"Yeah, and right now he's in that pizza shop with several like-minded folks, I think."

"What's our man look like?"

Jamie described the suspect and gave Mark the info on the building.

"How long you want to watch him before you move on him?"

"I want to give it two weeks, so we get his routine down pat."

"Good idea. Why don't you go home and I'll take it from here. I'll see you at six in the morning."

After two weeks Jamie knew the suspect's routine, the few places he regularly visited and had photos of him and his friends. It was time to introduce himself. When the hacker went to have pizza with his friends, Jamie left Mark outside in the car and went to the man's apartment door, quickly picked the locks and made entry. He lit the one bedroom apartment with his mini maglite.

He had been there several nights earlier to copy the hard drives in the computers and saw the small and dirty place hadn't changed. McDonald's sacks were stacked high in the one garbage can Jamie could see. Beer cans were stacked around the garbage can. The kitchen sink was full of glasses and cups. The living room area was aglow with a bank of computer screens. Three servers hummed and Jamie figured they were making the apartment as warm as it was. Judging from the electrical hookup, it looked like he was siphoning power from his neighbors. That would explain one reason why the CIA couldn't pinpoint him.

Jamie started searching drawers in the bedroom and found a rent receipt for a Stephan Gulasky for apartment six. In another drawer he found a birth certificate, social security card and a United States passport. The photo in the passport surprised Jamie. While he could see that it was the man he had been surveilling, the picture showed him clean shaven with a regular haircut and wearing a suit. Visa stamps in the passport showed the guy had been to England, Germany, Poland, Russia, China and Japan. The length of stay in China attracted Jamie's attention because it was long for a country not too fond of Americans. He started building a hunch.

He went to the closet, which was almost empty except for two clothes bags at one end. He unzipped one and found it contained two nice suits with shirts, ties and belts. The second bag contained casual clothes of a quality better than the suspect wore on a daily basis. Jamie checked his watch. He closed the closet door and picked a chair in the corner of the living room on the other side of the lit screens. He removed a Glock 19 from a shoulder holster and screwed on a suppressor. His cell phone vibrated.

"Yeah, Mark."

"He's coming your way," Mark said.

Jamie hung up.

A few minutes later Stephan came into his apartment and deposited a twelve pack of beer into his refrigerator while keeping one to drink. Without turning any lights on, he went to his computer screens. As he started to sit, he looked up and saw Jamie pointing his pistol at him.

"Don't move and you just might live to see tomorrow," Jamie said in a calm voice. He stood and walked over to Stephan.

The hacker's eyes opened wide showing his fear. "Who... who are you?"

"That's not important right now. The important thing is that you completely cooperate with me and tell me everything I want to know."

"What if I don't?"

"I'll kill you right here and now."

Stephan's body started trembling.

"Go ahead and sit down. Drink your beer and relax a little."

The young hacker tried to say something, but his dry mouth prevented him from forming the words.

"I wasn't lying when I told you that if you cooperate, you'll live to see tomorrow. You just need to make the right decisions. I also need to warn you not to pull any tricks like trying to destroy memory or hard drives and such. Everything was copied over the last three nights. Do we understand each other?"

"No. I want a lawyer."

"Stephan, I'm not with the government. I don't give a damn what you want. If you want to live, you will cooperate with me. Now, do we understand each other?"

Stephan fell into his desk chair. "Yes."

Jamie pulled up a dinette chair. He sat down and laid his pistol on his lap. "Is your name Stephan Gulasky?"

"Yes."

"How old are you?"

"Twenty-nine."

"Where are you from?"

"I was born in Aberdeen, Washington."

"What did your parents do for work?"

"Why do you want to know that?"

"I'm asking the questions, Stephan. You're answering them."

"Oh...okay." Stephan rubbed his head. "My dad was a fisherman. My mother worked as a chef at hunting lodges until my dad was killed and then she got a job as a secretary at the elementary school."

"Did your dad die fishing?"

"Yes."

"How old were you when that happened."

"Five."

Jamie was quiet for a moment. "That had to be tough."

The younger man looked down and Jamie thought he heard a sob.

"Go on."

"I didn't have much time with my dad because he was out on the fishing boat, but the times I remember were pretty great. I know I loved him and he loved me."

"Well, Stephan, there's a lot of sons who know their dads for decades and can't say that."

"I know."

"How did you get into computers?"

"I got into computers because I'm no good at anything else. After my dad died, mom realized she didn't have any marketable job skills. She used to be a lodge cook but she wanted to spend more time with me. She found out she could learn to type on a computer so she bought a Commodore 64 with some of the insurance money and started working on it. I started playing games and taught myself how to write code so I could cheat on games. I found out the technology of computers was easy for me to understand and work with. I became addicted to it because I'd finally found something I was good at."

"So you learned to write code early on, just when the personal computer thing was taking off. That must have attracted someone's attention."

Stephan shrugged. "Well, girls started talking to me. I would help them with their computer problems as computers became more popular."

"Using computers to score with girls. Good move, Stephan."

Stephan blushed. "Like I said, they talked to me. Well, one girl kissed me on the lips once."

Jamie's cell phone buzzed. "Yeah, Mark."

"Any reason to be worried about two tough-looking Asians that just entered the building?"

"Would Asians be looking for you?" Jamie asked Stephan.

"The Chinese hackers."

"Chinese hackers? There is no such thing unless they work for the government. Why would they be looking for you?"

"Because I agreed to work for them but changed my mind when I got home."

Jamie stood up. "Get up here, Mark. We've got problems." He hung up. "Stephan, get into the bedroom and be quiet."

Stephan, who had turned ashen, quickly followed Jamie's orders.

Jamie took up a position next to the door. He holstered his pistol and prepared for a fight. Although he'd been working with Burke on hand-to-hand combat, the thought of his disabilities turned his mouth dry and sweat started to bead on his forehead. Quiet footsteps approached the door and stopped. Jamie could hear whispers. Then Mark's voice interrupted the whispers.

"Hi, guys. Do you know what apartment Susie Osgood lives in?"

Jamie flung the door open and grabbed the nearest Chinese agent by the hair and the throat and slammed his forehead into the door jamb. The man fell to the floor on his hands and knees. Jamie smashed his left fist into the back of the man's head, knocking him out. He looked up to see Mark dragging the other man to the door.

"Let's get these bozos inside and cuff 'em up. Then we'll skedaddle with our boy," Jamie said.

"Roger that."

After cuffing the Chinese agents with plastic cuffs and relieving them of their weapons, ID and cell phones, Jamie went into Stephan's bedroom. "Come on out, Stephan."

"Why?" Stephan's muffled voice came from the closet.

"You're coming with me."

"I'm not going with you!"

"Stephan, you're lucky you're still alive. We gotta get you outta here."

Stephan stepped out and looked around. "Are they gone?"

Jamie gently but firmly pushed Stephan into the living room. "C'mon, we don't have time for twenty questions."

Stephan's eyes grew wide at seeing the two Chinese agents on the floor. "Who is that?" Stephan asked upon seeing Mark.

"My partner. Do you have a crash code?"

"Yes."

"Hit it. Don't worry, I've got all your info. Pull the hard drives first."

Stephan walked over to his computer and disconnected the six hard drives he used. He looked at Jamie with worried eyes, took a deep breath and hit three keys.

"Did that wipe it clean? You don't want anything left they can find."

"It's clean."

Jamie grabbed Stephan's passport and other documents and then the two Guardians ushered Stephan to the car and put him in the back seat. Jamie got in the back seat also, and Mark drove.

Stephan was quiet for about ten minutes and then asked, "Who are you guys?"

"I'm Jamie, he's Mark. We're now the best friends you have, Stephan. With us, you're safe. Without us, you're dead."

"What about my clothes and stuff?"

"We'll get whatever you need."

"My life is over."

"No, my newfound friend. I think your life is just beginning."

CHAPTER FIFTEEN

The next day, in Robin's company office, his voice raised up a notch. "Jamie, you're telling me you essentially burglarized an apartment, assaulted two Chinese agents, and kidnapped an American citizen in the City of Seattle, United States of America. Do you know how many crimes that amounts to?"

"I know, Rob, but you have to admit it was an emergency situation. If I hadn't gone into the apartment, Stephan would be dead now."

Robin thought for a minute. "Has there been any chatter about the agents?"

"Not that I've picked up, but I haven't queried the CIA, for obvious reasons."

"Where is this Stephan?"

"He's on the ship with Nikky."

"Christ, Nikky will probably scare the kid to death."

"You'd be surprised. He acts more like a stern grandfather than a Spetsnaz topkick. I think Stephan actually likes Nikky."

"Okay, now explain to me what you think this kid can do for us."

"He's not really a kid. He's twenty-nine, but socially clumsy. Once I got him calmed down and talking to me, it became clear to me that he is a genius—a real genius. He's focused all his intelligence into computers and the language of computers. In other words, he's a hacker and a damn good one."

"Pardon my ignorance, but what's a hacker?"

"Well, you know about people that steal people's credit card info and information off the Internet, right?"

"Yeah."

"Well, Stephan operates at about a hundred notches above that. He hacks into mainframes of large corporations and government agencies."

"What's he trying to steal?"

"He doesn't steal anything. He just likes to hack into a system and leave a message for the folks that he compromised their system. He does it for the challenge and the thrill of it."

"So you're thinking he could do that for us?"

"That's what I'm thinking, but you're going to have to convince him to do it for us."

"Why me?"

"Because you're the boss. He's very skeptical of government and big business. He sees us as both, but I've seen the change in you. I think you and Stephen may have a lot in common."

Robin was taken aback by Jamie's comment. "Am I doing something you don't like, Jamie?"

"It's not that, Rob. I think you're way ahead of the rest of us. We're all having our doubts about things we took for granted and believed in. It's kind of emotional for some of us."

"We'll have to discuss this more later. But I'll just say one thing now. If you or the others are thinking I'm losing my faith in this country, you're wrong. I *am* losing faith in our government, but I'm not losing faith in what this country stands for and I'll never lose faith in the American people."

Jamie smiled. "I think that's where we're all headed, Rob."

"All right, I'll talk to Stephan tomorrow around noon."

"I'll have Nikky put the meat pies on."

Robin laughed. "Great idea."

T hat evening the doorbell rang at the Marlette home. Robin looked through the security peephole and saw Chris Fleming standing at the door.

"Well, look what the cat dragged in." The two men hugged each other. "Karen, we have a visitor for dinner."

Karen came in and gave Chris a hug. "Hello, Chris. How are you doing?"

"I'm just an old retired guy now."

"You didn't bring Barbara?"

"No, she's up to her knees in grandkids, happy as a clam."

"Well, come to the dinner table. Robin, will you get our guest a drink?"

"What would you like, Chris?"

"Bourbon would be great, and please make it a double."

The three enjoyed a quiet dinner, the conversation carefully avoiding any mention of Beirut until Karen couldn't stand it anymore. "Why is it you men can't talk about things that need to be talked about?"

"What do you mean?" Chris asked.

"Beirut, Chris. You two haven't seen each other since the team got you out of there. Are you going to pretend there's nothing to talk about? Have you talked to anyone about it?"

Chris looked at his plate. "Just the formal debriefing and a visit with the psychologist."

"That's it?"

"Karen, they were just getting enough info to force me into retirement."

Karen stood, walked over to Chris and put her hand on his shoulder. "Chris, you have to talk about it. No one can go through what you did, keep it inside and remain sane."

Chris turned to Robin. "I do need to thank you, Rob. Somehow I knew you were coming and that thought kept me from giving up."

"What made you think we were coming?"

"It's just you. I knew if you found out I was kidnapped you'd come no matter what because that's just who you are. You would never abandon a friend. So, thank you."

"No thanks needed, brother."

"The bad thing about all of this is five good people died because of me."

"Five?"

"Five. In addition to Gary and Jason, a woman named Dialya and a taxi driver friend of hers were killed getting my report to the embassy. Then, of course, there's Steve Burns, the Beirut SAC. A heavy toll for my life. I don't think I'm worth it."

Robin got up and poured another bourbon for Chris and one for himself. He pulled a chair next to Chris.

Karen kissed Chris on the cheek and quietly walked away. "The truth is, Chris, you're not worth it. No one ever is. How do we justify trading one or more lives for another? It just can't be done. When such a thing happens, all the survivors can do is try to live the rest of their lives in a way that honors those who died. I think that's why Medal of Honor winners who survive say they wear the honor for those who didn't make it back. What else can you say?"

"None of that eases the pain."

"I didn't say it did. Watching Gary disappear in that flash is seared into my soul. It will haunt me for the rest of my days, and nights. But for us not to try to come get you was unthinkable. We all need to know that someone will at least try to help us if we are in a similar situation."

"I didn't see Dialya die, but her face haunts me at night. She comes first and then the others. It's getting to the point where I don't want to go to sleep anymore."

"Well, that's not going to work."

"You don't have to tell me."

"Chris, now that you're retired, you can come work with us."

"I would like to, but I've got to get to the bottom of something."

"What's that?"

"I need to find out more about the Nazi movement around the world and the full connection with Hezbollah."

"I thought you already knew there was a money connection."

"There's more to it, Rob. Something isn't right. I couldn't even get access to half the Nazi files maintained by the Bureau."

Robin tapped his fork on the table in a simple rhythm. "Chris, you've retired. You don't need to put yourself in the middle of something like this."

"Yes, I do. This all relates back to Beirut and, brother, I've got a grudge."

"Okay, we're working up a mission to learn more about all this. Your knowledge will be helpful. Join us."

Chris thought for a minute. "Did Ben give you the information from my interview?"

"Yes, he did. We're working with Mossad on this."

"Mossad is working with you guys?"

"Yep."

"You must have really impressed them. They don't normally work with people they don't know well."

"Let's just say they like the way we operate."

"Rob, you understand that when I say something isn't right, I'm talking about corruption. I smell a rat—a big one."

"We've been smelling the same rat, Chris. We've come across some very interesting shit the last couple of years. You'll be in good company."

Chris nodded. "I'll have to talk it over with Barbara."

"Hell, I insist you do."

"Thanks, Rob. Well, I'd better be going."

"You're out of your mind. You've had too much to drink. We have a guest house in back where you can stay. Everything you need is there."

Chris stood up and took an unsteady step. "Okay, you're right."

"Get your stuff and follow me." Robin led Chris to the guest house and showed him where to find what he needed.

"This is really nice, Rob. Thanks."

"Leave the window open a little so you can hear the waves. It may help you sleep. It does for me."

Chris nodded.

"Why don't you plan on spending the day with me tomorrow? I'd like to show you the company and give you an idea of what we do."

"I'd like that. I'll just have to check in with Barbara."

"You can use the phone over there."

"Thanks again."

"See you in the morning."

K aren was reading when Robin walked into their bedroom. She put down her book.

"Do you think Chris is all right?"

Robin thought for a moment. "No."

"What are you going to do about it?"

"Other than being there for him if he needs to talk, I don't know what else I could do about it. I'm not even sure if I'm the best person for the job."

"What about Kathleen?"

"Maybe later. Right now he's not too keen on mind doctors."

"I can't believe there's nobody."

"Well, actually there is—Barbara."

"Just because she's his wife you think she can solve his problems?"

Robin climbed into bed. "You do it for me. You're the best counselor I have."

"Really?"

"Really. You're my partner, best friend, lover, nurse and counselor—the one counselor that knows me better than anyone else and who I can trust with my heart and soul."

Karen laid her head on Robin's chest. "I do love you with all my heart, Robin."

"I love you that same way, Karen."

"We're so lucky."

"Yes we are."

T he next morning found Robin and Chris at the dock where the now imprisoned renegade General Picushkin's former ship was moored. The ship's name was changed to *Putinka* to honor the vodka drunk at the dinner where Robin and Alex Prokenzy, a Spetsnaz commander, had become friends.

"Wow, this is your ship, Rob?"

"It is."

"You guys must be doing very well."

"If you decide to join us, I'll tell the very interesting story of the ship and how it came to be ours."

As the men stepped on board, Nikky and Jamie greeted them at the gangway. Jamie waved at Chris.

"Captain Setchinko, this is Chris Fleming."

"Welcome aboard, Mr. Fleming," Nikky said, holding his hand out.

"Thank you, Captain." The men shook hands. "Jamie, how are you doing?"

"Couldn't be better. It's good to see you."

"Likewise."

Jamie turned to Robin. "Boss, you need to go to the com room. Grassley's on our secure line."

"Show Chris around, will you?"

"Will do."

Robin went to the com room, where Mark handed him a headset.

"Bill, you there?"

"Hi, Rob. I hear you need to talk to me."

"I do. We need some information."

"Before we get to business, how are you doing? I hope you've fully recovered."

"I'm good. Maria cleared us all for missions."

"So, now tell me how you really feel."

"We all still hurt in different places. You know how it goes. When you get shot, you tend to stay shot."

Bill let out a cynical laugh. "One of the great golden truths. So, how can I help you?"

"I need the location of Farrok Mokri and Hans Boorman."

Bill was silent for a moment. "What makes you think I know where they are?"

"I don't think that. I'm just asking if you have a way to find them."

"Why? If you're even slightly thinking about a revenge hit, you can forget it."

"This is not about a hit. Our goals are more strategic."

"I thought we gave you the strategic missions."

"You have one for us?"

"Not at the moment."

"Well, then this will have to do."

"You're such a goddamn pain in the ass, Rob. I'll get back to you."

CHAPTER SIXTEEN

R obin found Jamie showing Chris some of the more interesting equipment on the ship.

Chris looked impressed. "Jesus, Rob, this is one hell of a ship. You guys plan on fighting World War III?"

"Your top secret clearance is still good, isn't it?"

"For another eight months."

Robin handed Chris a manila envelope. "Fill out your renewal while Jamie and I take care of some business. It will take the government eight months to approve it."

Robin and Jamie started down to the staterooms.

"Hey, Stephan, I'd like you to meet Robin, our boss."

Robin held out his hand, but it took Stephan some time before he stood and shook hands with little enthusiasm.

"Thanks, Jamie. I got it from here."

"Okay, boss." Jamie left.

"Take a seat, Stephan," Robin said as he sat down. "Jamie has told me about you and what's going on. What do you think about all of this?"

"Boy, you get right to the point, don't you?"

"Unless I'm trying to bullshit somebody, and I have no intention of doing that with you."

"Why do I get special treatment?"

Robin looked directly at Stephan. "Because you're in a deadly serious predicament and you need straight info to make important decisions."

Stephan was quiet for a moment as he ran his fingers through his hair. "I can't believe I got myself into this mess."

Robin remained quiet, letting Stephan think.

Stephan stood up and started pacing. "Look, I'm scared. I'm scared of you guys, I'm scared of the Chinese and I'm scared of whoever else is looking for me."

"Who else would be looking for you?"

"I don't know. I didn't know about you guys or the Chinese until two nights ago."

Robin leaned back in his chair. "Well, you don't have to be afraid of us. We're not going to hurt you."

"Oh really? The first thing Jamie said to me was if I didn't cooperate, he'd shoot me on the spot."

Robin nodded. "That's when we had no idea who you were or what you were up to."

"Well, do you really shoot people?"

"Yes. We shoot members of drug cartels, hostage takers, terrorists, secret police types and people trying to detonate nuclear devices on innocent people."

"You're kidding me. Nuclear devices?"

"No joke," Robin replied.

"Do you guys work for the CIA?"

"No. We work for ourselves. But we do missions for the CIA if we like the mission and we've done work for other countries. We base our decision to take a mission on whether or not we are going after truly bad guys, not just some politically inconvenient person."

Stephan sat down. "Wow."

Robin leaned forward and looked at Stephan. "So the questions is, what am I going to do with you? Jamie thinks you could be an asset to our organization. He believes you're a genius with computers."

"I'm no genius. I'm a dunce with people. I've been told I'm a genius because of my IQ score, but I'm not convinced."

"Jamie says you learned your computer skills on your own."

"I did a lot of it, but I also have a PhD in computer science from the University of Washington."

Robin was surprised. "Jamie didn't tell me that."

"That's because I didn't tell him. It's not a great memory for me."

"Why?"

Stephan blew out a long breath of air. "After I got my PhD, I was offered an assistant professor position. I started teaching but it turned into a disaster. The students kept saying I was talking way over their heads and when I tried to make it simpler, I got all confused and just messed everything up. I got fired after that."

"Maybe you weren't cut out to be a teacher, but that doesn't mean you're not great at computers or any number of things."

"That's exactly what Professor Wong said."

A red flag went up in Robin's head. "Who's Professor Wong?"

"She's the one who sent me on the trip around the world. She bought me clothes and stuff and paid for everything. She only required that I go to China and talk to some people."

"Did she say why she was doing all that?"

"Yeah, she said I had a fine mind and needed exposure to other opportunities and possibilities."

"And that's how you got hooked up with Chinese intelligence," Robin said, almost to himself.

Stephan shook his head. "I didn't know they were Chinese intelligence. I met them at Jiaotong University in Shanghai. I thought they were professors and students. They never mentioned the government. They said they were forming a hacker's group to counter all oppression."

Rob saw an opening. "Are you really interested in fighting oppression?"

"I'm scared and confused. I don't know what I want."

Robin stood up and paced for a moment. "Okay, let me rephrase the question. Would you be *interested* in fighting oppression?"

Stephan looked at Robin, and in his eyes Robin saw a young man, alone and searching for a truth he could grab onto. "I would if I really believed that's what I was doing."

"All right, I'll show you what we do. I think you'll find that we are straight up guys that really do fight oppression and truly bad people. We could use your talents in our business."

"I don't want to be lied to."

"Stephan, if you join us, you'll be part of a family. An interesting family for sure, but a family. We don't lie to each other."

"Speaking of family, can I call my mother?"

Robin's internal alarm system lit up. "Where is your mother?"

"Aberdeen, Washington."

"Did this Professor Wong know about your mother?"

"Yes, she even met her a couple of times…" He bolted out of his chair. "Oh, no…you don't think…."

"Stay calm, Stephan. We'll figure this out."

CHAPTER SEVENTEEN

F arrok Mokri sipped tea at a corner cafe in the Plaka District of Athens, Greece. At his table, Lippio Kokinos, a commander in the militant arm of the Golden Dawn Nazi party, sipped a cup of coffee. The men surveyed the narrow street for anything out of place, anything that looked like a surveillance. Nothing was apparent.

Farrok breathed in the fresh afternoon spring air, filled with the fragrance of blooming flowers. *Not unlike spring in Tehran. Oh, how I wish they would call me back home.*

"The temperature is perfect today, Lippio."

"It usually is this time of year."

"Do you have the number of men we requested?"

"I do. All of them have had basic training and are eager to experience real operations."

"Were you able to obtain funding through your usual source?"

"Yes, the network is operating perfectly. Typical German efficiency."

"Excellent. Our Beirut friends are anxious for your arrival.

The additional manpower will allow more simultaneous operations."

"Are you leaving soon?"

"I am supposed to be in Austria tomorrow night, but I was thinking I'd like to enjoy the weather here for a few more days."

"Would Talia's company help you enjoy the weather?"

"Oh, well, if she is available and would like to see me, that would be wonderful."

"I'm sure Talia would enjoy your company again." Lippio leaned closer to Farrok. "My men are eager for the honor of killing Jews in the land they stole from the Palestinians."

Farrok patted Lippio's hand. "And you shall, my friend. You shall."

That afternoon, Emmett led a team of Mark, Willie and Doug and flew by helicopter to Aberdeen. They split up into pairs and took different routes to the address Stephan gave for his mother's house. When they arrived at the location, they didn't like what they saw.

Emmett signaled Mark and they pulled back from the area. He dialed Robin on the sat phone.

"Robin here."

"Hey, boss, we have problems. The local constabulary is crawling all over the house and talking to neighbors."

"I was afraid of that. Try to verify what's going on."

"Will do."

R obin had his hand on Stephan's shoulder as the man sobbed into his hands. "We're going to do everything we can to get her back, Stephan."

"It's all my fault. I'm such a goddamn stupid ass."

Robin sat down in front of the distraught young man. "Look at me, Stephan."

Stephan's bleary, tormented eyes met Robin's.

Robin's heart hurt for the man. "Stephan, you're far from stupid. We're very good at what we do, and we can get your mother back—and you can help. So, I need you to get over your guilt and get ready to fight with all your skills."

Stephan's eyes searched Robin's face in a way that made Robin think the kid was reading his mind. It felt a little spooky. "How do you know she's still alive?"

"Because she's no good to them dead."

Stephan inhaled deeply and straightened his back. "Tell me what to do. If we get my mother back, I'll do whatever you want me to for the company."

"We'll get your mother back, but I don't want you working for us because you feel obligated. I want you working for us because you believe in what we do. So, just hold that thought until we solve this problem."

"Okay, where do we start?"

"Jamie will take you to a computer store that has the equipment you want. There is no limit here. Get whatever equipment you even just dreamed about. I want you to be the most powerful hacker in the world. Does that work for you?"

Stephan's eyes were now shining. "I'm ready, Rob. Let's do it!"

M ark sat against a tree on a lawn at the University of
Washington in Seattle. He focused on the Electrical
Engineering and Computer Engineering Building. Mike
Collins, Doug Ariel, Willie Young and Lev Rogov were
watching other points, some in cars in case Professor Wong
went mobile. Robin had learned that, according to the CIA,
Professor Wong was a Chinese agent.

Doug's voice crackled in Mark's headset. "The subject is
leaving the parking lot in a Porsche 911, Washington plate
Echo One Seven Four Niner Charlie. She turned westbound.
We got the eye."

Mike Collins rolled up and Mark got in the car.

The professor drove through the University District, into
the Ballard District and made her way across the Aurora
Bridge. Then she headed west through Queen Anne and into
the Magnolia District. The team rotated the eyeball position,
but moving surveillance became difficult because of the light
traffic and predominately residential area. They lost the
professor for about fifteen seconds, but Willie sighted her just
as she turned into a waterfront house near Discovery Park.

Mark called Robin and reported the surveillance
information.

"Good job, Mark. I want you to head to Paine Field and
get one of the pilots to take you on an overflight of the
professor's house. Tell the rest of the team to head to
Anacortes and wait for us on *Putinka*."

"Will do, boss."

L ater that day, Robin stood at the top of the boarding and
deboarding stairs in Fatboy that led to the tarmac at
Paine Field. "I don't know how Bill managed to find out

Mokri is in Greece so fast, but remember, Ernie, we want to learn as much as we can about these guys' activities, but we don't want to get burned."

Ernie got a mischievous grin on his face. "Hell, Rob, I'm going to stretch this out as far as we can so I can have European vacation. Are you going to get Bill and the FBI involved in Stephan's mother's case?"

"I already alerted him. He agrees that if the Chinese have taken Stephan's mother, we'll have a better chance of finding her faster than the FBI can."

"Meaning play hard ball with Professor Wong."

"Unless you have a better lead."

"I don't know about doing that kind of op on our home turf. It could get sticky."

"We'll figure it out, Ernie. Quit worrying."

"All right. I'll just have fun in Greece."

"Well, then I'll just get my sorry ass off this plane."

Ernie waved and Robin headed down the stairs.

I n the early evening, Robin parked his car at Cap Sante Park in Anacortes. The park provided a breathtaking view of the Port of Anacortes from the marina across the shipping lanes to the San Juan Islands and the surrounding area. He walked to the edge of the overlook and stood next to Bill Grassley. Bill's most trusted security agent stood twenty feet away. Robin didn't see any of the others. "You didn't waste any time getting here, Bill."

Bill continued to take in the view for a few moments. "Things are getting more than a little strange in D.C., Rob."

Robin started to make a crack that D.C. was just strange, period, but thought better of it.

"Ever since Chris got onto this investigation about

Hezbollah and the Nazis, we have been tasked with some interesting operations by the National Security Council staff with increasing frequency. All of them ostensibly have to do with terrorism—and all of them are pure bullshit."

"Sounds like a smoke screen."

Bill smiled. "You've always been able to see through the smoke, and you're right about this smoke screen. With the exception of Ernie, what I'm about to tell is for your ears only. As things progress, that can change."

"Understood."

Bill took a deep breath. "We have a serious problem in our national security apparatus."

"Breach?"

"I wish it was that simple. It's not a breach, it's a movement—a movement I believe is designed to undermine the very principles upon which our nation was founded."

"And start the takeover of the country."

Bill gave Robin a surprised look. "I take it you've already figured this out."

"No, I'm just following the logic of your observation. Our founding principles were designed to prevent any one group from getting too much political power. If someone is trying to undermine those principles, their goal must be the takeover of the country."

"That seems to be the case. I'm not really sure who the suspect or suspects should be. There are people who have been appointed to national security positions that have no real national security or intelligence experience, but they've been put in positions to make decisions about the allocation of assets and to direct operations in terms of targets for investigation. Right now they're concentrating on signals intelligence and almost shutting down our human intelligence capability."

"Why would they shut down HUMINT assets and just rely on SIGINT?"

"My opinion is they can control the message better. With HUMINT assets there's always a loose end."

"The human. Why are you telling me this?"

"Mokri and Boorman. You've hit a nerve."

Now Robin was quiet. "So people know we're looking at him?"

"No, they think the CIA is. I'm stretching my authority giving you this information. You know the CIA cannot operate in this country. I have a very confidential informant, known only to me, who has given me information on this Mokri. There is some serious shit afloat, Rob. We need to know what it is and I need people I can trust to find it out."

"I understand, Bill." Robin smiled and put his hand on Bill's shoulder. "We'll get what you need." He nodded to Bill's security agent. "Is he the only one you can completely trust?"

"He's been with me from the start. So, at this point, yes. Him, Director Yates and you."

"What does Director Yates think about all this?"

"We seriously discussed resigning but have decided to stay to minimize damage as much as we can."

"Good call. Anything else?"

Bill was quiet for a few seconds. "I need you to use your best judgment, Rob, including about where this mission will take you. I can't be in contact with you on a regular basis."

"We're on it, Bill. We've started changing the scramble code on the sat phones every hour, instead of every four. That way you can talk to us on a secure line anytime."

"Thanks, Rob. That helps, but it will still be difficult for me to be in regular contact. I'm being watched and monitored."

Robin looked at his friend. "That's a dark sign, Bill. Why don't they just fire you?"

Bill just looked out over the water, and then shrugged. "They can, but they're not making any noises about doing so."

Robin looked at Bill. "This worries me. Maybe they don't want to fire you because they want to know where you are. Do you think you're in danger?"

"Yes. I just don't know who or why."

"You think this Iranian knows?"

"I'm told there's a good chance he does."

"If he knows, we'll find out."

"Thanks, Rob. I'll see you later tonight."

CHAPTER EIGHTEEN

Doug Ariel squared himself away in the rigid inflatable boat and looked at Robin standing on the rear deck of *Putinka* in the darkness. Lev Rogov, who had just finished his training, was with him, along with Mark. Willie, Mike and Rick were in another RIB. The night ocean air was cool and dense with moisture that clung to his face. A fog was building over Puget Sound and getting thicker.

"We're ready, boss."

"Roger. Away all boats." Robin and Nikky pushed the two RIBs into the sea. The SEAL modified engines started. The modifications made the engines much quieter. The two teams headed for the shore of Discovery Park, near Professor Wong's home. Doug was leading the mission and was a little nervous. They were to scout the professor's property for any sign of Stephan's mother. This meant absolutely no contact and no compromise of their presence. He knew it could get tricky, as the over flight showed the property had two homes and several outbuildings.

It was Robin's intention to have the FBI HRT do the actual

rescue, so the team had to learn enough information about the property and buildings to pass on to HRT for their planning, assuming they located Stephan's mom. If they did, Doug was to send an immediate coded message to *Putinka* with the word "Mother."

After ten minutes, Doug gave the signal to slow down. The light from West Point Lighthouse lit up the fog to his left with a ghostly glow. That told him they were on course. The boats were moving slow enough so the engines made almost no sound. *Thank God for SEAL ingenuity.* He swept the area with an infrared scope looking for heat signatures of people. The park was supposed to be closed, but Doug knew that didn't mean much to teenagers, insomniacs and lovers. It looked clear, so he waved the boats forward.

They rode the boats in on a small wave, jumped out and pulled them into a stand of brush and trees.

"Check weapons," Doug ordered in a whisper.

The teams were carrying suppressed pistols, only to be used in a life- threatening situation. Stealth was the word of the night. Weapons check completed, the men moved out along the brush line toward the property. They were all dressed in black wet suits, black balaclavas and rubber-soled booties. A tactical vest with a small backpack containing swim fins completed their equipment. If necessary, they could take to the sea to avoid detection and swim back to rendezvous with *Putinka*.

The six men blended into the brush and trees as they moved towards the property. It took two minutes for them to get there.

Doug surveyed the home and the area around it with night vision. He didn't see any people, but he could see surveillance cameras. He watched them for a few minutes and decided they were stationary. He knew, however, that movement sensors were probably on the property. He switched to the infrared scope and looked for light beams that would indicate perimeter sensors. He didn't see any. He turned to Mark and whispered, "Okay, brother, do your thing. They have video like you said, and that probably means motion sensors, but no laser or infrared."

Mark nodded and slipped off towards the main house.

Doug, Lev and Willie prepared to move on Mark's word. Mike and Rick were to hang back as a reaction force in case of trouble. Doug figured the fewer people wandering around the property, the better.

R obin spoke into his headset. "You awake, Bill?"
"Yes, I'm awake, smart ass."

Robin laughed. "Just making sure you haven't gone soft with that office job of yours."

"Thanks a lot."

"The team has inserted. We should know what the score is pretty soon. Doug reports no surprises on the layout so far."

"In that case, we're going to move into the area and get ready."

"Roger, but be careful. It's tight in that neighborhood."

"Understood."

M ark worked quickly once he got to the power box. He put a plastic tube with a plunger over the wire with an active transmitter and signal filter inside. It had an electrical connection to a battery. The system, built by Andy Jackson, was designed to turn off surveillance cameras and motion sensors. At the same time, it would freeze frame the receiver/recorder for a maximum of thirty minutes. It had worked in all the trials. Mark hoped to hell it would work tonight. He pushed the plunger, closed the panel door and moved behind a bush in a crouch. A full minute passed with no reaction.

"SpearTip Eight to SpearTip Seven...we're good."

"Roger, we're moving in."

D oug and Lev ghosted around the right side of the main house and headed for the rear cottage. They stopped briefly at the two out buildings, but only found lawn mowers and gardening equipment. They moved on to the cottage. Doug went left and Lev went to the right side.

Lev came to a door and listened. He could hear a man speaking with a harsh voice. He moved to the window and rose up along the edge. A woman who matched the picture of Mrs. Gulasky lay tied to a bed. A Chinese man was pacing back and forth, verbally berating her.

Mrs. Gulasky looked defiant. Lev heard her say, "How many times do I have to tell you? I don't know where my son is, but even if I knew, I wouldn't tell you a damn thing."

The man became more agitated.

Lev keyed his mic. "SpearTip Seven, SpearTip One Four, I found her. Come over to my side."

The Chinese man yelled at Mrs. Gulasky again. She spit on him and he hit her across the face with the back of his hand. He reached into his coat and pulled out a knife.

Lev reacted on pure instinct and training. He went through the door, drawing his Glock and confronted a man sitting in a chair. Lev's leg rose in a roundhouse kick that sent the man flying. Continuing through the door to Mrs. Gulasky, he came face to face with her tormentor and his knife. Lev side stepped and shot the man two times in the chest and two times in the head. The man fell forward in mid step. Lev spun around to face the sound behind him. It was Doug.

"Jesus, Lev," Doug blurted. "What the hell happened...? Oh, fuck it. Get Mrs. Gulasky." Doug keyed his mic. "SpearTip Eight to SpearTip, we have Mother and are moving out."

Lev untied a terrified Mrs. Gulasky. "It is okay, madam, we're taking you to Stephan."

Doug could see the woman was confused by Lev's Russian accent. "We're here to rescue you, Mrs. Gulasky and we gotta move now."

She took a step and her legs collapsed under her. "Damn, my legs are asleep." Lev gathered the woman in his arms, carrying her as they headed out.

Robin's voice was in Doug's headset. "What's the status, Eight?"

"We got Mother. She's safe. Our friends will have to handle a complication."

"How bad?"

"Terminal."

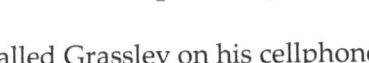

R obin called Grassley on his cellphone.
"Yeah, Rob."
"Better get in there, Bill. The team took Mother and apparently killed one or more of the bad guys."

"Goddammit, Rob!"

"Don't jump to conclusions, just get in there."

Grassley hung up.

T he team moved down the beach. As they neared the boats, they could see two young women standing by them. Mark approached them.

"Excuse me, ladies, you do know the park is closed don't you?"

"Who the hell are you?"

"United States Coast Guard. We're conducting a counter terrorism drill. I advise you to leave the park, as other law enforcement personnel are coming into the area."

The two women looked at each other and then hurried down the trail to the park entrance.

"Good line of bullshit, Mark," Doug commented.

"Thanks."

Mrs. Gulasky looked at the men and asked, "Who are you?"

"We're friends of your son," Doug replied.

"Are you really taking me to him?"

"Yes, ma'am. You'll see him in about twenty minutes." He put a blanket around her shoulders. "You're safe now, Mrs. Gulasky."

B ill Grassley watched intently as the Hostage Rescue Team banged on the front door of Professor Wong's residence.

"FBI, SEARCH WARRANT!"

After waiting ten seconds, an agent swung a battering ram and smashed open the door. The stack moved in and spread out through the house. Over the radio Bill heard calls of "Clear" as the house was methodically cleared. Two calls of "suspect in custody" followed. A call from the smaller house confirmed a body and one injured Asian man.

"Ready, Bill?" asked Pat Chaslin, the supervising special agent for the FBI Seattle office Counter Intelligence Unit.

"Yeah, let's go see who we have in there."

The men entered and were directed upstairs to the master bedroom. Bill went through the door and saw an Asian woman who matched the photograph. Her hair was askew and her mouth was bent in a frown. Her eyes hardened when she saw Pat and Bill, who were dressed in suits instead of tactical gear.

"I demand to know why my house has been invaded!"

"Good morning, Professor Wong...or should I say Captain Xiaoli Lin," Pat replied.

The professor stiffened. "I don't know what you're talking about. I'm Professor Elaine Wong with the University of Washington."

"Captain Lin, we know who you really are and that you work for Ministry of State Security under the Second and Tenth Bureaus."

"I demand the Chinese Embassy be contacted immediately."

"Certainly, Captain. You see, there is the matter of the kidnapping of Mrs. Gulasky and the death of one of your agents we need to discuss with the Ambassador."

Captain Lin turned and stared at the wall. Bill took no pleasure in seeing the blood drain from her face. She would be immediately sent back to China in exchange for a Japanese intelligence agent being held by the Chinese and their guarantee that Stephan and his mother would be left alone. The Chinese government would lose face. There was no doubt in Bill's mind that Captain Lin would disappear from the face of the earth.

"**M**om!"
"Oh, Stephan. Thank God."

Mother and son embraced, and Robin felt an immense weight lift off his shoulders. He noticed that Mrs. Gulasky was dressed in a flannel shirt and jeans that appeared a little too large for her small wiry frame. She wore good quality hiking boots. Her face was tan with laugh lines that indicated years outdoors. She didn't appear to be the shy, retiring type.

"Mom, your face...what happened?"

Mrs. Gulasky burst into tears. "Oh, Stephan, I was so worried about you. Where have you been?"

"We can talk about that later, Mom. Are you okay?"

"I was being held by some real bastards, son. One of them hit me just before these gentlemen rescued me," she said in a husky voice.

Willie came in with his medical bag. "Here, Mrs. Gulasky, sit down and let me have a look at that bruise."

"Oh, it's nothing, young man."

"Ma'am, I'm a medic and you've taken a solid hit there. How 'bout you just sit down and let me do my thing?"

Mrs. Gulasky looked at Willie with a bemused smile. "Well, I guess I could use a sit-down for a spell."

Stephan hovered around his mother while Willie finished giving her first aid.

"There you go, ma'am. I'll go make an ice bag for you to keep the swelling down."

"Thank you, sir."

"I'm Willie, ma'am. You don't have to call me sir."

"Thank you, Willie."

Stephan looked up at Robin. "Mom, I want you to meet the commander of this group."

Robin stepped over to Mrs. Gulasky. "Hello, Mrs. Gulasky. I'm Robin. We're very happy you're okay."

"Thank you so much for coming for me. I was a little worried about what those men might do to me."

"Well, they've been taken care of. You don't have to worry about them anymore."

Mrs. Gulasky looked over at Lev and rose up from her chair. She stepped over to him and put her arms around him. "Thank you so much. You saved me from that awful man."

"I am happy I was there in time, madam."

Willie came back with an ice pack. "Mrs. Gulasky why don't you come with me? I have a place ready for you to lie down and get some rest."

"I could use some sleep, Willie," Mrs. Gulasky said with a tired voice. "I'm afraid I'm exhausted."

Willie took her by the hand and Stephan followed them to the lower deck.

R obin looked over at Lev. "Okay, Lev, sit down and tell us what happened."

Lev dropped into a chair and rubbed his forehead. "I worked with Doug. We went to opposite sides of the small house. I heard some yelling and moved to the window. I saw Mrs. Gulasky on a bed and a Chinese agent interrogating her. He hit her and pulled out a knife." Lev took a deep breath. "The next thing I knew I was in the house. I knocked out a man in the front room. I went into the room where Mrs. Gulasky was, and the interrogator came at me with the knife. I did as I was trained. Two shots to center mass and two shots to the head.

"Doug came into the room and told me to take the hostage and move out." Lev seemed to slump when he finished.

"In retrospect, is there anything you could've done differently?"

Lev raised his head and looked at Robin, shrugged and shook his head.

"Neither do I." He looked at the team members present. "Any one see a problem?"

"Yeah, I do," Mark spoke up. He went over to Lev and put his hand on his shoulder. "Lev, you know you did the right thing, brother. Next time, act like you know it."

"Good job, Lev," Robin added. "All right guys, why don't you get a beer? Lev and I have another matter to discuss."

The other team members filed out of the salon.

"Lev, you have had the very unpleasant experience of killing a man for the first time. Tell me how you're feeling about that."

Lev thought for a moment. "The best word I can think of is confused. I felt anger and the desire to kill him when I pulled the trigger, but the reality of it all is my body acted like a machine. I reacted to what was in front of me. I'm confused because, at this moment, I wish I felt something when I shot him, but I don't think I really felt anything except fear." Lev tried to choke back the last word.

"How do you feel now?"

"Sick."

"Lev, everything you felt at the time of the shooting and what you're feeling now, including the fear, is normal. I know you're a good man, or you wouldn't be here. Good men don't like to hurt anyone, let alone kill someone. But you know as well as I do that some people, very bad people, need to die so they won't hurt others. That's what you did this morning. To be in this business and survive, psychologically, you have to have mental and emotional agility to sort things out."

Lev nodded. "They told us that in training."

"I'm going to set you up for a meeting with an Army psychiatrist. She's Burke's fiancé. I think you'll find it helpful to talk to her."

"Do you think I might go crazy?"

Robin laughed. "No, Lev. We've all talked to her at one time or another. She'll help you sort things out. She won't disclose what you say to her to anyone."

"Okay, Rob." Lev stared at the floor and rubbed his temples.

"Lev, what else is bothering you?"

Lev slowly looked up. "What do I tell Rada?"

"Ah, I don't think I can be any help there, brother, except that you need to tell her the truth."

"She is going to be very upset."

"Yep, you can count on that. She'll also be frightened. All natural reactions."

"How did Karen learn to accept you might have to kill someone?"

"She never has."

A breath left Lev's mouth with a whoosh. "Telling her about this is going to be difficult."

"It always is, Lev. Always."

After being up for thirty-six hours, Robin finally lay in bed trying to give in to sleep. His mind kept replaying the recent events like a looped video tape. Karen's even breathing gave some comfort, but he couldn't relax. His subconscious mind puzzled on something, trying to figure it out and bring it to light.

Finally, exhaustion started claiming its supremacy and pulling Robin into the dark world of sleep. As he slipped away the phrase, "Good men don't want to kill anyone," floated in his thoughts. A pure thought, but at the same time, a disquieting one.

CHAPTER NINETEEN

Carlos Casconda looked down the hall at Ernie who did a quick look around and gave Carlos the go-ahead signal. Carlos picked the lock on Farrok Mokri's suite at the Kivonos Hotel on Mykonos Island, Greece and entered the room, closing the door behind him. The room had already been cleaned by room service, so Carlos had to be careful not to leave anything looking out of place. The former Cuban intelligence agent's years of experience and recent training by American special ops teams made his search quick and efficient. A miniature Minolta camera captured information on the target and the woman staying with him, Talia Megalos. He smiled at the liquor and wine in the room. Apparently, Mr. Mokri was not exactly a devout Muslim.

He then planted several bugs in the room and in the phone. One more quick sweep and he was out, the room secured. Carlos made his way out of the hotel while Ernie went to the bar to sip on a beer for a while, so as to not appear connected to each other. Eventually, Ernie showed up at the car they were using.

"How'd it go?"

"Fine. It felt good to be operating again. I have a lot of photos we need to get developed."

"Anything of immediate interest?"

"Her name is Talia Megalos and she's a member of the Golden Dawn. I believe that's the Nazi party in Greece."

"Hmm, interesting, though not totally surprising since Muslims and Nazis both hate Jews. We know they were connected in Beirut. I wish we knew where Boorman went."

"Can't have everything, I guess."

"Did you run into any Nazis when you worked for Cuba?"

"When I worked in South America, before joining Rodriquez, I worked on locating concentrations of Nazis. The Cuban Communist Party thought it important to do since Nazis hate communists too. The party was always afraid the new Nazis would join forces with the US."

"I've heard there were Nazis in South America. Did you find a lot of them?"

"You would be surprised. There is actually quite a few, especially in Argentina, Brazil and Chile."

"Really? Do you mean real German Nazis or new wannabes?"

"Both."

"I guess you learn something new every day. As interesting as all that is, I doubt we'll be playing footsies with Nazis over this guy. He's just getting some ass on the Iranian government's dime."

Carlos shrugged. "You never know."

"Let's get that film to our man, Neo, so we can see what you found."

Neoptolemos Contos, known to the team as Neo, was the company's rep in Greece. He was medically retired from the Hellenic Air Force for injuries he suffered after ejecting from an F-16 fighter with catastrophic engine failure. Neo had jet black hair, a bushy mustache and a ready smile. Ernie and Carlos met him at the hotel at where he, Burke and Rick were staying. The owner was a native of Mykonos and an old friend of Neo's, so he helped the team get things quickly. They found all four men drinking coffee in the dining room.

"Damn, isn't it Miller time?" Ernie cracked.

"It should be, but you put us on the night shift," Rick groaned.

"Oh yeah, I forgot."

"Sure you did, boss."

"Hey, Neo. We need to get this film processed quickly. Any suggestions?"

Pali, the owner of the hotel stood and put out his hand. "Give it to me, and I'll have it back in an hour."

Carlos handed the film over to him and Pali walked out of the room.

Nine o'clock the next morning, Robin was talking to Ernie on the secure phone at his home.

"How's the surveillance going?"

"Pretty good, Rob. Mokri isn't doing much other than having a good time. We have no idea where Boorman is, but we got into Mokri's hotel room and learned some things."

"Like what?"

"His itinerary, for one. We may not know when he's going to these places because he seems to do what he pleases, but we know where he wants to go and in what order. He's going to be traveling for a while, at least four to six months."

"Damn, that could put a crimp in our style."

"I have a suggestion."

"Shoot."

"Let's get *Putinka* over here. Her capabilities would come in handy."

"It'll take about a month for her to get there, even with her new cruising speed," Robin pointed out.

"I know, but we'll have plenty of time to use her."

"You're right. It'll be a good test for her and her crew. I'll get them going on it today."

"If I know Nikky, he's ready to go now."

Robin laughed. "You're probably right about that. Well, you get some sleep, Ernie. And you guys keep your eyes peeled."

"Will do, Rob."

CHAPTER TWENTY

Burke finished connecting the bug to the car battery lead to the dashboard of Mokri's rental car. He lifted his head just high enough to look around the immediate area of the car in the hotel parking lot. He keyed his mic. "Am I clear to exit, Rick?"

The answer was a whispered, "Don't move."

Burke froze, which was painful for him because his six–two frame was scrunched up in the floorboard. His ears searched for any sound he could identify as a threat. He heard what sounded like a police radio. Then a light flitted around the car. *Oh, shit...cops.* The sound of a car engine slowly came closer. The search light kept moving around. The engine was now very near and not moving. A car door opened.

Burke took a deep breath and held it. Footsteps went by the car. Then a strange sound, like water hitting pavement. A smile came over Burke's face. The guy was taking a piss. The water stopped and footsteps went back to the police car. The door closed and the car drove away.

"Clear to exit," Rick said.

Burke spoke into the bug. "Can you hear me?"

"Loud and clear."

Burke opened the passenger door and snaked his body out. In a crouch, he moved over to Rick's car. He got in and was greeted by Rick's big grin.

"Bet your gonads were crawling back up."

"They were, right up until I heard the piss."

"Cops are the same everywhere."

"I don't recall us ever pissing in the parking lot of a classy hotel."

"Maybe not, but when ya gotta go, ya gotta go."

"Hey, Ernie, come here," Emmett said, pressing his earphones to his ears.

"What's up?"

"Our Iranian friend is getting chewed out by Boorman."

"What's he saying?"

"Boorman is telling Mokri to get his ass to Austria and how they need to meet with somebody named Felsa. Okay, the call is over...wait. He's dialing again. Ah, okay, he's making plane reservations to Vienna, Austria. The call from Boorman certainly lit a fire under him."

Ernie nodded. "Get that recording to Jaime so it can be fully transcribed."

"Will do." Emmett pushed the earphones closer. "It seems like Mokri and his lady are leaving the room now. I'll alert surveillance."

Burke put down his sat phone. "Emmett says our targets are coming out."

Rick keyed the mic to his radio. "Get ready to move. Targets are coming out. We'll have the eyeball."

Rocky and Marv acknowledged the call.

The couple came out and got into the car.

"Son of a bitch didn't even open the door for her," Burke noted.

"Women are second class citizens to many Muslims," Rick said.

"This guy ain't no devout Muslim."

Mokri started the car and the bugs turned on.

"...I don't think it's asking much from you, Farrok. I'm beginning to feel like the party whore instead of a contributing member of the Fourth Reich," Talia said.

"You mustn't feel that way, Talia. I like you very much and enjoy your company."

"Then show me some respect and tell Lippio to send me to Hezbollah with the commando team. I want to fight for the Reich."

An exasperated breath seemed to come from Mokri. "You can be a stubborn woman, Talia. All right, I'll tell Lippio to put you on the team."

"Thank you, Farrok." Talia's voice took on a husky tone. "I will really thank you when we get back to the room after dinner."

"Mmm, I think I made the correct decision."

The couple pulled into the parking lot of a small restaurant and the bugs went dead.

R obin sat in the conference room on board *Putinka* with Jamie, Stephan, Mrs. Gulasky and Nikky.

"Okay, Jamie, I've seen that look before," Robin said. "What have you got up your sleeve?"

"Boss, you know at this point we can't really let Mrs. Gulasky leave us without protection."

"I've thought about that."

"Well, this morning, we woke up to the greatest breakfast I've had in a long time."

Nikky nodded. "I affirm that assessment."

Robin looked over at Mrs. Gulasky. "I take it you're responsible for the gastric enthusiasm, ma'am. Do you have experience cooking for a group of hungry men?"

"First, please call me Liz. I'm not a formal person."

"Okay, Liz it is."

"Good. Before I married Stephan's father, I cooked on fishing boats and at hunting and fishing lodges during the different seasons. When Stephan was born, I just took him with me. I did it until Stephan started school. After Steve died, I couldn't go back to doing that kind of work because I would never be home."

"I think after the last couple of days you have an idea of what we do. While this ship is relatively unknown, there can be danger just being associated with her and us."

"I think you've already pointed out I'm in danger wherever I am. This would appear to be the safest place for me to be for now."

Robin sipped his coffee. "I've ordered Captain Setchinko to set sail for Europe. If you stay, it will be for the long haul."

"Actually, it sounds exciting. I love the sea."

"Then perhaps you've found a new home. I'll have some of the team get with you so we can secure your home and belongings."

"That will be fine, Robin. Thank you."

"Stephan, I trust you have everything you need now."

"I do, Rob. I never expected to have such wonderful equipment and software. You guys moved too fast for me to help finding mom, but I'm ready to help."

"Good. I have to talk to our team in Europe. I'll see you all later."

R obin stood in the com center on Fatboy listening to Ernie. "Those are very interesting intercepts. Do we have any idea when he's leaving for Austria?"

"In three days. I'm going to try to get someone on his flight, but it will help if you go to Vienna and cover the airport, boss."

"Roger that. Send the flight info to Jamie. What are you going to do about this commando unit going to Hezbollah?"

Ernie sighed. "I hope we can identify this Lippio guy. Then we'll see where we go from there. But considering Jamie couldn't find jack shit on this Felsa character, I'm not holding my breath."

"Jamie just tried to run that name, Lippio, but there's a couple of hundred Lippios running around there. We'll probably need a picture of the guy."

"We'll work on it." Ernie promised.

"Be safe, brother."

"You too."

T he man who called himself Jake Schmidt was frustrated. He had been to the house of his new target no less than twenty times in three days at different times of the day and night. His family was there, but Chris Fleming appeared to be nowhere around. He had chosen not to break into the house, because the neighborhood was well-to-do and it appeared many of the neighbors were retired. Too easy to be spotted.

He had chanced doing some surveillance around the Phoenix FBI office to see if the retired agent would visit there but had no luck. Other clients needed attention. He would have to tell the Raven to update the information on Fleming if he wanted quick results.

R obin knocked on the door of a home in Mulkiteo, Washington. Ellie Perkins, Gary's widow, opened the door and a sad smile graced her face as she hugged Robin.

"Oh, it's good to see you, Rob. Please come in. Would you like some coffee? The pot is fresh."

"That would hit the spot."

Ellie poured two cups of coffee and they went out to the back deck. The Perkins' home was set on a hillside with a grand view of Possession Sound and Whidbey Island.

"I want to thank you again for the beautiful service, Rob. It meant a lot to me and the family. I never dreamed Gary would be buried at Arlington and that he would be awarded the CIA star the Distinguished Service Cross."

"He died for his country, Ellie. He really deserves the Congressional Medal of Honor, but that would draw publicity. We just wanted to honor him." Robin sipped his coffee. "So, how are you getting along?"

"I'm all right. Each day gets a little easier..." The composure broke and tears started flowing down her cheeks. "I miss him so much."

Robin leaned forward and took Ellie's hands into his. "We all do, Ellie. Gary was a good man we all relied on."

"He loved working on the team. He said he never felt so alive, except when he was with me, of course." She smiled.

"He wasn't kidding about that, Ellie. He spoke of you often and the plans you had."

Ellie looked into Robin's eyes as if searching them. "What does the team feel about his death? Truthfully, Robin."

"He gave his life so we could live, Ellie. Our hearts and guts have been ripped out."

"Rocky and Ernie have told me some of the men blame you for his death."

"Some are questioning my judgment." Robin shrugged. "It comes with the territory."

"How do you feel about it?"

Robin thought for a moment. "As I sort through it, I'm humbled by Gary's bravery and love for the team. But make no mistake about it, part of me died in that horrible blast."

Ellie stood and led Robin to the edge of the deck. Cream-colored clouds floated against a shining blue sky. The water lay smooth and calm. "Gary loved to sit here and watch nature go by. Both of us were thankful this ended up being our home. His spirit is here, Rob, and he is at peace. Of all the men on the team, he had the most respect for you. He told me you always seemed to have a grasp of the situation and never ran out of ideas." Ellie turned and looked at Robin. "He also said you were haunted by the worry you might lose a member of the team. Now you have. Are you going to be all right?"

"You're a wonderful lady, Ellie. But I'm not as wonderful as Gary may have tried to portray me. I have a deep hurt that will never go away and I can't do much about that." Robin's voice turned cold. "But I also have a raging anger, and there are people who are going to eventually pay for Gary's death.

Not just the soldiers we killed in Beirut, but those who sent them. Then I'll be all right."

Ellie put her arms around Robin's neck, her lips close to his ear. "Find them, Rob. Find them and rip their hearts out — like they did to me."

CHAPTER TWENTY-ONE

Three days later, the surveillance following Mokri and Talia to Athens ended at a parking lot next to the Glyfada Arena and very close to the Ellinkon International Airport. It was an open area on one side and the team had to scramble to keep a visual and bug reception without being detected.

When Mokri parked, a man got out of another car and climbed into the back of his rental. Ernie gave thanks the day was warm so that Mokri kept the air conditioning going, which also kept the bugs the had team planted activated.

Mokri greeted the man. "Good afternoon, Lippio, how are you this fine day?"

"I'm good. What did you need to talk to me about?"

"I want you to allow Talia to join the commandos going to Lebanon."

"Farrok..."

Mokri raised his hand. "Come now, Lippio, Talia has been a loyal member of the party and she wants to fight for the Reich."

"I will have to talk to Xander about this."

Through the binoculars, Ernie could see Mokri turn and face Lippio.

"Excellent idea. Then I will not have to."

There was silence for a moment. "I hope you know what you are getting yourself into, Talia."

"I am not afraid, Lippio."

"That's unfortunate, because you should be."

"Good, it is settled then," said Mokri. "I will not forget this, Lippio. Now if you will help Talia with her baggage, I must get to the airport."

Ernie saw Lippio and Talia get out of the car and go to the trunk. They each took a bag out and then Talia went to the driver's window and kissed Mokri. Mokri waved and drove off.

"Okay, team, we'll stick with this Lippio and Talia," Ernie transmitted. "Carlos can handle Mokri at the airport."

Carlos sat in the terminal for the Lufthansa flight to Vienna. He had his briefcase in his lap and felt the vibration of his sat phone. He opened the case and saw a message telling him Mokri was on his way to the airport. He closed his case and folded his arms over it. Now all he had to do was make sure he got off the plane quick enough to keep track of Mokri.

A few minutes later, Mokri came into the terminal and took a seat. He busied himself by reading a magazine until the flight was announced with the call for first-class passengers. Carlos stood and noticed Mokri also stood up. He waited to make sure Mokri was in line ahead of him.

When the line got to the cabin of the plane, Carlos was surprised and pleased that he would be sitting next to Mokri. This was going to be a golden opportunity and Carlos would do his best to exploit it. It was a good day to fly.

I t became apparent to the rest of the team following Lippio that he was an experienced operator. He made counter surveillance moves at least every five minutes. This included pulling over to the side of the road, making quick turns without signaling and blowing stop signs or lights. Although good moves, they didn't take into account the team members paralleling the surveillance on side roads. Whenever he pulled one of these maneuvers, causing the eyeball cars to break off, the parallel cars would take over the lead position while the eyeball cars became the parallel cars. It was a system in which the Guardians were well practiced.

Lippio drove to a large plaza Ernie's map identified as Omonoia Square. He then went west where Ernie noticed the buildings were rundown and a rougher looking populace walked the streets. Lippio went into frenzied driving but stayed within a one mile radius. Ernie knew they were close to Lippio's destination, but it wouldn't be long before the suspicious eyes on the street would peg them as intruders, even as the day was fading into night.

"All units, put a man on foot," Ernie ordered. Marv, Rocky, and Burke all got out onto the streets at different locations.

The mobile units were able to follow Lippio for three more minutes before they lost him. Ernie keyed his mic. "Subject was last seen about a quarter mile west of the square."

"SpearTip Three, I'm in that area," Burke replied.

"I'm out of pocket," Marv said.

"SpearTip Nine, I'll catch up to you, Three," Rocky said. He started moving at a trot and turned down an alley. Three men stood in a group in the middle of the narrow passage. Rocky started to their right. They saw him and moved to head him off. Rocky slowed to a walk. One of them said something in Greek in a threatening voice.

"Hey, guys, I don't want any trouble," Rocky said in a calm steady voice.

"American!" the man closest to him said in English. "You have money. Give it to us."

Rocky shook his head. "Nope."

The man pulled a knife and stepped closer to Rocky, jabbing at him. Rocky fended off the knife with his forearm, stepped into his assailant and at the same time used his left arm to trap the man's knife hand against his hip with a circular motion. He smashed two quick punches into the robber's throat and rotated his body to the right, along with the trapped arm, causing a crack to resound in the alley. The man uttered what would have been a scream—if his throat was still working—and collapsed. The other two men looked at their companion with wide eyes and hesitated for a moment, turned and ran down the alley. Rocky resumed his trot to back up Burke.

After two blocks, Rocky called Burke on his radio. "Three, where are you?"

"I don't know. I don't understand the street signs."

"Check your GPS."

"Standby…" Burke then read off his coordinates.

"Got it. I'm close," Rocky acknowledged.

"Okay, come until you're a block away. There's security all over the place."

"Cops?"

"Negative."

"Oh, roger," Rocky said realizing Burke meant other bad guys.

Rocky made his way to within a block of Burke's location. "I'm here, Three."

"Okay, work your way east on the north side of the street. I'll come west on the south side. Their car is parked on the south side, but I don't know what building they went into. That's what we have to figure out. Do you see the security?"

"Roger that. Some on the roof also," Rocky noted.

"Roger. Be prepared to bullshit or haul ass. If we have to run, we'll head northwest. The neighborhood looks better over there."

"Copy."

The two men began their walk. Burke could see Rocky sauntering along the opposite side of the street. Burke took his time, looking at the building as he walked. He came up on Lippio's car and glanced inside. Suddenly two men burst out of the door the car was parked in front of and grabbed Burke.

"Hey, what the hell is going on?" Burke demanded.

"Who are you?" one of the men asked in thickly accented English.

"Who are you?"

The man stuck a gun in Burke's face. "Answer me or I'll kill you." He started frisking Burke.

Burke saw Rocky cross the street and move in behind the men. A man yelled something from a roof. Burke grabbed the gun and twisted it out of the man's hand as he kneed him in the groin. A punch behind the ear finished the thug. Rocky had taken care of the other man.

"Time to go!" Burke said.

They ran down the street, calling Ernie to come pick them up. A few shots rang out, but no bullets came near. Running at full speed, they made several turns and ended up in a small rundown park. They crouched behind some bushes and waited for a car to pick them up. It didn't appear anyone was following them.

Rocky started laughing.

"What's so funny?"

"You."

"What are you talking about?"

"You jack Rob up about planning on the fly and what did you just do?"

Burke didn't answer right away. He drew a deep breath. "I know, I know. I just don't want to die."

"Well, then don't."

Burke laughed. "Good advice."

Ernie arrived at the park and the men got in the car.

"You guys okay?"

"Yeah, we're fine," Burke replied. "I want to go back tomorrow night to see what's going on there."

"We're going to Vienna in the morning."

"Dammit, Ernie, there's some serious shit going on there. They've got armed security all over the place."

"And it isn't too well hidden either," Rocky added. "Makes me think the fix is in with the local cops."

"There are no local cops working that area," Ernie said.

"Why?" Burke asked.

"Because it's too dangerous. The only patrol is an armored SWAT van that moves in and about the streets trying to keep a lid on it. This area is full of drug addicts, radical college students and anarchists."

Rocky leaned closer to the front seat. "Speaking of drug addicts, Ernie, I had to lay one out when I was running to back up Burke. He tried to rob me with a knife."

"What do you mean lay him out? Is he dead?"

"Maybe."

Ernie groaned.

Burke grinned at Rocky. Then he turned back to Ernie. "Boss, we need to learn more about these guys. If they're going to Syria, we need to uncover their contacts. They may give us leads to the people who need to pay for Gary."

Ernie sighed. "I'm sorry, guys, we need you on this op. I'll get this info to Ben. I'm sure they have assets here that can take over."

"But...." Rocky started.

Ernie's stare cut him off. "Okay, boss."

CHAPTER TWENTY-TWO

Robin leaned against the wall at the exit from the Austrian Airlines gates at Vienna Airport. Mark was seated and pretending to read a newspaper. Robin saw Mokri coming through and had to suppress a grin. Carlos was walking next to Mokri and they were engrossed in what seemed to be a friendly, animated conversation.

The men walked a few yards until a man dressed like a chauffeur walked up to them and took Mokri's bag. Mokri shook hands with Carlos and they parted. Robin signaled Mark to follow Mokri and the chauffer while he moved to make contact with Carlos. Carlos stopped at a kiosk.

Robin came up to him, pretending to look at flyers. "I see you made a new friend."

"Hello, Rob. Yes, sort of. I did get some info, but he is no pushover. Lots of talk but commits to very little."

"Let's get to the car and catch up with the surveillance."

They hurried to the parking lot and got in the car. Carlos turned on the portable radio. The surveillance chatter was ongoing.

"Say the license again," Doug said.

"It's a large, black Mercedes sedan, license Wilco One Four Two Sierra Papa," Mark answered.

"Okay, that vehicle has not come out of the airport yet."

"SpearTip Twelve, we have the eyeball and are still making our way out of the parking lot, Seven," Willie advised.

"Good work, Twelve. We're waiting for you," Doug replied.

"Carlos, ask if anyone sees any possible counter-surveillance."

Carlos relayed the inquiry and all units responded that no counter-surveillance was evident. The surveillance moved from the airport to a freeway and went north for fifteen minutes and then headed west toward the mountains. Robin's mind was working ten miles ahead. If they stayed in the metropolitan area, surveillance wouldn't be a problem. If they headed into the mountains with narrow, winding roads, it could be a big problem. After another fifteen minutes of driving, it became apparent they were headed into the mountains.

"Carlos, set the phone for conference, get everybody on and hand it to me."

Carlos did as Robin asked.

Robin held the phone on his lap. "Heads up, all units. Doug, when I give the command, I want you to pass the target and stay ahead of it by about three miles from our location updates. Mark, take over the eye. Willie, pull over and have Lev trade with Carlos when I stop with you, then hang back unless we need you. Everybody copy?" Everyone answered in the affirmative. "Mark, ready to take the eye?"

"Roger, boss."

"Okay, execute the moves."

Four minutes later the surveillance was rolling in its new

configuration. They went by Vosendorf, Kaltenleutbegen and Woglerin, all Tyrolean picture card towns.

"Target just turned left on a smaller road. I'm going to have to hang back," Mark advised.

Robin passed Mark. "We got the eye."

"I'm turning around," Doug said.

"He's still headed west from the junction going into Gruberau," Robin said after a few minutes. "We're breaking off."

"I'll take the eye," Doug called in. Several minutes later Doug came on the radio. "Everyone, don't come in this area. I'm being confronted by security types."

"Fuck," Robin said under his breath. "All cars drop your passenger off for foot surveillance, then head back to Wolgerin." He stopped so Lev could get out. Then he headed back.

Robin parked back in the trees just outside Wolgerin. He fidgeted with the car's radio as he waited for word from Doug or the men on foot surveillance. He saw Doug's car turn towards Wolgerin from the Gruberau road. Another car with four tough looking men was right behind him, but they turned around and headed back towards Gruberau.

His sat phone buzzed. "Rob here."

"Where are you, boss?"

"Turn around and come just past the road to Gruberau. I'll be in the trees to the left."

A few minutes later, Doug parked next to Robin.

Robin rolled down his window. "Apparently, you met the neighbors."

"Man, they swarmed all over me. Ugly guys, everyone with scars all over their faces."

"Really? Wonder what that's all about."

A cynical smile formed on Doug's mouth. "I didn't think it would be prudent to ask."

"What did they say?"

"They asked me what I was doing. I had my car set up for the bird watcher cover. They seemed to buy it, but basically told me to stay the hell out."

"Why did they escort you out?"

"I guess they wanted to make sure I was gone."

"Well, that doesn't sound that bad."

"There is one bad thing, Rob."

"What's that?"

"They took a picture of me and the car."

"That's bad. All right, turn in your car and go to Fatboy."

"Okay."

L ev moved through the forest, a ghost leaving no trail, no disturbance, one with his surroundings. The birds didn't interrupt their songs and animals didn't sound the alarm. His senses were acutely alert and he never felt more alive. Robin had warned him that it was easy to get addicted to the adrenalin rush of being a special ops operator. Lev knew it was just possible he already was.

He had worked his way to within one hundred yards of the back of the large home on the property and crawled into a thick row of foliage and brush. No one had come out of the house since Mokri had arrived except for the guards patrolling the grounds. But Lev had soaked up his training and he knew patience was paramount. Time went by with Lev only moving to do a security check on his position.

After an hour, Mokri, a man he recognized as Boorman and an older man came out onto the deck and sat down at a table with drinks in their hands. Lev had the sun to his back, so he didn't worry about a reflection off of the four- hundred-millimeter lens attached to his camera. He began snapping pictures of the three men and the security personnel in the area. Then he took extensive pictures of the back of the home and looked for the best places for covert entry.

The sun was beginning to seek the horizon and Lev knew he had to get moving. He mentally prepared himself as he was taught, then he resumed his ghostly attitude—a wisp weaving through the forest.

R obin was worried. All of the ground team had returned, reporting they couldn't penetrate the security agents without getting spotted. All of the team except Lev. Robin had sent everyone back to Vienna because he didn't want locals getting interested in the new group of people in the area. He didn't know how well they were connected to Mokri's host.

More time went by and darkness was settling in. Robin's shoulder muscles felt like they were in knots. His sat phone buzzed.

"Rob here."

"I am ready to be picked up, Rob," Lev said.

Robin let out a long breath. "Where are you?"

"I am on the road heading towards Wolgerin."

"I'll be there in a couple of minutes."

Robin started his car and drove at a slow speed until he spotted Lev. Lev got into the car and when Robin looked into his eyes he could see the excitement in them. The dome light went out.

"You all right?"

"Yes, sir, I am."

"Did you get spotted?"

"No, sir, I did not."

Robin turned the car around and headed back to Vienna. "Okay, tell me what happened."

"I was able to get pictures of Mokri, Boorman and an older gentleman I assume is Felsa from our briefing. I also took pictures of the security men and of the home."

Robin was quiet for a moment. "Well, Lev, you accomplished what no one else on the ground team could. I'd call that damn good work." The glow from the instrument panel reflected off of Lev's teeth, showing through the proud grin on his face.

In a small log home nestled in the deep forests of the Virginia, part of the Washington National Forest, FBI agent Harry Meridan was stretched out on his bed with his back against pillows and the headboard, reading FBI reports. June Ellerton, assistant secretary to the director of the FBI, stepped out of the bathroom and got into the bed. "Which report are you reading?"

"A report about Jeff Hall."

"You need to read the one from the Beirut office."

Harry flipped through the stack of reports and pulled it out. He started reading and after a minute he jumped out of bed. "Chris Fleming was on to Nazis and Hezbollah working together on money transfers? June, this is important. Where's the rest of the file?"

"It's been classified top secret, need to know only."

"How did you get this?"

"I copied it before it got diverted when I saw the reference to Nazis. Do you want me to try to copy the secret file?"

"No, no, June. That's too risky. I need to talk to Fleming. He may be in danger."

"He retired, you know."

"You mean he was forced out. Yeah, I know. I'll have to track him down."

"I can get his contact information for you."

Harry looked at June for a moment then tossed the report on the night stand and got back in bed. He pulled June to him and held her. "I owe you so much, June, and I'm afraid what I've been able to give in return doesn't come close. You've risked your job for ten years getting reports you thought would help me out and have never complained."

"I believe in what you're doing—and I love you. All I ask is for you to love me."

"Is there any doubt in your mind?"

"No. Marriage would've been nice, but I know why we can't and I appreciate you looking out for me."

Harry looked into her eyes. "I consider us to be married, June. I always have. I treasure the moments we share in this cabin. I think I would've gone insane if I didn't have you." He gave June a long kiss.

"Maybe you and Chris can team up. He's a good man."

"He has a family. It would be too dangerous."

June rose up on her elbow. "You know, Harry, someone went in and got Chris out of Beirut. It wasn't the military. Some HRT guys went rogue and were involved in the rescue. A disciplinary investigation was started, but it was quashed very quickly."

"What are you getting at?"

"Somewhere out there is a team of operators that have to be damn good to have pulled off that rescue. Maybe they're the ones you need to be talking to."

"Interesting thought. I'll have to ask Chris about that."

"Good. Now I would like you to concentrate on me."

June's hand went inside Harry's robe and started wandering.

"Hmm, I think I can be persuaded."

K aren and Barbara Fleming sat at the Marlettes' kitchen table drinking coffee.

"I appreciate all the help you've been giving us, Karen."

Karen smiled. "Don't worry about it. It seems to have become my job with the team to help new members become settled in the area."

Barbara ran her finger around the edge of her cup.

"You seem concerned about this move, Barbara. Do you want to talk about it?"

"I-I don't know. In the Bureau, one didn't...."

"This isn't the FBI. Robin wants every member and their families to feel free to talk, among ourselves that is, and bring up things that may be bothering us. So if you want to talk, I'm here."

Barbara sat quiet for a moment. "Chris has always been dedicated to his work, but I have never seen him like this. He seems driven, almost obsessed with Beirut, the Iranians, the Nazis, and the money laundering. When he told me he wanted to join the team and move here, I was stunned. I thought we were retiring, but I couldn't object. I could see in his eyes it wouldn't do any good."

Karen reached over and put her hand on Barbara's. "Barbara, you need to tell Chris how you feel. It isn't good for you, for Chris, or for the team."

"How can I? He's on his way to Vienna."

"Robin is going to rotate the guys back home one or two at a time so they can have time with their families. When Chris comes back, you need to tell him."

"What about moving here?" Barbara asked.

"The company owns several homes in the area just for this reason. As long as Chris is working with the team, you should be here for security reasons. You and Chris can decide about whether or not to buy later, but everything is run through the company for security reasons…That reminds me. Have you used a credit card in this area?"

"Yes, for the ferry and lunch."

"Before you leave, I'll give you a company credit card. Use it for everything."

"I don't know about doing all of this. I feel like I'm betraying Chris."

"Nonsense. You two are married. You have an equal say in things. Besides, he dumped the move on you and went to Vienna. I say you're running the move and make the decisions."

"I don't want you to get the wrong impression. Chris is a good husband and he does treat me like an equal partner. It's just this whole affair has seemed to have taken control of him."

"Have you two talked about Beirut?"

"Yes, of course. He told me about the torture, the people who died helping him and how the team rescued him. But there's something he isn't telling me and I think it's only because he doesn't know himself. Does Robin tell you everything?"

"Yes. We tell each other everything. It took a while for us to get to that point, but the honesty keeps us strong."

"Thank you so much, Karen. I don't know what I'd be doing without your help."

"This is the time to roll with the flow. You can work out the rest when Chris gets back."

Robin picked up his sat phone. "This is Rob."

"Hey, Rob."

"Chucky, my good man. Where art thou?" Chucky was a

reformed international criminal and old informant of Robin's, whose talents and connections still proved useful to the team.

"Hanging out in Paris, like you told me."

"Ready to go to work?"

"Hell, yes!"

"I need sources who don't like terrorists or Nazis, but who do business with them. Right now I need them to be operating in or around Austria and Germany, particularly Vienna."

Chucky remained silent for a moment. "I can do this, but we'll be dealing with some of the most hardcore criminal elements in Europe—and their help will be expensive."

"Can they be trusted to keep their mouths shut?"

"They are the most tight-lipped of them all. They're Roma."

"Gypsies? Will they talk to me?"

"To be honest, my friend, that will depend on how you impress them. No guarantees."

"Get me hooked up with them. I'll take care of the rest."

"Okay, Rob. I'll get back to you in a week, two tops."

"Make it a week. I think we're getting into deep shit here."

"A week it is."

"Adios."

CHAPTER TWENTY-THREE

Chris waited for Harry Meridan to pick up the phone.

"Hello?"

"Hi, Harry, it's Chris Fleming. My wife told me you needed to talk to me."

"Hey Chris, I'm damn glad you called. I need to meet with you to discuss some very important matters."

"Can you tell me what this is about?"

"Not over the phone."

"Barbara said you retired."

"I did."

"So this isn't FBI business?"

"It should be, but it isn't."

Chris's mind was whirring.

"Look, Chris, I know this is coming out of the blue, but let me just tell you two things. First, I've read reports of your last investigation. Second, your life and those close to you are in danger."

"Jesus, Harry, what in the hell are you talking about?"

"The stuff you uncovered in your last investigation is just

scratching the surface. I've been investigating the same thing for years on my own. It's a much, much more pervasive operation than you can imagine. I can't say anymore over the phone. We need to talk in person."

Chris let out the breath he had been holding. "I'll get back to you shortly."

Rob walked into the conference room on Fatboy. "What's going on, Chris?"

Chris took a deep breath and repeated what Harry Meridan had told him. "He's got me spooked, Rob."

"How well do you know Harry?"

"Shit, I've known him for thirty years. We've worked together on and off. Harry has always been a damn good agent. He was trained by one the legends."

"Who was that?"

"Jonas Carrington."

"What made him a legend?"

"He did a lot of the mafia investigations in the early days. Took down some of the big ones. Hell, he even was an investigator during the Nuremburg trials."

Robin's head snapped up. "Nuremburg! Goddamn, Chris." Robin's mind worked the puzzle. He considered that this information, although totally unexpected, was another piece. "Tell Mr. Meridan to fly into Prague. Get an alias for him so we can pick him up there."

"Are you sure, Rob? I mean, I haven't seen Harry for years."

"He knows something we don't. The main thrust of your investigation in Beirut was money flowing through certain banks to Hezbollah. He said you were only scratching the surface and that he had been investigating the same thing on his own. Now you tell me he was mentored by an agent who as an investigator in Nuremburg. We have terrorists and Nazis dancing together here. I'm seeing a connection."

"But, Rob, it's kind of suspicious that he's been investigating these things on his own."

"Really? What are you doing now?"

Chris's face turned red. "I'll call him."

Leonard Moreland, third vice president for the credit department at Barclays Bank, was pleased he could help out Mr. Felsa. "Yes, sir, I found a credit card charge for a ferry and lunch in Washington State, both for Mrs. Fleming. I also found a credit card purchase for travel under Mr. Fleming's name."

"What was Mr. Fleming's destination?"

"Vienna, sir."

Moreland heard a grunt on the other end. "Thank you, Leonard. Do you have an area in Washington?"

"Yes, sir, the charges were made in connection with Whidbey Island."

"Please send me the information you have by fax. You will be rewarded, Leonard."

"Thank you, sir."

"Took you long enough to get here," Robin said.

Ernie flashed a Cheshire grin at Robin. He and his team had just arrived in Vienna from Greece. He came immediately to Robin at has hotel. "We had to act like tourists, so we wouldn't attract attention."

"I bet you guys did a hell of an acting job."

"Academy Award stuff, my brother. So what's been going on?"

Robin was quiet for a moment. "I'm getting a bad feeling about this whole thing."

"Oh, Jesus, please don't tell me that." Ernie let out a long breath. "Why?"

"Well, we've followed Mokri to a righteous Nazi named Schinner, straight from Himmler's personal security unit, who is surrounded by a bunch of little Nazis."

"That's interesting, but why does that bother you other than it's scary we have a lot of Nazis running around?" Ernie asked.

"Those little Nazis blew Doug's cover and they have the resources to find him here. I had Jamie take him to Fatboy for now."

"Smart move."

"The other problem is the house where Mokri is staying is a nightmare for surveillance. We need to work up a surveillance and covert entry plan for it now that we have almost everyone here."

"Why do we need to get in there? Aren't we just supposed to find out who Mokri is contacting?"

"We need to find out what's in there for our information."

"Oh shit, Rob, you're worried about a bigger problem than this, aren't you?"

"I'm only trying to answer questions I have and prepare in case I don't like the answers."

"You going to tell me what your concern is?"

"Not yet. I don't want you to think I'm getting paranoid."

Ernie smiled. "That's not a bad trait in this business. What did you mean by we have *almost* everyone here?"

"I sent Mike and Rick with *Putinka*."

"That was also a smart thing to do."

"I'm glad you approve."

Robin leaned back in his chair. "We need to begin the rotation back home. Start with the guys you brought over."

"I'll send Emmett and Burke back first."

Robin was quiet for a moment.

"You don't agree, Rob?"

"No, that's fine. I was just thinking how important those two are, but I'd probably say the same about any two you chose."

Ernie laughed. "That is more than just probable, Rob."

N ikky followed the US Naval tugboat to a covered dock in between two Ticonderoga-class cruisers in the San Diego Naval Yard. He watched as Mike and Rick threw lines to the sailors on the dock and felt a pang of sadness that it wasn't his adopted sons Ahmed and Bacla. They were seasoned sailors now, but they were too young for this kind of work. While Karen had them safely tucked under her care, Eddie, Robin's son, and Ilya, Lev's son, were also good friends with the boys and they all stuck together in school.

With docking completed, two Naval officers came up the gangway. "Permission to come aboard, Captain?"

"Permission granted."

The older of the two officers held out his hand which Nikky grasped amicably. "I'm Commander Rollins, Naval Intelligence and this is Lt. Commander Gasgar, deputy commander of the maintenance group here."

Nikky shook the other man's hand. "Welcome aboard, both of you."

"We've been instructed to extend every courtesy to you and your crew," Rawlings said. "Commander Gasgar stands ready to have maintenance experts go over the ship to check all systems, which I understand are all new."

"Most of the systems are new and this is our first extended voyage," Nikky pointed out.

"That is our understanding."

"Very well. My crew and I do not require any special treatment, Commander Rollins, but thank you for your offer. I assume you are aware of the full capabilities of this vessel."

"We are, Captain, and fully aware of the secret nature of this vessel," Gasgar replied. "My crews are ready to start and look forward to taking a look at our Bremerton brothers' handiwork—maybe even offering some suggestions for improvement."

Nikky smiled. "A little competition is a healthy thing, Commander Gasgar. You can start immediately if you like. You have full access to the ship. I would just ask that if you need access to any stateroom, please check with us first."

"Of course. We'll get right to it."

After picking up Harry Meridan at the Prague airport passenger terminal along with several large file boxes, Robin took him to Fatboy parked at the cargo area. During the short drive, neither man said much. They carried the boxes into the conference room where Chris was waiting.

Chris noticed Harry's brown hair was thinning and sprinkled with grey, but he still appeared fit. He rose from his seat and offered his hand. "Hello, Harry. It's been a long time."

"Yes, it has. Too long, I think."

Robin brought out a bottle of Jack Daniels and three glasses. He poured two fingers worth of whiskey in each.

Chris motioned for Harry to sit down. "I assume Robin introduced himself."

"I told Harry my first name. I saved the rest for this discussion." Robin looked at Harry. "At this particular time, I prefer not to go into detail about me or the group I work with. Chris works with us now. We are concerned with his safety and are interested in the same things he is. Your phone call has captured our attention as well as Chris's. We would like to hear more."

"You are the guys that got Chris out of Beirut?"

Robin nodded. "We are."

Harry took a deep breath and looked directly at Chris. "I hear your retirement wasn't exactly voluntary."

Robin could tell Chris was taken aback by Harry's directness. Not that many people knew he really hadn't wanted to retire.

"They fed me the bullshit that my injuries from the Beirut incident plus my age made me medically unfit for duty."

"I know it was bullshit too, Chris. You're too good an agent to be treated like that."

"What the hell is going on, Harry? I don't see you for ten years, you call me and say you need to see me and then you start off with this crap."

Harry took a sip from his glass. "I suppose I could've eased into this, but quite frankly I don't have time—and neither do you." Harry leaned over and lifted one of the boxes he had brought to the table. He opened it and handed what looked like a letter to Chris.

Chris started reading. "Is Jonas, Jonas Carrington?"

"The one and only."

Chris finished reading and looked into Harry's steel gray eyes. "So he passed all of this on to you?"

"About half of it. The rest is the work I've done."

"Is this really about crime committed by the most powerful people in the world?"

"It is. Jonas told me he was passing me a curse. He was more right than he could ever know, God rest his soul."

Chris looked at his glass. "So where do I fit in all of this?"

"As you read in the letter, my options are to pass the curse on, or take action. According to my information, you were hitting some sensitive nerves with your investigation into the passing of money to Hezbollah and some of their Nazi friends. One of those nerves you hit was an indication that some elements of the Federal Reserve may have been involved, correct?"

"Yes, but only as a conduit for money transmitted from the Bank for International Settlements in Basel, Switzerland."

"Right. What do you know about the Bank for International Settlements?"

"Not much. I didn't receive clearance to expand the investigation that far."

"You wouldn't have made much progress since everything that bank does is completely secret."

"Secret! How can that be when all it handles is money from governments?"

"Well, I'm sure you know that much of what the Federal Reserve does is also secret."

"Yes, but the Fed has to report to Congress on a regular basis."

"They have to report some things, but there's also a lot they don't report. And I'm sure you know that the Fed is a privately owned bank, as is the Bank for International Settlements."

"I do, but according to them, Congress doesn't appropriate any money to them and they don't make a profit."

"It's true Congress doesn't appropriate money to the Fed, but that doesn't mean taxpayer money doesn't fund the Fed. Simply stated, the Fed controls currency policy by releasing dollars into the economy, balanced by purchasing treasury bonds."

"And the taxpayer funds treasury bonds."

"Exactly. And of course, when the Fed releases dollars into

the economy, taxpayer purchasing power is diminished. In fact, the purchasing power of the dollar has steadily decreased since the Fed came into existence. Both the BIS and the Fed make a profit. The shareholders of the Fed, which are, of course, banks, get a six percent dividend which is set by statute. You can't have a dividend without a profit."

"What about the BIS?"

"The two men who started that bank, Hjalmar Schacht and Montagu Norman, stated it was not the intention for the bank to make a profit, yet it made over eleven million dollars in its first year of operation in 1930...during the Depression."

Chris rubbed his head. "I feel my blood pressure going sky high."

"I'll give you a few more facts, even though there is much, much more. During World War II, the BIS continued processing international transactions for Nazi Germany. This included the transfer of gold bullion the BIS knew was stolen from Czechoslovakia, Poland and France. Just think how much shorter the war would've been had the BIS cut them off. This is even more criminal given the fact that the BIS was set up for the expressed purpose of processing reparation payments from Germany to the Allies for World War I. To this day, Germany has never made a payment."

Robin leaned forward on the table. He could feel anger rising in him. "You mean to tell me they did this while sixty million people were being killed around the world...while my father was flying P-51s in combat over Germany?"

"It's a fact. Schacht made sure that BIS staff was well infiltrated with Nazis and I suspect it still is. The current situation is that there is a group of bankers, investment groups, multi-national corporations and corrupt politicians that control the world's economy, or at least think they do. Their excuse is that governments are too inept to do it, so they are saving the world from economic destruction. The reality is they control the economy to ensure their profits and wealth at the expense of the average Joe."

"This is all fucking unbelievable. Our own government betraying us." Robin said.

Harry turned to Chris. "The way I see it, since we are retired, we are now free agents. We have the knowledge, the skills and the desire to investigate these assholes, get the evidence and hammer them."

"If they're as powerful as you say, what government is going to prosecute?" Chris asked.

"I'm not talking about prosecution. I'm talking about going public."

Robin looked at both men. "That could get dangerous—very dangerous."

Harry took a deep breath. "It already is, as Chris experienced firsthand. We will have to be very careful and operate under the radar. We will also need help. We won't be able to do this by ourselves." He turned to Robin. "Are you possibly that help?"

"We very well could be."

"I kinda thought so."

"Harry, can I ask you a personal question?" said Chris.

"You can ask, but I won't promise I'll answer."

"Is all of this why you never married?"

A haunted look filled Harry's face, followed by a cynical chuckle. "The rumors that I'm gay are highly exaggerated. Yes, the curse is why I never married. A few years after Jonas died, I knew I couldn't pass this along anymore. I have to do something about these fuckers. I couldn't subject a family to the danger. Plus, over the years, I've done things a little less than legal to get additional evidence on these people. I could've been fired anytime and probably prosecuted. Wouldn't make for a happy family life."

"You've lived a lonely life."

A sly smile curved Harry's lips. "I'm a trained covert operator. It hasn't been all lonely and there is an upside."

"What's that?"

"I've saved a lot of money and made good investments. We have the finances to get this done."

The men sat silently for a while and sipped their whiskey. Then Chris said, "I bet you miss Jonas."

Harry's eyes turned sad. "Yes, I do."

"I never heard how he died."

"He was murdered. Someone, someone in the FBI, put a radioactive isotope in something he ate or drank."

"Harry, that's crazy. Who would do something like that?"

"I think it was someone connected to the people we're talking about."

"Did he suffer before he died?"

"I spent his last three days in the hospital with him. Every time he felt pain, I pushed the morphine button...I kept pushing it..." Harry lowered his head. "I kept pushing it... until he...he... didn't hurt anymore." Harry raised his head and wiped his eyes.

Chris put his hand on Harry's arm. "I'm sorry, Harry. I know you were close."

Robin picked up his glass. "I raise my glass to the memory of Jonas Carrington. May he rest in peace and may we find the person who killed him...and exact justice."

The other men raised their glasses and drank.

Then Harry pulled a stack of floppy disks out of one the boxes.

"All of the documents in these boxes are on these disks. You guys need to read them."

Robin and Chris nodded. "I'll take the disks, Chris. You read the originals with Harry here so you can   ask questions."

"Sounds good to me," Chris replied.

Robin put one the photographs Lev had taken on the table and slid it over to Harry. "Recognize any of these people?"

"That's Boorman on the left. He's the new head of the Fourth Reich, sort of."

"Why do you say sort of?" Robin asked.

"Because as far as I know, it hasn't been proven he is a descendant of Martin Boorman but these Nazis keep him around because of his name. That looks like Schinner in the middle. Jonas really hated that guy. I don't know who the other man is." He handed the photograph back. "Gentlemen," Harry said in a serious tone, "this really is a curse. If you join me, it will turn your life upside down."

Robin leaned forward on the table. "Why don't we concentrate on turning these assholes' lives upside down?"

Harry raised his glass again.

"Have we made any progress on the surveillance of Schinner 's place?" Robin asked Ernie.

"You were right. This location is a bitch to do much with. Frankly, I think we ought to stick to our assignment and follow this guy around until we think he's leaving Europe and snatch his ass. The risk of us getting caught in that house is too great. I'm not even sure we could make it across the surrounding space to get to the house."

Robin rested his chin on his palm. "Maybe you're right. Let's rotate teams in and around the area to find out if there's anything we can develop. Have Lev get into his observation point every couple of days."

"We do have one bright star."

"What's that?"

"Burke found the junction box for the phone line."

"Have him get on that and get a tap set up."

"It's already being done. So, where are you going?"

"Budapest."

"What the hell are you going to do there?"

"Chucky has some new friends for us to meet. I'm going to do the screening."

"Are you taking someone with you?"

"No. I'm just feeling the situation out."

"You be careful, Rob."

"If I was careful, I'd have been an accountant."

The excitement was building in Lippio as the Hezbollah convoy moved along the Syrian/Israeli border. He knew it wouldn't be long before he would see combat. The convoy was comprised of four pickups, with a mix of Lippio's team and Hezbollah fighters in each vehicle. Talia was sitting in the front passenger seat of their pickup, the second vehicle in the convoy. The Hezbollah man driving was obviously enamored with her.

A thundering whoosh engulfed Lippio, and the lead pickup vaporized in fire and smoke. The staccato of an automatic cannon was followed by explosions tearing Lippio's pickup apart, ejecting him out of the vehicle and onto the ground. He lay stunned for a minute and then rolled to the right to try to get up. He screamed and starting retching when saw Talia, her legs and lower torso gone and entrails laying bared to the sun. Her eyes stared at the sky. Her jaws opening and closing as she gasped for air. Lippio tried to stand, but his legs were useless. He kept staring at Talia. He heard helicopters and saw Israeli Apaches flying a circular pattern over the destroyed convoy.

A man walked up to Talia. He wore Israeli battledress. He stared at Talia for a moment and then shot her in the head with a pistol. He turned and walked over to Lippio. The man's eyes were devoid of emotion and he had a scar down his left cheek. He bent down. "Well, Lippio, it looks like you survived." He stood and said to other soldiers, "Keep this one alive and get him to the Jerusalem headquarters."

The SLAMRAAM surface to air missile left the launcher on *Putinka's* aft deck. Mike had the target drone locked on his fire control radar which transmitted the information to the missile. The missile locked on the target at twenty-two nautical miles and closing fast. Four seconds later, the target disappeared from Mike's scope.

"Eee haaw! Target destroyed," he announced.

"Good kill, good kill," confirmed the controller on board the Frigate *USS Gary*.

Commander Rollins shook Nikky's hand. "Congratulations, Captain, all systems are operational."

"Thank you, Commander. I would like to head back to port, top off our provisions and head for the Panama Canal."

"That's probably wise. The longer you're at San Diego Naval Station, the more people get interested in you."

"My thoughts exactly."

CHAPTER TWENTY-FOUR

Robin had the car windows down to enjoy the fragrance of the air even though the June day was warm. He mused how plains and farmland looked the same no matter where you go. These thoughts and others ran through his mind as he drove the M1 Expressway between Vienna and Budapest. He had worked late into the night reading the information on the disks Harry had given him. The information made him furious when he read it, but that fury had distilled to a cold resolve.

The disks contained much more information on how the Bank for International Settlements, American politicians, bankers and industrialists all provided services to the Nazis or looked the other way during the war. He particularly fumed when he read how IBM provided punch cards for the Nazis to manage the Holocaust. And that was just one large American company of several that did business with the Nazis during the war.

The investigations by Harry and Jonas Carrington showed Martin Boorman had set up a global mechanism of over seven hundred and fifty banks and corporations to move hundreds of millions of dollars in gold, cash and other valuable items out of Germany at the end of the war. The goal was to have funding to continue Hitler's dream in a Fourth Reich. Robin knew Boorman couldn't accomplish this without the assistance of international bankers and businessmen. In total, the information convinced him a definite connection existed between their current mission and Harry's investigation. The scope of the problem intimidated even him.

When he came to the Hungarian border, Robin noticed a change. The ravages of the recently evicted Soviet state were still evident in the dingy buildings along the highway. The road itself had turned from a smooth road in Austria to one rough with potholes.

The Hungarians had dismantled the razor wire border in 1989 but left the guard towers intact. The Soviets were not happy about this but did nothing because they knew the system was collapsing. The Soviets had been gone only one short year. He was seeing the leftover effects of communism. The closer he got to Budapest, the worse things became.

When he arrived in Budapest, the inherent beauty of the city was still evident. Although cleanup was in progress, dirt and grime built up during the communist reign still stained buildings and the infrastructure of the city. Some buildings were still scarred from the battles of World War II and the Soviet invasion.

Robin negotiated the narrow streets, following Chucky's directions to his hotel. He parked the car and went into the lobby. The hotel was a small but clean establishment. Robin went up the stairs to the second floor.

S chinner, Boorman, and Mokri sat on the large back veranda of Schinner's home. The men were dressed in light clothes and enjoyed the warm day. They sipped chilled Rhine wine.

Boorman put his wine glass on the table. "I am pleased to hear the movement is gaining strength, Hermann."

"Our hard work is paying off handsomely. Our cells all over the world grow in size and number. Ordinary people are sick and tired of their countries being turned upside down. They yearn for the structure of the Third Reich. The Fuhrer has been proved right time and time again. Our return to power is inevitable."

Mokri patted Schinner's arm. "I told you before I am proud of Iran's alliance with Germany and the Reich for over a century. Our goal of purifying the earth by ridding the world of undesirables is worthy only of men such as us."

Boorman chimed in. "Along with the goal of conquering the United States and its allies. They must pay for the destruction they rained upon the fatherland and your country. They must pay for their occupation of both our lands."

Mokri's fist hit the table. "They shall, gentlemen. We have Hezbollah and our own agents in the US. We are selling drugs and siphoning off their riches for our cause. We are taking over EU countries by immigration, infiltration and best of all...birthrate."

Boorman smiled "I know. It is good work, Farrok. It also shows the impotence of the Americans and their allies. I know you tire of the travel you must do, but you are invaluable to the network. No one has been as successful as you in transporting money and operational orders."

"Diplomatic credentials help."

"True, but others with those credentials have been

intercepted, with serious consequence, I might add," Schinner said.

"I regret your prison time, Hermann."

"Nonsense. A small price for the rise of the Fourth Reich."

"You are a hero of the Fourth Reich."

"As you are, my friends."

The three men toasted each other.

Schinner put his glass down. "The operation orders you are delivering on the rest of your trip are most important, Farrok. They set out a coordinated operation to attack enemy intelligence and law enforcement operatives. If one delivery fails, the operation will fail."

"They will be delivered. Is the amount of cash I'm delivering to each cell the amount they are expecting?"

"Yes. We do not want a repeat of the last fiasco. That was an unnecessary disruption to our operations."

Mokri nodded. "I hope you have sufficiently calmed the dissident cell leader."

"Oh, he is quite calm. He is dead."

"Very efficient."

"We are known for efficiency."

The men toasted each other again and laughed.

R obin knocked on the door to Chucky's hotel room. A moment later Chucky opened the door.

"Hey, Rob, come on in."

Robin put his hand on Chucky's shoulder. "Good to see you, too, Chucky."

"Oh, c'mon, man, you know I'm always glad to see you."

"Just makin' sure."

Chucky closed the door as Robin surveyed the room. "You sure you want to do this?"

Robin turned and looked at Chucky. "I'm sure, as long as they're as tight-lipped as you say."

"Oh, they're tight-lipped all right. They're Roma."

"Are these guys we're meeting the best of the den of thieves?"

"Rob, these guys are on a whole different level than the gypsies you arrested in Arizona. This is organized crime at its best. These Roma are sophisticated criminals. They know what they are doing and they're ruthless. So much so that even though the Roma are looked down upon and generally treated very poorly here, no one messes with these guys—well, with one exception."

"What's that?"

"The KGB."

"I thought the Soviets were gone."

"They are, but many Russians stationed here decided this was a better place to live than home. Members of the KGB were no exception. They stayed and became another criminal group and therefore competitors with the guys we're going to meet."

"What do the Roma think about that?"

"They take care of business."

"My kind of guys. How did you meet them?"

Chucky looked down at the floor. "I've always enjoyed Europe. I worked some deals with them in my younger years."

"Don't be embarrassed, Chucky. We've known each other too long for that. I know you've gone straight. Besides, look how valuable these contacts turned out to be."

Chucky looked up and smiled. "Thanks, Rob, but remember, these guys are no pushovers. They'll be demanding."

"I'll handle it. Did you check out?"

"Yeah, I'm packed."

"Good, shall we get on with this rodeo?"

"Let's go. We can walk."

"No, let's drive."

"But, Rob it's only a couple blocks away."

"I have my reasons."

"Okay."

Robin and Chucky got into the car and Robin reached under the seat and handed Chucky a package.

"What's this?"

"Cash. If these guys are what you say they are, I have to play by their rules, which means there are no rules. You just follow my lead."

"You're making me nervous."

Chucky directed Robin to an alley a few blocks from the hotel to the back of a restaurant. The air was filled with the rich aroma of marinated meat on a grill. They approached a door and Chucky knocked. A large man with dark complexion and slicked black hair answered the door. He nodded to Chucky and looked Robin over with cold eyes. He stepped back, allowing the men to pass, and they walked through a kitchen to a room off the side from the main restaurant. There were two men seated at the table and four standing, one in each corner.

The man seated at the head of the table waved them to chairs. He also was a large man, with a lighter complexion and inquisitive eyes that seemed to sparkle. His face broke out in a grin. "Welcome, Kappi. Who is your friend?"

"Cato, this is Robin. Robin, Cato."

"Good to meet you, Cato."

"I assure you, the pleasure is all mine, Robin. Would you like some coffee?"

"I would."

Instantly a young woman appeared with a tray of cups

that steamed with the aroma of strong coffee. She quickly served the men at the table.

Robin sipped his and enjoyed the strong, deep flavor.

"I understand you have a business proposition for us," Cato said.

"I do, if we can agree that certain services can be provided."

"What did you have in mind?"

"I understand that nothing happens in this part of Europe without you knowing about it."

Cato stared at Robin with measuring eyes. "That is a possibility. Why would you want to know such information?"

"I'm hunting certain people and those supporting them, which includes Nazis."

Cato's eyebrows twitched at the mention of Nazis. "Are you the police?"

"No."

Cato drummed his fingers on the table for a moment. "Before we go any further, I need to see cash—American dollars."

Robin stood. "I have to go to my car for a minute."

C hucky's gut tightened. He had trusted Robin with his life several times, but this was just a little crazy. As Robin walked out the door, Chucky forced himself to stay still and maintain a poker face. As soon as Robin left, Cato nodded to the man who had greeted Chucky and Robin at the door, who quickly went after Robin. Chucky still didn't move. "You seem worried about your friend, Kappi," Cato observed with a sinister smile.

"Oh, I'm not worried about Robin. I'm worried about your man."

Suddenly, a commotion erupted in the kitchen followed by the door crashing open and Cato's man flying through it and landing on the floor like a rag doll. Robin calmly followed him in. Chucky smiled.

R obin walked up to Cato. "I didn't come here to be your friend, so I don't expect hugs and kisses. I came here to do business. But I won't do business with someone who wants to stab me in the back, or even worse, who sends someone else to do his dirty work." Robin held out his hand to Chucky, who handed him the package of cash. Robin dropped it in front of Cato. "Do we understand each other or do I take my money and look for someone else to give it to?"

Cato opened the package and glanced at the cash. He leaned back in the chair and with a wave ordered his men out of the room. The last man closed the broken door as well as he could. Cato tapped the cash with this finger. "Are you CIA?"

"No."

"Do you work for any government?"

"Sometimes."

Cato nodded with a grunt. "What do you want to do to the Nazis?"

"We will kill some of them, but we really want to destroy their ability to operate."

"I think you may be very naive. Even now the Nazis are powerful worldwide."

"I'm not as naive as you think I am. I know a lot about the Nazis, but I need to know more and I'm willing to pay for it."

"Do you know the history of my people and the Nazis?"

"I know enough to know you have every right to hate them."

Cato leaned forward again. "That is so. I do hate them. They murdered hundreds of thousands of my people, including some from my family... including my father. And today, they still consider us less than human." Cato shrugged. "But they can be useful to me from time to time."

"I get your point. What about terrorists?"

"Such people need commodities that are difficult to obtain. They often come to me to solve their problems. It is a lucrative trade."

"What if the terrorists are Iranian or backed by Iran?"

Cato's eyes narrowed. "I do believe you are not as naive as I first thought. The Iranians think of us like the Nazis. I have no love for them."

"So, you make money off of the Nazis; you make money off of terrorists. Both of them look down on you as less than human. I, on the other hand, consider you an equal. We both look for opportunity and advantage. So, how about you continue to make money off the Nazis and terrorists *and* make money off of me by keeping your ears open and passing me the information I need, with the initial payment of the fifty thousand dollars in the package?"

"It is something to consider. First we must eat."

Immediately, the young lady who had brought the coffee and two others brought in large wooden plates filled with grilled veal, beef, pork cutlets and thick slices of bacon. They also brought a large plate of cabbage and another of thick sliced fried potatoes along with a large bowl of tomatoes, cucumbers and onion. The aroma of a marinade consisting mostly of garlic and paprika filled the room.

Another woman brought in a large decanter of a dark red wine and poured glasses for the three men. Cato raised his glass. "Before we eat, we toast with Bull's Blood."

"What are we toasting to?" Robin asked.

Cato looked into Robin's eyes as if he were searching for something. "I think you were wrong about one thing."

"What was that?"

"I think we could be friends in time—yes, in time. We drink to that day."

Robin raised his glass and the two men nodded to each other. Robin savored the taste of the full-bodied wine. "Excellent wine, Cato."

Cato started to pass the food around and the men began to eat.

"So, Robin, you must have some people you are already interested in."

"I do. Do you know Hermann Schinner?"

Cato nodded.

"Do you do business with him?"

Cato wiped his mouth. "No one does business with Schinner—at least no one like me. He has his scar-faced boys do his business for him. What is your interest?"

"I want to get close to him. I want to find out what is in his house."

Cato pondered his wine for a moment. "I will make some inquiries."

"Do you know how he finances his operations?"

"All I know is that I smuggle weapons and cash for him."

"To him or from him?"

"Neither. I get the weapons and deliver them to whoever he wants to be delivered to. As for the cash, I go to a designated bank and get gold and then I deliver money on his behalf after keeping my fee."

"Gold?"

"Yes, gold. I suspect it is gold from the Third Reich."

"That's very interesting. How many banks have you drawn gold from?"

"Many different ones all over the world."

"All right, you will have information I need." Robin reached over and handed Cato a card with a phone number on it. "You can reach me at this number."

Cato put the card in his shirt pocket.

Robin leaned back in his chair. "Cato, I think this is the beginning of a profitable relationship."

The two men raised their glasses.

obin and Chucky got into the car. Robin drove half a block and turned left.

"Hang on, Chucky." Robin hit the accelerator and the BMW took off. Robin put the car through its paces as if he were driving the Le Mans road race, doing frequent high-speed turns and racing down straightaways. Then he braked hard and pulled over.

"Get the luggage, Chucky." With that statement Robin jumped out of the car and ran up to a taxi that had just let a passenger off. He walked up to the driver's window.

"I need to hire your car."

"I'm sorry, Mr. American, I have been already dispatched to another pick up."

Robin stuck a one-hundred-dollar bill in front of the man's face. "I need to get to the river passenger pier."

The driver looked at the bill for a moment. He gingerly took it. "Please get in."

Robin and a huffing and puffing Chucky got into the taxi.

When the taxi arrived at the pier, a river cruise ship floated next to it. Robin led Chucky up the gang plank to where a uniformed crewman waited.

"Good evening. I'm Mr. Marlette and this is Mr. Osgood."

"Yes, sir, we've been expecting you. Welcome aboard."

An hour later, the two men were sitting on the balcony of Robin's stateroom enjoying a drink.

"You've been quiet, Chucky. What's up?"

"What was all that crazy driving all about?"

"For now, I want to appear and disappear at my choosing with these guys. I'm playing on their superstitions a little bit."

"What about the car?"

"Don't worry, Chucky. It's all taken care of."

"Like the reservations on this boat?"

"Yep. As you well know, money does have its advantages."

Chucky took a deep breath and slowly blew it out. "The way you handled Cato...for a minute there, I thought we were dead."

"Why?"

"I've never seen anyone talk to him like you did and get away with it."

"You did notice I first showed him I was no pushover and I did have cash resources."

"Thank God. You did hit a nerve on the Nazi and Iranian attitude towards the Roma, though. How did you know all that?"

"Research, my boy. History is our greatest teacher."

A moment of silence passed between the two men. "The look on his face when you told him you considered him your equal amazed me, Rob. I think he'll do anything for you."

A cynical laugh escaped Robin's throat. "Yeah, as long as there's a profit in it."

"Yeah, there is the money thing."

"That brings us to a question I have for you."

"What?"

"Have you ever met some of the big money people?"

"Like who?"

"The Rockefellers, Vanderbilts, Hearsts, those kinds of old money people?"

"Considering my family is 'old money people,' yes, I have."

"How about the Bornsteins?"

"Rob, I don't know where you're going with this, but I think you're treading on dangerous grounds."

"I've seemed to hit one of *your* nerves, Chucky. I'm not accusing you or your family of anything. I'm trying to understand about the world economy."

"What? All that crap about the Bornsteins and the others you mentioned controlling the world economy?"

"I've seen evidence from reliable sources that it isn't just a load of crap."

Chucky turned in his chair and looked directly at Robin. "You know, you've changed, Rob."

"What do you mean?"

"You've become harder—more cynical."

"Christ, are you turning into my psychiatrist now?"

"Oh no, I'm the last one to try to figure anyone out. I'm just telling you so you know—so *you* can figure it out."

"I take it you don't want to talk about old money."

"I'll talk about it, just not now. I'm tired and you just unloaded this on me."

"Hey, bud, I'm not ragging you. By the way, we've never talked about this, but you do realize you're not my informant anymore."

A frightened look came over Chucky's face. "You're firing me?"

"Oh c'mon, you know better than that. No, Chucky, you're not fired. You're officially a member of the team. And what's more, we're no longer going to call you Chucky. We'll call you by your proper name."

A giant grin broke out on Chucky's face. "Thanks, Rob. I

appreciate that. But if it's all the same to you, Chucky works just fine for me. I've gotten used to it."

"If that's the way you want it." Robin drained his glass. "Whaddya say we turn in? It's been a long day."

"Nice try."

"What?"

"At avoiding my observation."

"Okay, go ahead and finish your observation."

"Just be careful when you go home. Don't be hard and cynical to them."

Robin looked out at sleeping Budapest. "That's a wise and good thought, Chucky. Thanks."

"Now, I am tired and I'm heading for my pillow."

"Amen."

After checking into his Vienna hotel, Helmut Jurgens reviewed the target package. The man was a retired FBI agent named Christopher Fleming. Jurgens studied the picture in the file. A kaleidoscope of faces flashed before him, law enforcement officers who'd met untimely deaths. Deaths he had arranged.

Of course, Jurgens had to first find Mr. Fleming, and Vienna was a big city of over a million and a half people. No credit card purchases had been detected in the city or the immediate area. The Burschenschaften were looking for him, but so far without success. This started Jurgens wondering, *Why would a retired FBI agent be interested in disappearing?*

Jurgens decided he needed to approach this matter from a fresh direction. He also decided he needed to be extremely alert for hostile action.

"Hey, babe."

"Rob!" The word stifled a sob.

"Karen, it's all right. Everything is fine."

"It's just been so long since I've heard from you. What else can I do but go crazy with worry?"

"I'm sorry for not calling sooner. This situation is complicated and has me bouncing all over Europe. But I'm okay. How are you doing?"

"I miss you."

"I miss you, too."

Silence reigned for a moment.

"How are Laurie and Eddie?"

"They're doing fine other than missing you, too. How long is this mission going to last?"

Robin felt his insides twist with guilt. "I don't know. It doesn't look like it's going to be over anytime soon. But sweetheart, I've started the rotation for guys to go home for a couple of weeks. Emmett and Burke should be home soon."

"As usual you'll be the last one in the rotation." Karen's voice had a bite to it.

"You know that's the way it has to be. I'm the commander."

"I know. I don't like it, but I know. Well at least we got Barbara settled."

"She doing okay?"

"Seems to be, but she and Chris are going to have to talk."

"Yeah, I figured that to be the case."

"Have you talked to him about it?"

"Hon, that's their business. As long as what's between them doesn't affect the team, I'd just as soon stay out it."

"Maybe that's best. We'll have to see."

"Right now I'm just missing you, Karen. This whole thing

is hard on all the families. I realize that. There's not much I can do about it."

"I hope they will consider the debt paid sometime in the not-too-distant future. They can't make us go through this forever."

"Hell, *we* can't do this forever. Our bodies are getting beat up, and when we're operating we're under constant strain. The most important problem is I'm away from you. I can't take this forever and I know the team can't either."

"Please be careful, Rob."

"I am, Karen. I am. And I'll make it a point to call more."

"Please do, Rob, so I won't worry too much."

CHAPTER TWENTY-FIVE

B
ill Grassley finished reading the report he'd received from Robin. Robin had posed several questions about the operation. The questions bothered him. It wasn't that Bill didn't want to answer them. Rather, he was bothered because he didn't have the answers.

The real problem was Robin's concern for the Nazi connection, especially someone like Schinner. Bill didn't know what to tell Robin. Of course, the CIA knew about the connections between terrorists and Nazis. The wrinkle was the CIA had used Nazis for their own purposes ever since the end of World War II.

Besides helping the Nazis escape Germany and the Russians, the CIA had protected certain Nazis because they were valuable intelligence assets, scientists for the space program and other more nefarious talents. The world wasn't less dangerous just because the war ended, alliances just readjusted. Experienced intelligence agents were even more valuable at that time because many threats went covert after seeing the might of the United States unleashed on Germany, Italy and Japan.

Nazis had first been used by the CIA to run covert operations against communist aggression. The Nazis hated communists and communists hated Nazis. A match made in heaven—or hell, depending on your point of view. The CIA used Nazi SS troopers who were left in the Middle East to help get the Muslim Brotherhood organized into direct action teams and intelligence assets against Soviet expansion in the area. The net result was the Muslim Brotherhood may not have liked the Soviets very much, but they also became a powerful force, against Israel and the West, especially the United States. And now the US was playing catch up on radical Islamic terrorism. Robin has probably figured this out by now. Bill didn't think he would take it well.

Robin had been a hard-charging cop before the Rodriquez incident. He always played it straight and followed the law. But Bill saw changes in Robin that impressed him...and worried him. Robin demonstrated the willingness to do the hard things necessary in covert operations, including killing the enemy. But when he worked with the Russians to go after Picushkin, he was freelancing beyond anything contemplated in the agreement between the Guardians and the CIA. While Bill could see the logic in Robin's thinking, it also showed that the CIA did not have complete control over him and his men. This caused great concern in the White House and the Department of Justice. At least one DOJ lawyer wanted the team prosecuted for treason. Robin's willingness to take out Chapple, the former acting director of the CIA, placed him in the good graces of the President, who told DOJ to back off and avoided identifying Robin or the team. The taking out of Chapple also had a downside in Bill's mind. It showed that Robin had become ruthless—and extremely dangerous.

A week of wiretap on Schinner's lines produced nothing of importance. They had to be communicating by another means. Robin and Rocky rented a private plane and flew over the area. Rocky did the spotting. Robin maintained a high altitude because he didn't want to alarm Schinner's security. Rocky surveyed the area through 20x80 Steiner binoculars with a gyro stabilizer attached.

"Rob, we're going to have to get closer. There are a couple of areas that look like they could hide a satellite dish array, but I can't get the angle, even at this altitude."

"What the hell do I pay you for?"

"You pay me to tell you shit like this so we get things done right."

Robin faked a sigh. "Oh, all right. I'm going to set us up so we fly over the house at about three angels."

"Aren't you worried they'll spot us?"

"Oh, ye of little faith. Watch and be amazed."

Robin flew out to ten miles from Schinner's home, made a 180° turn, and started the Cessna 172 in a power on glide with a slight tail wind. He was aiming to be over the house at three thousand feet. He did the final trim and looked over at Rocky, who was grinning from ear to ear.

"You da man, boss."

"Flattery will get you everywhere. Just pay attention and find me the communication system."

"Roger."

Even though the plane was traveling at sixty knots, the house seemed to creep closer. Finally, the details of the house became defined and the ground started passing by more quickly. Rocky raised the binoculars and swept the area as the gyro stabilizer whined.

"Rob, come left and put that garden just to the right of the nose. A little more...little more...there. Hold it. Son of a bitch."

"What?"

"It's a garden all right—a satellite dish garden. Two large dishes and three smaller dishes."

"Great," Robin said with a dejected voice.

"What? Now we know how they're communicating."

"Yeah, but we're going to have to get into that house to figure out how to intercept the transmissions. Otherwise it could take months to figure out what satellites they're using." Robin applied power to the plane's engine as they flew out of hearing range of the house.

"How are we going to do that?"

"I'm going to have to give my friend Cato some incentive to speed up."

Putinka was one hour out of Colon, Panama when Mike handed the message to the captain.

"Hmm, it seems we are to get special treatment through the canal."

"Won't that attract attention?"

"I do not think so. Grassley has arranged for a retired US Navy officer to be our pilot."

"That's probably not a bad idea considering none of us has done it before."

"I have transited the canal before, but only as a passenger. The help will be appreciated."

An hour later, Nikky guided the ship into the waiting area for ships preparing to pass through the canal. Soon after they set anchor, a small motorboat pulled up to the port side. A man with definite military bearing threw a line to Rick. The man climbed the boarding ladder and Rick pointed to Nikky and Mike standing on the deck.

Mike, who wore dive gear, noticed the approaching navy man had wavy silver hair, ruddy complexion and ready smile.

"Permission to come aboard, Captain."

"Permission granted."

"Thank you, sir."

"Please call me Nikky. This is Mike."

The navy man shook their hands. "A pleasure, gentlemen. I'm Tom. Can I have a tour of the bridge please?"

"Follow me," Nikky answered.

Nikky briefed Tom on the ship's propulsion and steering systems.

"I see you have the latest technology. It will make the transit that much easier." Tom turned to Nikky with a serious look. "There's been buzz about you guys ever since you left San Diego. Your arrival here wasn't unexpected by folks who aren't exactly our friends. Do you have enough people for twenty-four hour watch?"

"Not without stretching us thin."

"We can't let that happen. There is a growing Chinese intelligence operation here and the Russians are *very* interested in you folks. I'll get some help from the 7th Special Forces Group at Fort Davis."

"When you say the Russians are interested in us, what do you mean?"

"Mainly because they can't identify the origin of your ship. They're not sure, but they think this ship belonged to one of their generals but has been highly modified. Their main interest is to find a guy named Robin."

"I guess Rob really did piss 'em off," Mike quipped.

"I can assure you he did so," Nikky replied.

"Do you have a lock-out trunk?"

"We do on the centerline of our ship."

"Good. The SF guys will want to use it. I'll send you their ETA by coded message."

"You're not staying on board?"

"No. I have to finish our transit arrangements. I'm negotiating for a 1500 hours' start tomorrow."

"Do you need some cash?" Nikky asked.

"No thanks. The agency has you covered on this one. It's easier that way."

Nikky nodded.

Tom looked at Mike. "I take it you're about to do underwater security."

"Yes, sir. SOP in an unsecured port."

"They told me you guys were pros. It'll be a pleasure working with you."

M ike exited the lock-out trunk for his fifth security check of the day. The sun had just dipped below the horizon, making the water darker than his last dive, but the lights from the ship gave off a glow. He started a quick 360, looking back to the stern first. His heart rammed into this throat. A diver was doing something to the props with an object in his hands.

Mike lunged forward in a fast swim to the intruder. The other diver reacted when he was twenty-five feet away. Mike charged ahead, his legs and arms working furiously to propel him through the water. The intruder had what looked like a mine in his hands.

Mike drew his Russian SPP-1 underwater pistol that fired darts. The diver didn't seem to be trying to get away. An arm snaking around Mike's neck told him why. A knife ripped through his air hose. Fighting panic, Mike kicked his right leg back into his attacker's groin. The man's grip loosened and Mike spun and grabbed his attacker's knife hand with his left and pumped two rounds in the assailant's chest.

Air...Mike needed air. He started for the surface when the other intruder grabbed his ankle. He looked down as he tried to kick free and saw a flash of the blade of a knife. He pointed his pistol at the man, when a swarm of divers were all around him and attacking the intruder. One diver offered Mike his mouthpiece and they started buddy breathing. Mike could see the American flag patch on his buddy's shoulder. He started to calm down.

◆ ◆ ◆

Just after nightfall, Rick stood by the hatch on the lockout trunk listening for the prearranged signal from the Green Berets. Then he heard a light tapping in Morse code that said, "SEALs are pussies." He chuckled as he opened the hydraulically operated outer door and thought, *I'm not getting in the middle of that argument.*

A video screen confirmed water flooding into the compartment along with the divers. Rick was surprised to see what looked like half an "A" team. One of the men raised his hand in a thumbs up signal. Rick pushed a button on the console and a programmed sequence of light signals started until a red light flashed. Then the outer door started to close. At the same time the door closed and locked, the system began purging the sea water from the trunk and filling it with oxygen. When that operation was completed, Rick opened the hatch.

"Welcome, gentlemen. Sorry you had to come through the back door."

The first man through the hatch laughed. "We're used to it."

"Here, help your teammate up. He's had a go of it."

"Mike! Are you all right?"

Mike just patted Rick's arm and crawled over to a corner and sat down with his head on his crossed arms.

More men climbed out. Then Rick looked in the trunk and saw other operators searching two dead bodies. "Holy shit! What happened?"

"Don't worry, they're not ours. Your teammate found

them messin' with your ship." The SF soldier held up a couple of underwater cameras.

Rick swallowed hard.

"It's a damn good thing you guys had security up."

Rick swallowed hard again.

While Rick called Nikky on the bridge to brief him, the SF soldier walked over to Mike. "Hey, bud, are you going to be all right?"

Mike looked up. "Yeah, I'm okay."

The soldier knelt down. "I'm Justin Malenky," he said holding out his hand.

Mike shook it. "Mike Collins."

"What happened out there?"

"Tunnel vision. I saw the diver at the stern and just went for him...didn't clear my six."

"You're not the first one to make that mistake. The good thing is you lived to talk about it."

Mike nodded.

"Sure you're going to be all right?"

"Yeah, I always take time to debrief myself on close calls."

Justin patted Mike on the shoulder. "That's a healthy practice."

Justin stood. "Sanders!" he yelled down to one of the men checking the bodies."

"Yo, Chief."

"Whaddya got down there?"

"Two dead Asian guys. No identification. One dead from two hits from a dart gun, the other from knife wounds."

"How long before you're done?"

"Were taking photos and fingerprints and then we'll be done."

"Where'd you get the fingerprint kit?"

"Our friends have them."

Justin turned to Rick. "Well, you guys are quite the professionals."

"We try hard."

"While they're finishing, how about taking me to your captain?"

"Follow me."

Rick and Justin walked into the bridge as Nikky turned to face them.

"Captain Setchinko, this is Chief Warrant Officer Malenky. He's in command of the SF team helping us out," Rick announced.

"Welcome aboard, Chief."

"Thank you, Captain."

"We owe your team a debt of gratitude for getting Mike out of a dangerous situation."

"I'm glad we got there in time, although I think he was about to put some darts into that last guy's face mask."

"That would be Mike," Rick noted. "He certainly wouldn't stop fighting."

The men nodded in agreement.

"Chief, since your people make up the bulk of the security team, I'll leave it to you to make the schedule and assignments. Fit Rick and Mike in where you need them."

"Thank you, Captain, that's very kind of you."

"I'll keep you posted of any intelligence we may receive in the meantime. We'll all meet again when our pilot for the transit arrives."

"Sounds good. I'll get busy."

CHAPTER TWENTY-SIX

Emmett leaned back in his chair, holding his stomach. "Man, I'm full. Eddie, your steaks rival that of your dad's."

"Thanks, Uncle Emmett, he taught me."

"He did a good job."

"I second that," Burke chimed in. "Whaddya say we take a walk?"

"Splendid idea, my man."

Karen, Kathleen, and Irma, Emmett's wife, looked at each other and shook their heads.

"If you men are really going to ditch cleaning up, you might as well take King with you and save Eddie the trip," Karen said.

"We can do that. Where's his leash."

"Hanging inside the back door."

The men put on parkas to ward off the wind coming in off the strait. They leashed up the big German shepherd and started their walk.

The sun was making its last peek over the horizon and the men headed down the road.

"Wonder why Barbara didn't come to dinner?" Burke asked.

"She thinks she's the odd man out right now. I mean we all know her, but not as well as we know each other. I don't think she feels comfortable just yet."

"Yeah, she doesn't seem to feel sure about the whole thing. At any rate, why don't we go by and check on her?"

"Good idea, but we'll only knock if there's a light on."

"Okee dokee."

The men walked for another fifteen minutes when they came around the corner before Barbara's house.

"What the hell?" Emmett exclaimed at the sight of a sheriff's car with the engine running, the door open, but no deputy.

B arbara's heart felt like it would explode out of her chest. She sat on her bed, her hands and feet were bound, tied by a man wearing all black, including a balaclava that covered his face. He spoke with a deep and measured voice. His businesslike demeanor frightened her the most.

"I hope you're not too uncomfortable, Mrs. Fleming. This is definitely one of the more disagreeable aspects of my work. I've been tasked with finding your husband's location. We don't have much time. I had to deal with a law enforcement officer. Unfortunately, he's dead. I'm going to remove the gag and then you're going to tell me exactly where your husband is. I already know he is in Vienna, but I need to know exactly where. After that I will kill you, but I assure it will be painless. If you don't immediately tell me, I will be forced to inflict great pain. Do we understand each other?"

Barbara had been sobbing, but she started to force herself to calm down. She knew the situation was desperate and she had to stall. This man must be part of the money laundering scheme. Chris mentioned something about a bank in Switzerland he had to investigate. She turned her head, looked into the man's eyes and nodded her head.

He removed the gag. "Where is your husband?"

She gulped a couple of large breaths. "He's in Basel, Switzerland," she said with a hoarse voice.

"Basel! He's getting too close. What hotel is he at?"

Her mind raced. *There must be a Hilton.* "The Hilton."

"What Hilton? There are two of them."

"I...I don't know. I didn't know there were two Hiltons."

When Emmett and Burke found the sheriff's car, Burke got on the radio. "Citizen calling Island County Sheriff."

"Go ahead, citizen."

"We've found a sheriff's car on West Beach Road with the engine running and lights on. You'd better send some other units."

"Citizen, we will send units. Stay with the car."

"What's their ETA?"

"We should have a deputy there in twenty minutes."

"Sorry, ma'am. We're going to look for your deputy."

"Sir, it is too dangerous for you."

"We have experience in these matters."

Burke threw the mic on the seat. "Let's go, pard."

The men headed for Barbara's house. After about twenty-five yards, King started pulling at the leash. "He's on to something," Emmett said.

They went another ten yards. "Shit!" Burke bent over the deputy's body. "Emmett, he still has a pulse. Give me King and you start doing your medic magic. I'm heading straight for Barbara."

T he man seemed to relax. "There *is* only one Hilton in Basel. I was only testing you. Goodbye, Mrs. Fleming."

He stood and came toward her, a syringe in his hand.

"No, no please!" Barbara screamed.

In her terror, Barbara could barely comprehend the bedroom door crashing open and a large growling dog attacking the man. She involuntarily yelled, "Burke!" when she saw Burke Jamison come in right behind the dog. The man drew a gun but the German Shepherd chomped on the man's hand and he dropped the gun. Burke slammed into the intruder and they smashed through the bedroom window in an explosion of glass shards and framing material.

J ake Schmidt rolled to his feet and sprinted toward the sea. Footsteps pounded behind him. *Why am I running? No one can beat me. Specially a simple neighbor walking his dog.* Schmidt turned to face his stalker. *Kill with my knife in the true tradition of the SS.* Even though Schmidt had to use his left hand, he was not worried.

His pursuer slowed to a stop in front of him. Security lights had come on. A calm voice, laced with anger and steel, said, "So, you wanna party, shit head? Let's get it on." To Schmidt's surprise, the man drew a knife.

Schmidt feinted a charge and slashed. He moved to the left, feinted another charge and slashed. To his frustration, his opponent did not react, but kept circling. Schmidt feinted once more, but when he slashed, the other man's knife flicked out with a flash. Schmidt thought the man had missed, until he saw blood dripping from his own left arm.

Fear crept in to replace hubris. His opponents face showed no emotion, the eyes were cold and determined. Schmidt knew he had strike or die. He moved left, then right...then lunged. Before he understood what was happening, he no longer had control of his knife hand. Then he heard a loud crack and all he felt was searing pain in his arm, and he heard himself scream. The man put the knife to Schmidt's throat.

"I'm not afraid to die," Schmidt gasped.

"Oh, you're not going to die yet. I need you alive."

The man dropped him to the ground on his stomach, put his knee on Schmidt's neck and grabbed the hair on the front of his head.

"Who are you?" the man asked.

Schmidt didn't answer. His right hand lay by his face. He slowly moved it to his collar.

The man started searching Schmidt's pockets. Schmidt's fingers grasped a capsule from a slit in the collar in his shirt. He put it in his mouth and bit down.

"Fuck!" Burke jumped back from the man.

"Sheriff's Department! Don't move!" A deputy covered Burke with a gun.

Burke raised his hands.

"What's your name?"

"Burke Jamison."

The deputy holstered his firearm. "Sorry, sir. Had to be sure."

"No problem, deputy. How's your fellow deputy?"

"He's still alive, thanks to your friend."

"Do you have people with the lady inside?"

"Your friend is in there."

Burke nodded.

The deputy stepped closer.

"Deputy, I wouldn't get any closer for a couple of reasons, one of which is the guy just took cyanide."

"I'll decide how close I'll get."

Burke stood. "I'm not challenging your authority. I'm trying to help you. Please call Sheriff Stewart and ask him to come out. Tell him I'm here. This problem is way above your pay grade. Here... use this phone."

The deputy hesitated, then took the phone.

"Sheriff, this Terry Cole. I'm out at a scene on West Beach Road. I have a Burke Jamison here. He just killed a guy who attacked a woman...yes, sir. 1192 Beach Road, sir. Yes, sir.

"I...I'm sorry Mr. Jamison. I didn't mean to come on strong. The sheriff will be right here. He said to follow your orders."

"Call me Burke, Terry. Don't worry about it. Could you bring your flashlight over here?"

Terry walked over to Burke.

"Just hold it over the body while I search it." Burke found a wallet. "The ID in here is all fake, but good stuff. This guy was one arrogant son of a bitch."

"Why do you say that?"

"He tried to take me on hand to hand even though his right hand was injured." Burke shook his head. "Underestimating your opponent will always get you killed."

"Why do you think he was here?"

Burke looked at Terry. "You want some good training?"

"Sure."

"This guy is a hit man for some very serious people. No traceable ID and gun, a handmade custom combat knife. He's well financed."

"But why this lady?"

"That I can't tell you, my friend."

Ten minutes later, the sheriff arrived. "Thanks, Terry. You don't write anything until I have a chance to talk to you."

"Yes, sir."

"And don't talk about this to anyone except me and those I authorize you to talk to. Please go help with the scene at the house."

"Yes, sir."

"What do you want to do, Burke?"

"How 'bout the guy who caused this mayhem fell into the sea and you're looking for him. We'll get NAS Whidbey to send a chopper. It'll look like it's participating in the search, but we'll move the body to the base until we decide where it's going from there."

"Sounds like a plan. Let's get this scene cleaned up so I can get to my wounded deputy."

"You got it."

K aren and Maria came out of the guest cottage at the Marlette house.

"How is she?" Emmett asked.

"I gave her a sedative to help her sleep," Maria answered. "She's terrified."

Emmett could see both women had serious worry etched on their faces. His phone vibrated. "That's Robin."

"What's up, Emmett?" Robin's voice was scratchy.

"We just had a bad incident. Barbara Fleming was attacked by a hit man."

"Goddammit! Is she all right?"

"Yeah, Burke and King rescued her, but she's badly shaken. Maria is taking care of her and we have a Marine squad pulling security in plain clothes."

"Prepare to copy."

"Just a minute...okay, shoot."

Robin gave Emmett grid coordinates. "Pack up everyone and get them to that location. Everything you need is there."

Emmett looked at the women in front of him. These women, who had been through so much, were made of steel. Yet their eyes were wide with worry and Emmett could almost smell the fear emanating from them. "How shall we transport?"

"Get to NAS Whidbey. A military transport will be waiting. And Emmett, *Putinka* was attacked in Panama. We have a security breach somewhere."

"Are our guys okay?"

"Yeah, they're fine. We've supplemented them with an SF A team."

"Who did the attack?"

"I'm waiting to hear what they find out."

"Okay, boss, we're movin'."

CHAPTER TWENTY-SEVEN

Nikky, Mike and Justin stood looking at photographs laid out on the chart table. The pictures showed matching tattoos on the attacking divers. The tattoos were on each diver's abdomen.

"I recognize the gang tattoos of the Triads," Mike commented, "and I know they're connected to Chinese intelligence."

"You are correct," Nikky answered.

"So why are these fuckers after you guys?" asked Justin.

Mike's lips formed a wry smile. "Oh, let's just say that we've interfered with some of Chinese intelligence's best laid plans."

"Really? You guys keep rising in my warrior rankings."

"Why thank you, kind sir."

Nikky's face was stern. "There are more questions than answers here. Did they really know it's us? If so, how did they know? How did they find us?"

"Those are questions someone else is going to get the answers to, I guess," Justin said. "Right now, we have to get this ship through the canal in one piece."

"Yes, Justin, you are quite right," Nikky acknowledged.

R obin had his head in his hand as he listened to Burke. His stomach was churning with concern for his family and the team members and their families.

"King is going to be okay. He needed some stitches, but the vet says he should heal just fine."

"That's a relief. What about the attacker?"

"This guy has SS markings along with other symbols over his heart, Rob. Chris has Nazis looking for him."

"Shit. Well, just to let you know, *Putinka* was probed in Panama."

"What the hell...?"

"We have a security breach, which has happened before, and it shouldn't surprise us. Plus, once we brought Chris on the team, we inherited his problems, too."

"I don't like this, Rob. Our families are in danger. If there is a deep breach, it won't matter where we try to hide."

"One step at a time, Burke. Your next step is to hook up with Emmett."

"That's the other problem."

"What do you mean?"

"Emmett is still here."

"Why?"

"We're dealing with a rebellion, Rob. The families are refusing to leave."

"Who the hell is leading that charge?"

"Karen."

Nikky had *Putinka* cruising in a random pattern on Lake Gatun while the team waited for the final canal passage. This minimized the chance of an underwater attack. Transiting the final locks presented another problem. The crew would have to be on deck working and vulnerable to sniper attack.

Nikky expressed his concern to Tom, the canal pilot.

"I know it's a concern, but the risk is low. The area around the locks is always crowded with people. There's not much chance of pulling out a rifle and not being spotted because few Panamanians have guns. Just the same, I have agents in the area. I suggest you have snipers in the crow's nest. If our agents spot something, they'll alert us over these radios." He handed one to Nikky. "The snipers should be able to suppress an attack."

At four o'clock in the morning, Tom guided *Putinka* to the entrance of the Gatun locks and the process of transiting began. Sunrise was a little more than two hours away, and the ship was not well lit by the lock lights, which pointed to the working sides of the locks and not on the ship. Tom maneuvered *Putinka* to the approach wall, where line handlers threw the lines from the locomotives to the crew, who tied them to the ship. The locomotives were on each side of the lock and pulled the ship through the locks, with the ship assisting with its own power.

As *Putinka* entered the second chamber, one of Tom's agents called in suspicious activity. Rick manned the crow's nest, which had a thin cover around it. Perspiration poured off him in the muggy night as he scanned the reported area with his binoculars and spotted a man in the shadows holding something that could be a weapon. He brought his rifle up and put it through a slit in the cover. The man raised the item he was holding so that a tube was pointed at *Putinka*.

Rick made adjustments to his scope and then put the crosshairs on the man's forehead. He keyed his mic. "The guy is pointing something at us that looks like a tube of some sort. I have a shot, Nikky." Rick's finger rested on the trigger. He took a breath and started to let it out.

Nikky didn't immediately answer.

The voice of the breathless agent came over the radio. "Hold the shot. I think he has a camera with a long lens... yeah, that's what it is. I'll take care of this."

Rick noticed movement behind the man with the camera. Suddenly the man collapsed as a hand kept the camera from falling.

"The subject decided to take a nap. I have the camera."

Rick scanned the area and resumed his overwatch.

When *Putinka* cleared the locks, Nikky pushed the ship to fifteen knots. That was faster than *Putinka's* original specs, but nowhere near its new top speed. Nikky didn't want to attract any more attention. When they hit open sea, Nikky set a cruise speed of twenty knots.

Fifty miles offshore, *Putinka* made a rendezvous with a US Navy support ship Tom had arranged for refueling. The supply ship sent a helicopter over with three sailors who quickly set up pumps and hoses. Then the chopper started ferrying one-thousand-gallon fuel bladders back and forth.

Mike, Rick and Justin leaned on a rail watching the sailors do their work.

"Damn, I thought refueling was a simple thing to do," Mike commented. "Just throw a line over."

"Those guys make it look simple," Justin replied.

Tom came up behind them. "The guy taking our picture going through the lock wasn't Chinese. He was Russian."

"At least they didn't get any pictures of us," Mike replied. "There's a good chance someone took pictures of you leaving Bremerton or San Diego. All the major intelligence agencies on both sides monitor the major naval ports. You just need to keep a low profile."

"How in the hell do we do that? We can't even get through the canal without attracting a fan club," Mike quipped.

Tom smiled. "Oh, I think your captain knows what he's doing. You guys just need to stay sharp." He looked at the refueling operation. "This would take a lot more people if we had to use the normal refueling system with ship-to-ship hoses. Luckily you guys don't need more than five thousand gallons today."

Rick let out a long sigh. "All I gotta say is that it's great to have the support of the US Navy. I would've hated to have refueled in Panama."

Mike put his arm around his friend's shoulders. "Amen, brother. Amen."

K aren answered her phone.
"It's me, Karen." The sound of Robin's voice caused her heart to beat faster.

"Rob, don't be angry with me. I..."

"I'm not angry. Just tell me what your reasoning is."

"We...all of us...just can't keep running every time there's a threat. We all love living on the island. None of us want to leave."

"Honey, the people we're dealing with are very powerful and very dangerous."

"But what makes you think they know about us? They were after Barbara because they know about Chris. They were looking for him."

Rob thought for a minute. "Maybe you're right, but do you want to take that chance?"

"Rob, I'm not the shy young girl you married. You've taught me how to be strong and how to face things head on. I've talked to all the other wives, including Barbara. We would rather fight than run."

"What have I wrought?"

"A tough ol' broad."

"Okay, sweetheart. You win. Have Emmett take you over to see Ellie. You're going to have to talk her into moving to the island."

"Why? Rob, she's out of it. She's free. Let her be."

Again, Rob thought for a moment. "You're probably right about that, too. I'm going to have to check in with you more often."

"That would be nice."

"How are the kids doing?"

"Everyone is fine. Eddie is on full alert."

"I'll bet."

"The girls?"

"Cathy and Andy are busy with the twins. Andy is anxious to talk to you about some new gear he's developed. Laurie is getting adjusted to Stanford. She seems very happy."

"Good. Have you heard from Casey?"

"Just quick calls to let us know he's okay."

"Figures. He can't say much. His communication system is always under attack."

"And how are you?"

"I'm doing okay, babe. Just very busy. We have a tough nut to crack here...and I'm missing you."

"I miss you, Rob. I take it you're still a longways from coming home."

"I'm afraid so. I love you, Karen and I'll get home as soon as I can."

"I love you, Rob."

"I have to go."

"All right."

Rob hit the end button and stared at the phone for a moment. His heart was breaking. He missed his wife. He took a deep breath and made another call.

"Pat Stewart."

"Pat, it's Robin."

"Hi, Rob. What's up?"

"Thanks for the help on that incident the other night."

"No problem, my friend."

"I also wanted to tell you the funds in that trust account I told you about are now available. You can get the list of candidates from Tim Echoles."

"You know this will double my department. People will snoop to find out who the donor is," the sheriff warned.

"Let 'em snoop. The trust is impenetrable."

"Okay, Rob. I really appreciate this."

"I appreciate the extra security for our families."

"You got it."

"Thanks."

CHAPTER TWENTY-EIGHT

After a two and a half hour drive from Vienna, Robin entered a small cafe in Urkut, Hungary and took a chair at a table. Cato had given this address for their meeting. The cafe was empty. It was very neat and clean, with tables and chairs made of oak that appeared to be handmade by a true craftsman. The decor was light and airy. Almost immediately a woman with dark medium-length hair, olive skin and dark eyes brought a cup of coffee. She seemed to be sizing Robin up with a critical eye. Somewhat surprised, but pleased, Robin said, "How much?"

The woman held up her hand. "Not necessary." Her accent was British and she turned and walked to the back of the cafe. A minute later Cato emerged from the back.

"Robin, my friend," Cato's voice boomed as he walked over to the table.

Robin stood and Cato gave him a bear hug.

"It's good to see you, Cato."

"Sit down, my friend. We'll have a little meal before I introduce you to a person you will find enlightening."

The woman came out with two plates of various meats,

coarse dark bread and sauces. She went to the door of the cafe and locked it, flipping a sign on the door. She then retreated to the back.

The men began to eat. Cato took a large bite of bread and meat and chewed thoughtfully. He then swallowed and looked a Robin.

"I want to prepare you for this person."

Robin nodded.

"He is special to me. He was with my father when he died. I would have never known what happened to him otherwise. This man was held by the Nazis for six years. His woodworking skills kept him alive. He was kidnapped in Austria in 1939 to work for Himmler making fine furniture. Schinner was one of Himmler's assistants in Vienna.

"Although he was allowed to live, he nearly starved to death and was beaten. I suppose just to show what could happen if he did not do as he was told. I have heard rumors that Schinner did unspeakable things to him, but this I have not heard from the man himself. During the time he nearly starved, he shared food with my father, trying to keep him alive. But it was too little, too late." Cato leaned forward, his eyes narrow and dark. "Do you understand my concern, Robin?"

"Very much so, Cato. I won't ask questions beyond his willingness to answer. I didn't come here to interrogate anybody. I came to find out what I can, but certainly not at the expense of someone who suffered so much."

Cato nodded and sat back. "You are an interesting man. Kappi speaks very highly of you. He says you are a man of your word."

Robin shrugged. "It's the way I was raised." Robin leaned forward on his elbows and clasped his hands. "Why do you call my friend Kappi?"

"Because he earned our respect."

The woman stepped out and held the curtain back.

"Come, Robin. My friend is ready to meet you."

As they walked farther into the back, Robin realized the building was much larger than the restaurant. Soon he caught the aroma of newly cut wood. They emerged into a moderate-sized furniture shop. Robin had always wanted to work with wood but realized he simply didn't have the talent to produce fine pieces like he saw before him. A dark thought passed through him, recognizing his true talents. They went to the left and through a door into a home. It was comfortably furnished and decorated. A man who looked around eighty years old sat at a beautiful table.

The man was thin, bald, with a long, snow white beard. His eyes met Robin's without suspicion, but with twinkling curiosity. He rose from the table, smiled and offered his hand. Robin took it in a warm handshake.

The older man pointed to himself. "Pesha."

"Robin."

Pesha repeated the name and smiled.

"Please sit here," the woman said. "I will translate for you."

He sat in the indicated chair and was amazed at its comfort. "This is a beautiful and comfortable chair. You are truly gifted, Pesha."

After the woman translated, Pesha's face broke out in broad smile.

"When did you realize you had this great talent?"

Pesha began telling his story. He told Robin that even when he was very young, he could see the potential in every piece of wood. His eyes could see the flow of the grain on the outside and follow it in his mind's eye inside the wood. He started seriously working with wood when he was seven years old, and his talent allowed him access to the best woodworkers in southern Hungary. They helped him hone his craft and admitted him to their guild when he turned twelve.

The woman continued the translation. "The older woodworkers urged me to go to Vienna and apply to apprentice under Gunter Schroeder, who was world renowned for his work and highly respected by other woodworkers. The guild put together a petition for him to accept me as his apprentice. Everyone signed it and chipped in money to send me to see Herr Schroeder.

"My great adventure started when I was just fourteen. It began with a train ride to Vienna. I arrived just before dark and quickly became lost. I finally became so tired I lay down on a bench outside a large building. A policeman found me and asked me some questions. I showed him the petition and he told me to come with him. I thought I was going to jail, but he took me to his home and let me sleep there. In the morning, he took me to Herr Schroeder's shop."

The woman interrupted Pesha by saying something in Hungarian. She turned to Robin. "I told Papa, I do not think you are interested in all this, that you are interested in more important things."

"Excuse me, ma'am, but I am interested in Pesha's story. I'm in no hurry," Robin said. He noticed Cato lean back in his chair with a look of satisfaction.

The woman translated to Pesha.

Pesha smiled. "The policeman and Herr Schroeder seemed to know each other and Herr Schroeder agreed to see me when he saw the petition. He took me into his shop, to his office. I had small pieces of my work in my bag I showed him. Herr Schroeder closely inspected some of them. He looked at me and his great eyebrows rose high on his face. I almost laughed. He took me into the shop and handed me a small log that came from a thick branch of pine.

"'Make me something. Anything you like,' he told me."

"I pulled out my favorite whittling knife and quickly shaved the bark from the log. I looked over every centimeter of the shaved wood, immersing myself into the flow of the grain and the texture of the wood itself. Then I went to work. Using only my knife, I shaped the log into a canoe, working to make the curves of all sides, the bow and the stern appear to be one continuous flow.

"After an hour, I handed the canoe to Herr Schroeder. He shook his head. 'Pesha, I cannot accept you as an apprentice.' I was crushed and felt sick.

"Then he said, 'I can only accept you as a journeyman. You are far too talented and experienced to be an apprentice.'"

"I jumped to my feet. 'Really, Herr Schroeder?'"

"'Oh absolutely, my boy. I dare say it won't be long before you'll be called "master craftsman."'

"I worked happily from that day until..." Pesha stopped talking for a moment. The brightness left his face and it turned into a grim visage. He squirmed a little in his chair and looked at Robin with saddened eyes. The woman reached over and softly stroked his arm. He smiled at her, took a slow breath and continued.

"I worked happily with Herr Schroeder until the Nazis came soon after Germany annexed Austria. I had heard about Hitler but didn't pay much attention to all of that. I didn't think it had anything to do with me. They were all there: Hitler, Boorman, Goering, Himmler and their entourage of officials and SS men. One of them, who I later came to know was Schinner, kept looking at me in a way that made me feel dirty."

"What brought them to the shop?" Robin asked.

"They all wanted custom furniture. They were inspecting finished pieces built by Herr Schroeder when they came to one of mine. Hitler saw it first and commented that it was the most beautiful table he had ever seen. Then the others started saying the same thing."

"Of course," Robin replied, "You either agreed with Hitler or you died."

Pesha nodded. "I saw Herr Schroeder look at me and start to say something, but I interrupted and told Hitler that Herr Schroeder had spent many hours making the table just right. I do not know why I did it. Something inside of me told me it was not good for them to know it was my work."

"You have sound instincts, Pesha."

"Unfortunately, Herr Schroeder didn't understand my concern. He smiled, patted me on the shoulder and told Hitler I was a good boy who wanted my mentor to look good, but it was me who made the table. He then showed them more of my work.

"Hitler came up to me and also patted me on the shoulder and praised me for supporting Herr Schroeder." Pesha looked Robin in the eyes. "I could see evil madness in his eyes." Pesha stared off to a memory.

"Are you okay, Pesha?" Robin asked. "We can stop if you want to."

Pesha looked at Cato and then back at Robin. "Is it true you are after Schinner?"

"Yes, among others."

"What are you going to do with him."

Robin leaned forward, his hands folded on the table. "At the right time, we'll kill him."

Pesha studied Robin's face. "I do not see hatred nor murder in your eyes, but I see hardness."

"Do you see justice?"

"Ahh, that is what I see." He took a deep breath. "I will finish my story."

Robin nodded.

"After Hitler praised me, they all left. I was relieved but

puzzled as to why they did not order anything. Herr Schroeder did not say much. Then an hour later two SS men came and said I was to go with them. Herr Schroeder protested, but they knocked him to the ground. Then they put manacles and a blindfold on me and took me away to a large cave. I found out later, the cave is either under Schinner's house, or connected to it. I spent the next six years in that cave making furniture for Nazis. Except for those times Schinner would have me brought up to his home…for his enjoyment."

Robin held up his hand. "I don't need to hear any more details, Pesha. I used to be a police officer. I'm all too familiar with rape."

Relief flooded Pesha's face.

"Does that cave still exist?"

"Yes, but even if I told you where it is, you will never find it."

"Pesha, I need to get into that cave."

"I know. I said *you* will never find it." Pesha nodded to the woman. "My granddaughter knows where it is and how to get in. She will take you to it."

Robin turned to the woman. "I guess it's time I learn your name."

She held out her hand. "I am Asena. You can call me Sena."

Robin shook her hand. "Nice to meet you, Sena."

Cato spoke up. "Robin, you need not be concerned about Sena's ability to take care of herself. She worked as a British intelligence agent against the Soviets for twelve years until the Soviets left in 1989. She is well trained and escaped several close calls."

"Sena, it isn't safe for us to travel together. Can you get to Vienna?"

"Of course."

Robin took out his wallet and gave Sena money. "This should cover your expenses. Here is a number where you can reach me when you get there."

Sena took the money and nodded. The look on her face was all business. He stood. "Thank you for your hospitality and information, Pesha. I must get back to Vienna and make some arrangements." He shook the older man's hand. "Cato, can you walk me out?"

When they got to Robin's car, he reached in the trunk and handed Cato a package. "I have a question for you."

"What is that?"

"Why do you do things for Schinner when he killed your father?"

"I do it hoping to be close enough one day to kill him." Cato looked in the bag and then at Robin. "Are you really going to kill Schinner?"

Robin looked back at Pesha's home. "Yes, eventually."

Cato handed the bag back to Robin.

"Don't you want the money?"

"Kill Schinner. That will be payment enough."

Robin nodded and handed the bag back to Cato. "Then give it to Pesha."

Cato stood silent for a moment, then smiled. "One other thing my friend—to the Roma, you are now Gunari."

"What does that mean?"

"Warrior."

Robin paused. "I'm honored, Cato. Thank you."

The men shook hands and Robin headed back to Vienna.

CHAPTER TWENTY-NINE

Barbara stood at the door watching as Chris hurried to her from the Marlettes' driveway where Emmett had parked the car. He held out his arms and she collapsed into them.

"I love you, Barb. I'm so sorry for putting you into such danger."

She didn't answer. She just held on to him, her face buried in his chest, her body shaking.

Chris held her tighter, stroking her hair. Tears welled in his eyes. Moments later the shaking subsided.

Barbara loosened her hold and looked up at him. Her eyes were inquisitive, but also fearful. She touched his new beard. "I don't know if I'm going to like kissing you with all that hair on your face."

"Let's give it a try." The kiss was tentative at first, but then she could no longer hold back and great relief came over Chris.

"Hmm, it's not so bad. I guess I'll keep you."

"Hey, you two. Come in for some lunch," Karen gently said. She and Emmett were standing in the kitchen doorway.

Chris kissed Barbara again and they went in.

L ater that evening, Chris and Barb sat in chairs in the Marlette guest house facing a window that looked out over the water. The sun was giving its last light of the day in a dazzling display of broad strokes of blue, orange and purple over dancing crystals on the sea. Other than Chris's apology, they hadn't mentioned the attack on Barbara all afternoon and evening.

"Barb, we need to talk about the attack and what's going on with the mission."

Barbara didn't answer right away. Then she turned and looked at Chris. "I need answers to two questions. First, why are we involved in this? Second, if we are going to be involved in this, how do we stay alive?"

Chris looked at the fading sun and thought about his answers. "I'm involved in this because my investigation into banks funneling money to Hezbollah is worrying some very powerful people. The truth is, they think I knew more than I did."

"What do you mean more than you *did*?"

"I know much more now than I did back then."

"Just how dangerous are these very powerful people... never mind, I think I know. So how do we stay alive?"

"Rob has put in place a heavy security presence on the island. You're going to see a lot more deputies around everyone's homes. Don't be surprised if the deputies look a lot like former special operations guys. Rob is also making sure at least two team members are home at all times. I think you've already heard about the training for the families in firearms and other skills."

"The problem is I didn't ask for any of this. I thought we

were going to be retired, living a nice calm life. I gave over thirty-two years of service as the wife of an FBI agent. Don't you think I did my time?"

"Yes, I do. I thought the same thing. I didn't ask for this either. It's been forced on both of us. It's a curse. The only saving grace is that the team and Harry Meridan are in it with us voluntarily...to help us."

"Harry Meridan? We haven't seen him in years."

"I know. Do you remember Jonas Carrington?"

"How could I not? All you agents thought he was a legend."

"He was even more of a legend than we knew. He secretly investigated the same people we are investigating now, for many years. When he retired, he passed the investigation on to Harry. Harry gave up a normal life to carry on the work Jonas did."

"Is that why he stayed single?"

"Yes. He found out about my investigation and retired so he could help. He's with the team now. He's why I know so much more about these people."

"So you're telling me Harry, Rob, the team and the families are all in this to help us even though they don't have to?"

"That's how it shapes up."

Barbara was silent for a long pause. Then she slowly stood, stepped over to Chris and eased herself onto his lap. "You could've saved us both a lot of grief by keeping me informed of what's going on, Christopher Fleming. I didn't know any of this, partly because I've been a pouty bitch around here, but also because you treated me like a mushroom."

"I'm sorry. Things moved so fast, I was overwhelmed. I'll keep you up to date from now on."

"Is everyone overwhelmed?"

"No. The team is the most impressive special operations people I've ever seen. For sure, Robin is a force that seems to grow stronger every day. He was wasting his talents as a cop. He is truly in his element now."

Both were silent for another pause.

"Chris, I'm frightened. These people are after us and I don't think they'll stop until they get what they want. How can we stop these people?"

"Just before I left Vienna, Robin talked to me. He told me you would ask that question."

"He did?"

"Yep. He told me to tell you that we will make them stop by making it too expensive in blood and treasure to pursue us."

"That is a very scary thing to say."

"I think these people have no idea of the hell they have unleashed on themselves."

They were silent again.

"How long are you staying?"

"Willie and I are replacing Emmett and Burke, so I'm here for two weeks."

Barbara let out a long sigh. "Do we truly have a moment of peace now?"

"I believe so."

"Then let's stop talking about all this. I want you to make love to me."

"I thought you'd never ask."

R obin and Harry Meridan waited hidden in some forest ferns for Sena to appear. It was fifteen minutes after eleven in the evening. Robin was surveying the area with infrared goggles.

"I think I see her." Robin gave a low whistle.

The thermal image he was watching stopped, took two steps to the right, and then two steps to the left as Robin had previously instructed Sena to do.

"It's her. C'mon."

The two men walked over to Sena.

"Good to see you, Sena," Robin whispered.

"Good to see you, Robin."

"This is Harry." Both people nodded to each other.

"Let's move out."

Sena led the way to the cave. She and Harry were wearing night vision goggles while Robin still wore the infrared. The path Sena led them on was easy traveling at first. Then they entered thick foliage. How Sena stayed on the path was a mystery to Robin. He could not discern it, so he kept his eye on her. Then Sena held up her hand as a signal to stop. She handed Robin a coiled rope and tied one end to her wrist.

"We will be going through very thick brush for the next fifty meters. This is to make sure we don't get separated."

Robin nodded. He took one foot of rope and wrapped it around his wrist and handed Harry the rest of the coil. Harry signaled Robin he was ready and Robin did the same to Sena. They started moving again, but very slowly. After twenty minutes, Sena held up her hand again.

"We're here."

Robin could see they were at the base of a hill covered with thick brush taller than himself. He watched as Sena reached through one of the bushes. She moved her hand around and pulled. Robin barely heard a mechanism operating. Then Sena pulled him and Harry through an opening and into a cave. She pushed a lever, closing the opening.

She motioned the men closer and whispered to them. "This tunnel is an offshoot from the main cave. My father and other prisoners secretly built it. You are now among the few people who know about it."

"How far is the main cave?" Robin asked.

She pointed to a wall ten meters away and stepped over to it.

"When I open this wall, we will be in the main cave. From here on we must be very careful. I think it wise you take point since my father always made me stop here. He says we want to go left in the main cave."

Robin nodded. He pulled out a suppressed Glock 19 pistol. Harry did the same.

Robin pointed to his pack. "Sena, there is a pistol with suppressor for you in my pack. It's loaded and charged."

Sena reached into the pack and retrieved the pistol. Then she moved along the wall and pulled a lever. The wall opened up three feet.

Robin stepped into the main cave and the others followed. Sena closed the wall. Robin stood stock-still...listening. He didn't hear any human sounds. He looked up and around for surveillance cameras, sensors or wires. Nothing. They started moving slowly ahead.

The cave walls were rock. A net made of rebar covered the walls and provided more support. The floor was dirt. The air had a dank earthy smell with a faint scent of death, and Robin had the feeling that death long reigned here. Sena let out a muffled yelp when rats scurried away from them as they moved forward, which worried Robin. They could be a warning device on their own. Robin stopped short at the sight of three human skeletons piled up on each other. He tried to inspect them, but without ambient light he couldn't tell much about them except they seemed intact and old.

They penetrated deeper into the darkness for another fifteen minutes. There were occasional human bones lying around. Then Robin saw a faint glow of light. He lifted the infrared goggles and realized the equipment was amplifying the light. He wouldn't see it with his naked eyes until he got closer. He pressed on until the light was visible to him without the goggles. All three people took off their goggles so their eyes would get used to the light. Sena put his and her night vision in his pack. They moved on.

They came to a curve in the cave and Robin stopped. A wall made of brick stretched across the cave. A door was in the middle of the wall. A security light shone above the door. Robin looked for cameras or sensors but saw nothing. He took off his pack and retrieved a fiber optic scope. He motioned the others to stay put. He walked over to the door and inspected the edges of the door with the scope to see any signs of alarm connections. Nothing. Then he dropped down and inserted the eye of the scope under the door. He saw a hallway that led to a modern room with electronic equipment visible. Robin's heart beat a little faster. This could be what he was looking for.

He waved the others forward. "There's a hallway leading to a room where I can see some electronic equipment." He tried the door. It was locked. He pulled out his lock pick kit. A minute later he had the door unlocked.

"We'll all step in. Sena, please wait by the door. Harry will come with me but will stop at the end of the hallway until I see if the area is clear. If it is, Harry, you'll move in and look for your evidence. Sena, you'll move to the end of the hallway and cover us. We good?"

Both nodded.

"Okay, let's go. Remember, we're trying to get out of here without leaving any evidence of our incursion. Weapons are only the last resort."

The others nodded again, their faces reflecting the seriousness of the situation.

Robin and Harry moved forward. When they got to the

end of the hallway, Robin could see three separate rooms full of electronic equipment. There was another door between two of the rooms. The sound of something hitting the floor seemed like a thunderclap. A man cursed in German.

Robin pushed Harry back around the corner. Then he went into a low crouch and silently crept to the room where he'd heard the voice. He peeked around the corner of a counter and saw a man bent over a table. Robin pulled an automatic syringe from his vest and moved silently toward the man. The syringe had a very sharp needle that injected a combination of drugs developed by the CIA that caused unconsciousness, temporary amnesia and numbing around the injection area. The drug was supposedly undetectable after a short amount of time. He had to inject the man with the syringe without otherwise touching him, so the target would hopefully think he simply passed out. Just as he got within striking range, the man straightened up. Robin struck him an inch to the left of the lower spine. The man stiffened and then collapsed.

Robin remained perfectly still as the target struggled to maintain consciousness for a few seconds. When his breathing returned to normal and he stopped moving, Robin went to the hallway and waved Harry forward. Harry in turn waved Sena forward.

Robin spoke in a low voice. "You've got thirty minutes to search." Harry nodded.

Robin went to a room with a bank of IBM computers half of which were connected to twelve cables from a large gray conduit coming through the ceiling of the cave. Following the instructions sent by Stephan, Robin sat down in front of the first computer connected to two cables. The screen showed the computer was monitoring a satellite called Motron 7. Robin pulled a case of floppy disks from the day pack he carried and inserted one into the drive of the computer. The disk loaded and then automatically started software that launched communication with Stephan on *Putinka*. Robin removed the disk as Stephan's instructions told him to do. After ninety seconds, the program disappeared. Robin smiled. *Damn, Stephan, you're good.*

This procedure was performed on three more computers. Robin tried a fifth computer, but he couldn't get into it before his watch said it was time to go. He photographed all of the computers then went over to Harry.

"Pack up, Harry, we gotta go."

"Rob, I can't take pictures of these documents fast enough. Please let me take the documents. There's so many smoking guns here it boggles my mind."

Robin pointed to the other door. "I want to explore more myself, but you know the drill, Harry. Blowing our cover now would be stupid. We'll come back."

Harry let out a frustrated breath. "Jesus, Rob...oh hell, you're right. At least I got a lot of good stuff on film. Let's go."

The men made sure the offices were in the same condition as when they'd entered and then went down the hallway. Sena made an inquisitive look to Robin and he made a thumbs up gesture.

The trio made their way back to the false wall. The faint smell of death still lingered in the air.

"You two go through the wall," Robin instructed. "I'm going to check out the other end of this cave."

The other two didn't argue.

Still wearing night vision, Robin started moving quietly as he could with the rats scurrying around him. The cave was going deeper and seemed to bend to the left, and after about fifty yards, he saw a large metal door. He could hear the soft hum of an electric motor. He pushed on the lever handle, but it was locked. He started picking the lock but found it more difficult than the other door. Robin lightened his touch and concentrated on the feel of his tools. He felt the lock mechanism give and cautiously opened the door. At first the image he saw confused him. Then an ice-cold grip of horror wrapped around his spine. He stood before a bank of cremation ovens. Looking to his left, he saw two bodies laid out on metal table—young black men. He looked to his right and saw a large refrigeration unit and next to that was a rack with strips of something hanging on it. He put his hand on the handle of the refrigeration unit and took a deep breath. He pulled and swallowed down bile. Four dead bodies: a man, two women and young girl lay on racks. He looked at one of the women and could see ligature marks on her neck. All had strips of their flesh cut out. He closed the door as he realized what was on the rack. He looked at the strips of skin. Just underneath the rack was a small table with watches and jewelry. One piece was a necklace with the Star of David. There was a membership card to a Jewish community center. The picture on it appeared to be the young girl. A tumultuous flow of horrendous emotions ran through Robin. He wanted to cry, to throw up...but most of all he wanted to kill.

He pulled out his camera and photographed everything. As he was backing up to get a wider shot, he noticed another door in an alcove slightly behind the ovens. He tried the handle and it moved. He took a deep breath, opened the door and slipped through.

He was standing on the landing of stairs that went down to another level. He could hear voices. He moved quietly down the stairs and stopped halfway to the bottom. He bent down to see as far as he could and stifled a gasp. The cave was enormous, stretching as far as Robin could see, filled with rows of military vehicles, including many tanks. Robin recognized the tanks as Tigers from World War II, but they had been modified to incorporate modern armor.

The voices Robin heard were moving away so he carefully moved down the stairs. He looked into several vehicles and could tell that they were vintage WWII vehicles only in appearance. They were full of modern communications equipment, targeting computers matched with up to date sights. His camera was working overtime. He popped in his third roll of film and worried he was going to run out. He moved to the other wall and found work benches filled with modern military parts. This operation was turning all of these old Nazi fighting vehicles into modern fighting vehicles.

Robin heard voices coming back. He looked and to his dismay, one of the men was closer than the others. Robin couldn't get to the stairs. He quietly climbed into the engine compartment hatch of one of the Tigers and squeezed himself in. Soon there were several voices in the area. Ten minutes went by. Metal engine parts were digging into Robin's body, but he couldn't do anything about it.

Two of the voices came closer until they sounded like they were just outside the hatch door. The voices turned to whispers. Robin prepared himself to fight. The whispering stopped and Robin's body was coiled to spring out. Then the men yelled and started laughing. Another man started cursing. *Fuck! They were just playing a prank on another worker.*

Robin rubbed his head where he'd thumped it when the men yelled. Soon all three men were laughing and moving away. He realized he must move out. He slowly climbed out of the hatch, crouched down behind the tank and listened. The voices were fading away. He stood and when he turned around, he could see a smaller tunnel with a concrete walkway leading towards Schinner's house. *So that's it. They don't use the cave much anymore. They use this to get back and forth.* He now had critical information that had to get to Bill Grassley ASAP. He made his way back up the stairs and out through the crematorium.

He had barely closed that door when a horde of rats came flooding into the area and started climbing onto his boots and onto his pants. A combination of fear and revulsion churned through Robin. He viciously kicked them off and trotted back to the wall. He pulled the lever and slipped through with a couple of rats. They started climbing on his boots again. He kicked them off, but they started back. He stomped them to death. Disgust shivered through his body. He walked to the other false wall and pulled the lever and slipped back out into the night.

Harry gently caught his arm. "What did you find?" he whispered.

Robin sucked deep breaths of fresh air for a minute. "An army being built, rats and dead bodies."

"Dead bodies?"

"Yeah, it looks like the fucking Holocaust, just on a smaller scale." Robin shivered again, gagged and then spat. "Fuck!"

"You all right, Rob?"

"I'll be all right when we come back and kill every one of these mother fuckers. But right now I need a hot shower and a stiff drink. Let's get outta here."

CHAPTER THIRTY

The phone by Robin's berth on Fatboy rang. He let it go for a couple more times before he answered. "What?"

"Rob, it's Ernie. I know you need more shut eye, but you'll want to see this."

Robin looked at the clock on the wall. He had slept for only two hours. He sighed. "Okay. Just don't dare come in here without a cup of coffee."

A minute later there was a knock on Robin's door. "Come in, Ernie."

Ernie put a tray with a carafe and two cups on the table in Robin's berth. He looked at Robin, shook his head and poured two cups of coffee.

"You look rough, brother."

"No sleep and one too many glasses of bourbon tend to do that to me."

"I'm sure this didn't help." Ernie slid eight by ten photos to Robin.

Robin turned the pictures of the bodies on their face.

"What are we going to do about all this, Rob?"

"We're going to tell Bill what we've found and we'll get Klaus involved in this shindig." Klaus was the company's representative in Berlin. A former member of the German anti-terrorist team, the GSG 9, another team member had accidentally shot him during a training exercise, shattering the upper part of the left arm, leaving him with only partial use of the arm and hand.

"Rob, we're talking about a large-scale insurrection and ongoing mass murder here. We can't put this off."

"Now just what do you think the authorities here in Austria are going to do about it?"

"Oh c'mon, Rob. No one can ignore this."

"You're telling me, Ernie? I saw the bodies and smelled the rot. It's forever burned into my brain. I agree we have to move fast to try to save lives, but we also have to move smart. Let's say they arrest Schinner. What's he going to say?"

"Well, I'm sure he'll deny it but how can he? It's his cave."

"The problem is Schinner is a true believer and he'll never talk."

"So we need to find out who else is involved before we move..." Ernie's voice trailed off. "Jesus, Rob, what are we going to do? This could blow up in our faces."

"Calm down. Schinner will be taken care of. What's Stephan getting off the satellite feed?"

"Oh shit, I forgot about that. Mokri slipped through our surveillance."

"I figured that might happen. Anything from Grassley on his location?"

"Nope, but the traffic on the satellites says he's in Zurich."

"Zurich! Goddammit! That's only an hour from Basel and the Bank for International Settlements"

"I know, Rob. I've already sent Rocky and Harry there. They'll hang tight until we get a better location."

"How are we going to do that? Phone numbers trace?"

"No. IP address for the server."

"I have no idea what you're talking about."

"Neither do I. I'm just repeating what Stephan told me."

"I'm sorry, Ernie. I should've known you'd handle it. How did you get Harry awake?"

"He never went to sleep. He was waiting for his photos to process when I told the guys what was going on. He volunteered to go with Rock because he knows that area from his solo ops and he knows what some of the players from Basel look like."

"Okay, let me shave and get dressed and we'll get a plan going."

"Oh, you got a lot more than that to do. We're not just getting info from one satellite. We're getting it from four. Stephan and Jamie can't handle it all."

"Damn, that's good news. I'm awake now. Give me ten minutes and we'll get it all worked out."

"Roger, boss."

R obin, Ernie and Jamie sat around the table in Robin's office. Stephan and Nikky were on speaker phone from *Putinka.*

"It's like an overflowing river, Robin," Stephan said. "I can't keep up with sending all of it to Jamie. It doesn't do any good for me to read it all because I don't really know what to look for."

"I know, Stephan. Don't feel bad. You've already done outstanding work hacking into their system."

"But you don't understand. There are many more channels we could hack through these new portals. Based on what Jamie has told me, I'm sure we would discover a whole lot of nasty stuff."

"Stephan's right, Rob," Jamie said. "We could be getting even more great intelligence if we could do more hacks. We need more geeks."

Robin rubbed his eyes. "Where are we going to find people we can trust?" He put his hands down and looked at Jamie. "I've seen that look before, Jamie. What are you cooking up?"

Jamie leaned toward the speaker phone. "Tell Rob your idea, Stephan."

"Well, I was thinking we could recruit my old hacker group. I've known them all for years. They're good people, Robin, and I know once I tell them what kind of work we're doing, they'd love to help."

"Stephan, you know full well how dangerous working for us can be. Would they be willing to take this risk? Would you want to subject your friends to the possibility of getting hurt or killed?"

"I can only tell you that I would have never thought I would be doing what I'm doing for you. I don't like governments. But I had no idea how much evil is in the world until I started working here. I had no idea people like you guys existed and the work you're doing to protect people from the evil. I'm proud to be part of it and I think they'll agree with me."

Robin leaned back in his chair and closed his eyes. "Nikky, when will you make port in France?"

"We'll dock in Brest, France tonight."

"That fast?"

Ernie leaned forward and put his folded hands on the table. "I told Nikky to make all possible speed and get to Europe."

"I take it *Putinka* did well, Nikky?"

"She did, Rob. We did have to refuel at sea again. The US Navy has been very good to us."

"Why Brest?"

Ernie spoke again. "The main reason is Chucky has a contact that got us a secure docking area. The second reason is that Brest has a full-service airport that can handle Fatboy." Robin smiled at Ernie. "You're a good man, Ernest Jackson."

"We got it covered, boss."

"Okay, get Mark on Fatboy and pick up Stephan in Brest. Get them back to the states and round up Stephan's buddies. Get a shopping list from Stephan and install a hacking setup in one of the three empty rooms in the headquarters basement. You got to move fast so we minimize the loss of information."

"What if Stephan's friends don't want to play?" Ernie asked.

"Make them an offer so it's not an option."

Later that evening, Robin and Ernie were reviewing the information intercepted from the satellites. They had been reading for several hours when Ernie spoke up.

"Are you seeing a trend in your messages?"

"Yes, and I don't like it. It looks like the operation mentioned in that conference call is coming to fruition."

"It certainly looks like they're planning some kind of simultaneous op."

"It has to be the op we've been seeing for the last couple of weeks, but what really bothers me is the different sources supplying the content of some of the messages." Robin looked up. "Ernie, these guys have penetrated intelligence and law enforcement agencies in many European countries.

We're going to need some help sorting out who can be allies and who we should avoid."

"Grassley?"

"No. I trust Bill, but not some of those around him. We need to get our French Foreign Legion friend Jonathan and our SAS friend Colin back in Europe and start sorting through this with their Legion and SAS contacts. Those two were a great help in Pakistan on our last go around."

"Good idea. Did you see anything else interesting in your messages?"

"Yeah." Robin handed Ernie one of the messages. "It's from Mokri yesterday."

"He says, 'No surveillance observed.'"

"That's good and bad. Good because he's not spooked and bad because we're not on him."

"What do you think is going on?"

"I think we'll know in a day or two."

"Have you told Bill we've lost Mokri?"

"No."

"Are you going to tell him?"

Robin shrugged. "If I have to...in a day or two."

Ernie's chin dropped to his chest. "Goddammit."

"What?"

"When you started talking about something not feeling right about this op, I thought you were being a little paranoid. Now with this...I hate it when you're right."

"We don't know that I'm right yet."

Ernie took a deep breath. "Oh, yes we do."

The next afternoon, Robin received a call from Bill Grassley.

"Where is Mokri now?"

"Zurich."

"Shit. My source didn't inform me of his move."

"Call him and ask him why."

"It's a one-way deal…she calls in, but we can't contact her."

"Is this person a he or her?" Robin asked.

"That's really none of your business."

"I see."

"Well, where in Zurich is our Iranian friend?" Bill asked.

"We don't know."

"Rob, you are telling me *everything* that's going on, aren't you?"

"No, because I don't know everything that's going on."

"Dammit, Rob, you're playing your semantic games again."

"No, I'm telling you the truth."

"Yeah, but you're not telling me everything you know."

"I am telling you everything I know, just not everything I suspect."

"Jesus, Rob." The aggravation was evident in Bill's voice.

"Bill, haven't I always done right by you?"

"Yeah, but you've gone rogue a couple of times to get things done, and that creates giant headaches for me."

"Take two aspirin and call me in the morning."

"Asshole," Bill said with an exasperated voice.

"You're going to get a report from us that's going to send your stress level sky high…and we're just getting started."

"About what?"

"Call me when you get it. Later, Bill."

Robin placed the receiver down on the cradle as Ernie came in.

"What did Grassley have to say?"

"He hasn't heard from his informant. He's really on edge."

"Why don't we tell Bill we're done and pack up and go

home? This is getting a little too complicated and hairy. This is very dangerous, Rob."

"I'm inclined to agree with you."

Ernie sighed. "Okay, give me the 'but.'"

"'But' for what we found in the cave for a starter. And then the messages about what appears to be a coordinated op somewhere in Europe. And 'but' for the info Chris and Harry have. No, we can't back out. We have to see this through...but we do need some help."

Chief Inspector Alden Worthing rubbed his forehead, as if trying to massage a hidden, annoying thought to the front of his mind. His Scotland Yard Counter Terrorism Unit had been surveilling a suspect for a week and things just didn't seem right to the tough chief inspector. The suspect had been passed off by the counter-terrorism arm of the Moroccan Directorate of Surveillance. The suspect's behavior alternated between acting like he knew he was being followed to seeming blithely unaware...very dangerous for an operative and unexpected for a supposedly experienced one. The Moroccan agents reported no such behavior. So, why this change? The inspector's instincts were making that little voice in his subconscious start to get insistent. Al, as his friends called him, couldn't figure out why—just yet.

Mark and Stephan walked into Stephan's old pizza haunt on Capitol Hill in Seattle. His friends were at the same table they always occupied, intently looking at their computer screens. Stephan's chair was empty, as if they were saving it for him. Jamie hung back as Stephan quietly slipped into the chair.

"Stephan!" the female member of the group jumped up and hugged Stephan. His face flushed crimson midst her breasts pushed against it. The other members of the group gathered around him, slapping him on the back and shaking his hand. They flooded him with questions.

"Okay, okay, calm down. I'm fine."

"But what happened to you?"

Stephan signaled the group to quiet down. Then he spoke in a low voice. "I want to tell you everything, but I can't here. If you all trust me, I need you to pack up and come with me and that gentlemen over there." He pointed to Mark.

Mark nodded to the group.

"If you come with us, you will have the opportunity to do the work we all have talked about with the most powerful equipment in existence...and I'm not talking about the government."

"C'mon, Stephan, you're really sounding creepy," the girl said.

Stephan leaned closer to his friends. "These people saved my life and saved my mother's life from some very dangerous people. I'm now helping them save other people. But we need more help. I've recommended you guys to be that help. That's all I can tell you right now, but if you're interested, you need to follow me out to the van parked out front. Everything will be explained to you. If you don't like the setup, you will be immediately brought back here. No questions asked."

"You expect us to believe they're going to tell us secrets and then let us go? That's crazy, Stephan," a man with a bushy dark beard said.

"Not really, because once you hear the offer, I know all of you will want to join me."

The group was quiet for a moment, then the girl started packing up her computer. "I'll go with you, Stephan. I trust you."

"Squeaky, don't be an idiot," the man with the beard warned.

Squeaky smiled. "We all trusted Stephan before this. Why shouldn't we trust him now?"

A man who dressed like he didn't know that colors were supposed to match started packing up. "I trust Stephan and I'm interested in finding out what this is all about."

The other woman and one of the other men also began packing up.

The man with the beard said, "This is nuts! Are we all going crazy?" Then with a sigh, he started packing his computer.

R obin picked up his phone on Fatboy. "Yeah, Jamie."
"I'm connecting Jonathan and Colin."
"Robin here."

"Hello, Rob. Jonathan here and the Old English Dog, Colin, is with me. We're in Paris."

"I don't care how you two sweethearts work this, but I need you to contact your Legion sources and Colin to contact his SAS sources. Find out what intel surveillance ops on known terrorists are in motion in Europe. It appears that some ops are setups for hits. This has to stay strictly confidential between you and them for the time being. If you have to, tell them we've uncovered several security breaches."

"Mon Dieu, this is not good." Jonathan repeated the info to Colin. They had a brief conversation. "Robin, we'll get working on it. We'll report back as soon as we learn anything."

"Thank you, gentlemen." Robin hit the end button and smiled. *Those two old goats pretend they don't like each other even though they love each other like brothers. We are so lucky to have found such men.*

CHAPTER THIRTY-ONE

Harry Meridan folded the paper under his arm and started to cross the street and walk back to the hotel he and Rocky were staying at in Zurich. Then he saw a man he recognized as Heinrich Hessel, an upper level staff member at the Bank for International Settlements. Harry also knew Hessel was a Nazi. Instead of crossing the street he walked parallel to Hessel. Harry walked a little behind Hessel and kept him in his peripheral vision. He picked up a hesitation in Hessel's gait and ducked into a door alcove of a clothing store. Through a corner window and several mannequins, Harry could see Hessel checking for a tail. *Son of a bitch.*

Hessel continued on his way and Harry followed him to the Storchen Hotel. He hurried across the street. He had to follow Hessel as far as he could. Hessel approached the front desk.

"Mr. Hessel, so good to see you, sir. What can I do for you?" a clerk asked."

"Hello, Fred. Mr. Mokri's room number please."

"Of course…" The clerk lowered his voice. "It's 321."

"Thank you," Hessel said as he handed Fred folded currency. He then went to the elevators.

Harry walked over to the pay phones and called Rocky.

"Where have you been?" Rocky asked when he answered.

"No time to explain. Just start heading south towards the Storchen Hotel along the river. That's where our jackpot is, plus a bonus."

"On my way."

"Bring a camera and radios."

"Roger."

Harry sat in a corner of the lobby and pretended to be reading the paper so he could keep an eye on the elevators. Twenty minutes went by and Rocky showed up. Rocky glanced at Harry and walked over to the brochure stand. After looking at a few brochures, he walked into the gift shop. Harry followed him. Rocky moved to a clear aisle. Harry walked to the aisle and Rocky passed a radio to him.

"Watch for Mokri and another man," Harry whispered as he went by. He left the gift shop and into the men's room near the lobby and set up the radio surveillance kit under his sport coat. He walked out and he met Rocky's eyes for an instant. Rocky stepped outside. Harry sat down and started looking at his newspaper.

A few minutes later, Mokri and Hessel came out of the elevator. Mokri's eyes were narrowed and his lips tight. *He's pissed about something.* The two men headed for the main entrance of the hotel and Harry pushed his transmit button to break squelch once. A double squelch break sounded in his earpiece confirmed Rocky was set to follow the pair. He waited for the men to exit and then headed out behind them.

"We're headed north. Take the east side," Rocky radioed.

Harry moved to the east side of the street. The men were moving at a good pace and soon they came to Lindenhof Hill. This was a park and the two men went to a somewhat secluded area where an older gentleman was sitting on a bench with a folding table set up with a chess board and opposing chair. Hessel sat on the bench next to the older man while Mokri sat in the chair.

"Do you see them?" Rocky asked.

Harry replied with a squelch break. He faded into a treed area and pulled out a pair of small binoculars. Acting like he was just surveying the area, he briefly glassed the older man. He didn't recognize him. He pretended to be looking at other things when he got a bad feeling. He put the glasses down and started moving. Out of the corner of his eye he saw the source of his concern. A man leaning nonchalantly against a pole was definitely scoping the area. He pressed his transmit button.

"Rock, we have counter-surveillance in the area. If you have the pictures move out."

Rocky answered with a squelch break.

The standard plan was to go their separate ways for an hour before heading back to the hotel, if clear. Harry walked at an easy pace, looking like a tourist. He stepped into a wine shop, and while looking for a bottle to purchase, he pulled out his earpiece. He made his purchase, walked back out to the sidewalk and immediately saw the man from the park standing across the street. Upon seeing Harry, he turned and looked out over the Limmat River. Harry took a deep breath and crossed the street.

A cafe with outside tables was close to where the man was standing, and Harry picked a table in clear view of the man—and Harry had a clear view of him. Harry ordered a claret and a pastry from a waitress and went back to his reliable newspaper. The waitress returned with his order, and as he thanked her, the man threw his cigarette into the river with an air of disgust and walked away. Harry watched him in his peripheral vision. The man stopped momentarily and looked back. Then he shook his head and kept on going.

Harry leisurely finished his wine and pastry for the next forty-five minutes. Then he walked for another half an hour while checking for a tail. Finally, he headed for the hotel.

"Where you been?" Rocky asked Harry when he got back.

"Dealing with a tail."

"Was he definitely counter-surveillance?"

Harry looked at Rocky. "Definitely, which means I can't do surveillance in this area until I change my appearance. He got a good look at me, but I think I made him believe it was just a coincidence. Still, we can't take the chance."

"Harry, did you recognize the older guy?"

"Nope."

Rocky called Robin, put him on speaker phone and told him what had happened.

"Did you get compromised?" Robin asked.

"No, I didn't see anyone giving me the eye or following me."

"Okay, Harry, you need to go to headquarters and work with Stephan's group until you can change your appearance enough. You can give them a good education while you're there."

"So, Stephan and Jamie talked them into working with us?"

"Yeah, they did, Rock. They like what we do, and they're excited about the equipment they'll be using. The salary didn't hurt either."

Rocky laughed. "Man, I would love to be a fly on the wall listening to this elderly FBI agent and those geeks hash it out."

"Oh, fuck you, Rock," Harry groaned.

Rocky's voice became serious. "Rob, you have any idea why Mokri was so pissed?"

"As a matter of fact, I do. He called Schinner and raised holy hell about having that meeting on such short notice. Schinner told him to calm down because his sources were not aware of any surveillance."

"Well, if Harry hadn't spotted Hessel, we wouldn't have been following them." Rocky punched Harry in the shoulder. "Good work, you ol' fart."

"It's the end result that counts, gentlemen. Harry, Fatboy will pick you up there in Zurich. They're bringing Emmett and Burke back. Burke will stay there and work with you, Rock."

"Roger that, boss."

"By the way, Harry, Mokri named the other guy in that meeting as Felsa. That name ring a bell?"

"No, it doesn't, Rob."

"Okay, guys. I'll catch you later."

R obin's phone rang. "Robin, Colin here. I picked up a bit of information concerning a counter-terrorism team from Scotland Yard currently following a subject who has their internal radar pinging."

"That sounds promising. How do I get in touch with them?"

"The team commander and an agent from MI6 are willing to meet us in London."

"Tell them I'll be there first thing in the morning. I'll call you with my flight information."

"Right, I'll make the meeting arrangements."

The next morning, Robin walked through Heathrow Airport and came to the security exit. He saw Colin waiting for him.

"Morning, Colin. You're looking well."

"Bollocks, Robin. I'm old and ugly." Colin nodded to the exit. "We go this way."

The men walked out of the airport to the taxi stand.

"Where to, gentlemen?" The man in the booth asked."

"The Stanley Club," Colin told him.

"Oh, of course, sir." The man signaled a taxi, which pulled up to the curb. Robin tipped the man and they got into the cab. The booth man leaned into the front passenger window and said, "Take these gentlemen to the Stanley Club."

"Right, guvner."

The trip took thirty minutes, during which time Colin made it clear he was very familiar with Heathrow and had taken a cab many times. When they arrived at the Stanley Club, there was no discussion about the fare. The two men walked into the club and a tall trim lady with medium length brown hair walked up to them. She gave Colin a warm hug.

"Colin, it's so good to see you again, Dary."

"It's always a pleasure to see you. Robin this is Darelle. This is my friend, Robin."

She held out her hand. "Nice to meet you, Robin."

"Nice to meet you, Darelle."

"Please call me Dary. Come this way."

Dary led them across the large main room to an elevator that took them up to the third floor. They went down a hall a few doors until Dary opened one and they went in.

A tall square-jawed man with keen blue eyes stood up from a small round conference table. The man appeared to be in excellent physical condition.

"Gentlemen, this is Chief Inspector Alden Worthing from Scotland Yard."

Robin held out his hand. "Good to meet you, Chief Inspector. I'm Robin Marlette." Robin nodded to Colin. "This is Colin Blakely, retired SAS." After the introductions the group sat at the table.

"Al," Dary began, "Robin commands a covert team. They have come up with information that indicates a planned coordinated attack on counter-terrorism operatives in different countries. Your current operation seems to be suspect in this regard." She turned to Robin. "Robin, Al's team is our most important counter-terrorism asset in the UK —and Europe, for that matter."

"That makes me very concerned for you and your team, Chief Inspector. Was this assigned to you as a surveillance operation?"

"Yes."

"Is the subject or subjects acting strangely?"

"Yes."

"I think it's highly likely you are one of the targets we're getting information about."

The inspector didn't answer right away. Instead he seemed to be studying Robin's face. He leaned forward. "How did you come by this information?"

"I'm sorry, I can't divulge that information. I can tell you the source is very reliable."

"Will the source ever be available to testify in a prosecution?"

"No, Chief Inspector. I know that doesn't help you. I used to be in law enforcement myself, but that's the way it is."

"If you were in law enforcement, then you know I just can't arrest someone based on this information alone."

"I do. I'm passing this information on to help you to be

alert to the possibility you're the target so you can take the appropriate safety precautions."

The chief inspector leaned back in his chair and drummed his fingers on the table. "We'll have to bring in more people."

Robin took a deep breath. "I wouldn't do that right now. The information we're getting indicates security breaches in intelligence and law enforcement services throughout Europe. I think if you check, you'll find your suspect's actions coincide with your reports to your superiors. If you need more people, I can provide some."

The Chief Inspector's eyes flashed. "I beg your pardon, Mr. Marlette, but I hope you're not making that accusation recklessly."

Robin's jaws tighten. His words came slow and measured. "You have the information. You have my offer to help. Whatever you do, is up to you."

Dary broke into the conversation. "Gentlemen, I think we need to back up somewhat. Robin, can you tell us who is behind this plan?"

"All we know at this time is we are dealing with Iranian-backed terrorists working with Nazis based out of Vienna."

The chief inspector sat straight up.

"Did we get your attention, Chief Inspector?" Robin asked.

"Can you tell me what you know about this connection?" Al asked.

"Hell, next you'll be asking me about the largest international banks funneling money to terrorists."

The chief inspector's serious face slowly broke into a smile. "It does appear we are on the same page, Robin. Please excuse my earlier skepticism."

"No apologies necessary, Chief Inspector..."

The chief inspector held up his hand. "Please call me Al."

Robin smiled and nodded. "We need a plan, Al. I can give four men to work with you."

"What level of capabilities?"

"We're former police detectives who have graduated to special ops Tier One."

Al slowly nodded. "All right then, let's get working on a plan."

CHAPTER THIRTY-TWO

R obin looked at the recent satellite info from Jamie. He rubbed his forehead. *We don't have enough manpower to keep up this waiting for the bad guys to make the move. I need to think of a way to make things happen or find more men…wait. Who says I need men?*

Robin stood and started pacing, turning over ideas in his head, considering the pros and cons of each. None of the ideas were perfect. Some were definitely sophisticated, but complicated, and Robin preferred to keep things simple. He finally settled on a plan. If it worked, it would be a smooth op. If it didn't, it would be a disaster.

He needed to call Colin and Jonathan—and Sena.

M ark watched the screens that showed him the information the hacking team was mining. The amount of information was bewildering. Stephan and another man were working on setting search parameters on the mainframe to try and pare down the bulk information to a workable size relevant to their mission. Mark fed them key names and words and they were working their magic, developing what they called algorithms. Mark didn't have a clue what that meant. He wished Jamie babysat these folks instead of him. His phone rang. It was Robin.

"Hi, boss."

"How are things progressing, Mark?"

"Stephan is setting up something called algorithms that are supposed to automatically find info we're interested in."

"I see. Are you learning anything?"

"This stuff is for geeks, Rob."

"Well, get geeky."

"Oh no you don't. I'm an operator, not a computer guy. I belong in the field. Don't even think of making this assignment permanent."

"Mark, I need Jamie here right now until we get this system seamless. Stephan knows you and is comfortable with you. Information is our lifeblood and we've hit a treasure trove. We need to exploit it to its fullest. I need you there. Besides, Harry will be coming and can help you out."

"Can't the CIA send some people over here?"

"If the CIA found out about this, they would shut us down in a heartbeat. Besides, this way we do our research and get the unfiltered information we need. Sometimes the CIA doesn't like us to have the whole truth."

"Okay, Rob, just don't let this keep me out of the field too long."

"I'll get you back as soon as I can."

A l Worthing involuntarily ground his teeth. Robin was right. As a test, Robin asked Al to report they had lost the suspect. Within twenty-four hours, they received information on his location. Al had some comfort that the four men Robin assigned to him were top-notch, no-nonsense operators. He especially like Ernie, Robin's second in command.

For now, he ordered the surveillance to loosen up to keep the suspect and his handlers guessing, and to give his team a little bit of an upper hand. Still, Al was uneasy. Even with Robin's info, things didn't add up. It made him even more uneasy that Robin agreed with him.

F arrok Mokri sat at the Storchen bar sipping a martini.

"Excuse me," a woman...a very attractive woman said, as she slipped onto the bar stool next to him. It was the only one available, so Mokri didn't think much of it.

"My pleasure, fraulein."

"Ah, a gentleman. That is very refreshing."

Mokri bowed slightly in her direction. "My name is Farrok. I would be happy to buy you a drink in return for some conversation. Staring at my glass doesn't suit me at all."

"That seems to be a reasonable offer. I'm Adrienne. I'd like a Stolichnaya Vodka with a twist of lime, on the rocks, please."

Mokri ordered the drink. He looked into the woman's eyes and set about another conquest.

M okri could feel his blood heating up as Adrienne slipped her key card in the door to her suite and pushed it open. He was carrying drinks they'd brought up from the bar.

"Make yourself comfortable, Farrok. I'm going to slip into

something more comfortable." She walked to the bedroom door, stopped, raised her skirt and removed her panties before closing the door.

Farrok forgot to breathe for a moment. He set the drinks on the table in the room and sat down. He surveyed the room and appreciated the French Baroque furniture carefully painted white with gold trim and fine linen curtains on the windows. *Ah, I do so love the finer things in life.*

A few minutes later, his anticipation leapt as the door to the bedroom opened...and was quickly dashed by two armed men wearing black balaclavas rushing at him. Before he could move, he was staring at a suppressed pistol held by one of the men while the other removed a pistol from under his coat and a knife from his ankle. He saw "Adrienne" slip out of the suite.

"Mr. Mokri, how are you this evening?" the man with the pistol asked.

With only a brief pause, Mokri replied, "Well, I must admit I am very disappointed."

"Ah, perfectly understandable. She is attractive, isn't she?"

"Quite."

"On the other hand, she is also extremely dangerous to those of your political persuasion, so perhaps this is a better outcome."

"Am I to understand *you* are not going to kill me?"

"Mr. Mokri, you are a professional. You know at this point you're much more valuable alive."

"To whom would I be of value, if I may ask?"

"You may, but first you must answer a question for me." Mokri nodded.

"Would you consider changing your allegiance, if the circumstances were appropriate?"

"Certainly you are not asking me to betray my country?"

"It depends. I'm sure you've given some thought as to what the Ayatollah would think of your love for all things western."

Mokri felt his sphincter tighten. He maintained a poker face, but he knew his eyes were betraying him.

"You don't need to answer."

The man with the pistol motioned the other man to leave. He unscrewed the suppressor from his pistol and placed both in a shoulder holster. Then he lifted the balaclava from his head. The man had black hair and ice blue eyes in a determined face. He was obviously in much better shape than Farrok. A chill shot through Mokri as he realized this man could kill him without a second thought.

The man walked over to the room bar. He turned to Farrok. "Scotch or bourbon?"

"Scotch please."

"Ice?"

Farrok nodded.

The man poured the drinks and then sat down, placing the glasses on the table. The man looked at him. "Do you mind if I call you Farrok?"

"Not at all."

"I'm Robin." The man held out his hand and Mokri shook hands.

"You do know, Robin, Muslims are allowed to engage in the sins of western culture to further Jihad."

"Oh, I didn't know you were slated for a suicide mission."

Mokri smiled.

"Farrok, this is not a time for games. I doubt very seriously the Ayatollah would condone your conduct, which we have on video, but even the mere suspicion of your activity would get you executed. You're going to tell me what your mission is, who is running the show, who is involved and what's the expected outcome. In return, you will be given a very lucrative offer to work as our intelligence asset in the Iranian government until you're either about to be compromised or we deem it time for you to retire in a country of your choosing with a guaranteed ample income under a new identity."

"What could you have on video? I didn't touch Adrienne. If you showed a tape to someone, Adrienne would be compromised." Farrok sipped his scotch with a hint of smugness.

"You did a lot more than just touch Talia."

Farrok almost choked on his scotch. It took a moment, but he regained his composure. "Well, then Talia will be compromised."

"Talia and her friends were caught in an Israeli ambush on the Syrian/Israeli border. The only survivor was Lippio. And by the way, Lippio spoke fondly of you during his interrogation by Mossad. Another thing that might upset the Ayatollah and maybe cast suspicion on you, if the tapes we have were to fall in the wrong hands."

Farrok could feel the blood draining from his face. He took a slow sip of his drink and then took a deep breath. "Talia was a good girl."

Robin's glare sent an icy spear down Farrok's spine. "Talia was a Nazi whore. Her death and that of her friends makes the world a better place."

At this point, Mokri understood the predicament he was in. "I assume you represent the United States."

"Your assumption is incorrect. You'd be working for my organization."

"I don't understand."

"How long do you think you'd last working for the CIA? You know there are holes in their security, just like there are holes in yours. We don't have those problems."

"Well, what is your organization?"

"Your worst nightmare, if you're not on our side."

Farrok stroked his beard while in thought. "What is the alternative?"

"There is no alternative. No negotiation. If you don't take the deal or if you renege, you'll be dead within seventy-two hours, no matter where you are, killed by us or the Iranian government, who I suspect will also kill your wife." Without skipping a beat, Robin produced a tape recorder. "Shall we begin?"

"I admire your style, Robin, but as you said, I'm a professional. You cannot make empty threats and expect me to comply with your little scheme."

Robin picked up the phone receiver, turned on the speaker phone and dialed a number.

"This is the Embassy of Iran emergency number, may I help you?" a voice said in English.

Farrok reached over and cut the call. He raised his glass. Robin raised his. The two men took a sip. Farrok swallowed, enjoying the taste and warmth of the drink. He smiled. "We haven't settled on a price."

"We know you're very valuable to us. I have a number, but why don't you impress me to go higher?"

Farrok smiled. "I *do* like your style." He savored another sip of scotch. "Where do we start?"

CHAPTER THIRTY-THREE

A l Worthing let out long breath. "This information from Robin is staggering. I can't believe these people would think they could get away with such acts."

"This plot we just found out about is merely a symptom of the disease." Ernie slid a stack of floppy disks across the table to Al. "Robin believes you need to know the information contained on these disks. We wouldn't be giving these to you unless we had the utmost faith in your integrity. The information contained on them is extremely dangerous to any honest law enforcement officer in possession of them. Only take them if you're prepared to deal with that reality."

The corners of Al's mouth curved into a slight, cynical smile. "You wouldn't be exaggerating a bit, would you, Ernie?"

Ernie put his clasped hands on the table and leaned forward. He could feel the hardness in his face and eyes. "I wish to Jesus Christ I never knew those disks existed. The FBI agent that secretly started this whole thing called this information a curse."

"Why?"

"Because we're damned if we do anything about it and damned if we don't."

"Then why do you want me to get involved in this curse?"

"We need allies. Allies with the utmost integrity and the desire to fight to make the world a better place for the average guy in the street. The guy who goes to work every day and busts his butt to make a better life for himself and his family. These guys," Ernie said pointing at the disks, "through banking laws, finance laws and corrupt politicians just siphon off the average guy's money by insidious means. Sometimes they do it by pure criminality up to and including murder. We want to stop them if we can. We want your help."

Al's eyes shifted between Ernie and the disks for a moment. Then he reached to the disks and took them in his hand, stared at them for a long moment, and slipped them in his coat pocket. His eyes met Ernie's. "Well, I guess we should get our plans in order for the coming operation."

Ernie smiled. "Time to earn our pay."

Two weeks went by without any unusual movement of communication by the terrorists or the Nazis. The surveillances proceeded as normal except that Robin only ordered light coverage on Farrok, as the Iranian checked in every evening and gave Robin an update. Farrok's information and the satellite intercepts were painting a detailed picture of the terrorist and Nazi organizations in Europe and abroad. Mokri believed Felsa was second in command of the Nazi side, but he had no idea who the top was. He'd dealt with Felsa off and on, but he mainly worked with Schinner and Boorman on the Nazi side.

Finally, Robin received a call from Bill Grassley. "Hi, Rob. I'm just checking in."

"Glad you did. Are you planning on coming to Europe any time soon, like maybe Paris?"

"Okay, Rob how do you know that?"

"I didn't. I just know that's where Mokri is headed and info we're getting is that's where this coordinated op is supposed to go down."

"So, I *am* the target."

"One of them. We believe the other is Chief Inspector William Worthing of Scotland Yard."

"I know Al Worthing. He runs one of the best counterintelligence teams in the world. But why us? Why Paris?"

"I haven't figured that out yet. Keep me posted on your travel and ETA to Paris when you can. Above all, don't make contact with anyone in Paris until we check out the who and where of the meeting."

"I'll do my best, Rob."

"Bill, if you don't, you're dead."

"Don't forget, Rob, I have my own security."

"And you don't forget the only people you know you can trust one hundred percent is us."

"I know, Rob." Rob could hear Bill rustling paper. "This report you sent me about the cave is extremely disturbing. I'm having a difficult time justifying delaying action on it."

"I know it's difficult. I was there. But if we move now, it could cost more lives than in the long run. We have to at least take out the leadership cell of the organization before we make a major move, otherwise we won't know the full extent of the conspiracy. We can't do it yet, Bill."

"The director and I are in a tight spot, Rob. The president needs to know about this."

"I disagree. You've already told me there are serious

problems with the national security apparatus. What is important is that we know about this situation. You have a copy in case something happens to us. I'm sure you gave Director Yates a copy. Right now, that's where it should stop. After all, Bill, who would you give this investigation to if you just discovered it?"

Bill was quiet for a moment. "You."

"Then trust us to do what is necessary."

"Okay, Rob. I'll have to confirm this with the director, but if you don't hear from me, we're doing it your way."

"Thanks, Bill."

T hat night Farrok told Robin some news.

"I was told today my part of the operation is to eliminate William Grassley."

"Do you know who Grassley is?"

"Of course. He's the Deputy Director for Operations at the CIA."

"And why do you think they want him dead?"

"Well, he is one of the best men the CIA has ever had. He is very effective in his job and has caused many problems."

"And you think that's enough to kill him?"

Farrok's voice turned cold. "Yes, but no more than any other effective head of an intelligence organization."

"You didn't know this before?"

"As I told you during the debrief, I knew we were setting someone up, but I didn't know who."

"Any ideas why Grassley is the target?"

"Not really. I told you this operation is driven by the Nazi side of our group."

"Don't you find it strange that Tehran isn't telling you more?"

"Operational security."

"You still don't know what your role is?"

"I am just the coordinator."

"The plan has been set in motion. Why do they want you in Paris?"

"I have not yet been told."

"You know, Farrok, it's a good thing you've come over to us."

Farrok gave a cynical smile. "I am still not convinced of the wisdom of my move."

"Be convinced, my friend. I'm guessing you're the bait in this shindig, and you know what happens to bait."

The blood drained from Mokri's face. "I...I don't understand."

"Any competent, determined assassination team could kill Grassley. It wouldn't be easy, but it could be done. So why now? Why Paris? And why you as the bait?" Robin leaned into Mokri's face. "Think about that."

⌐ ⌐

"Hey, Jamie, got any new intel for me?"

"Hi, Rob. We have a ton of intercepts on satellite messages, but they're in code and we haven't broken it yet. We have managed to figure out that there is a conference being held soon and a delivery is in progress, but that's it so far."

"What's Schinner saying?"

"His phone traffic is down to almost nothing."

"Operational security."

"That's what I figure. Something is going down soon."

Robin thought for a moment. "Jamie, reset the sat phone encoding."

"I just did it half an hour ago."

"Do it again."

"Okay." Jamie walked over to a small console and keyed in a new encoding. "It's reset."

Robin punched the keys on his sat phone.

"Grassley."

"Are you clear?"

"Yes, but I'm getting on a plane in a couple of minutes."

"Have you figured out that you're being set up for a hit?"

Bill took a long breath. "I figured that it was a setup from the beginning. Just wasn't sure who they wanted to take out. Why do you think I gave you the mission?"

"Then let's screw their plan up and you come to Brest instead of Paris."

"No. We're going to play this out. I have other business before I meet you, but I'm counting on you keeping me alive."

"How many in your security team?"

"My two best men are with me and a four-man team from the Paris station will be there."

"Dump the four-man team, we'll have you covered. I need to limit confusion." Robin paused. "You do know this whole thing still doesn't add up."

"I'm sure you'll figure it out."

The comment took Robin by surprise. He looked at his phone for a moment then raised it back to his ear. "I'm working on it. Exactly when and where are you meeting?"

"I'll let you know later, Rob."

"All right. I guess I'll be talking to you." Robin ended the call.

"What was that all about?" Jamie asked.

"He's afraid of a security breach, even on our system."

Jamie chuckled.

"What's so funny?"

"Well, you're afraid of a leak on our system too, or did you have me change the encoding just for fun?"

"I'm not worried about our side, but I am worried about people around Bill. Apparently, he is too."

"So what are we going to do?"

"Like he said…figure it out. I want you to find out everything that's going on in Paris in the next five days."

"Everything?"

"Everything. I don't care if it's a kid's birthday party or a girl planning to lose her virginity. I want to know about it."

Jamie grinned. "You have such a way with words. I'll get on it."

Robin dialed another number. "Hey, Chucky."

"Hi, Rob."

"You got us set up?"

"Yep. I've got a chateau just outside of Paris complete with helipad. I also have three apartments in downtown Paris in different locations. I sent the info to your phone."

"Great. Also, I want you to do some tours of Paris."

"What am I looking for?"

"Anything out of the ordinary or something that looks too ordinary."

"Got it. I'll keep in touch."

CHAPTER THIRTY-FOUR

July 2, 1992
The Chateau
1300 hours

The next day, all of the team commanders met at the chateau. The group included Robin, Ernie, Al, Colin and Jonathan. Robin addressed the group.

"Well, gentlemen, we're here to plan an op. The only problem is we have no idea where or when it's going to happen or *what* is really going to happen. This means we are one hundred percent tactical and flexibility is the key. At this time all teams have twenty-four-hour watches in place in different parts of central Paris. No suspicious activity has been identified.

"As far as my team's situation, I have a quick reaction team ready to roll. We won't be moving until we hear from

Grassley. I have my surveillance team in west central Paris. I have two snipers available. Al, what's your status?"

"We followed our target into Versailles this morning. We still have no idea what he is up to. I'm keeping my people around the suspect. I've released Ernie and his men back to you."

Robin nodded. He turned to Colin. "Colin, what's your status?"

"I have a six-man team, including two snipers. We have four vehicles and can move anywhere quickly. Right now, we are set covering north central Paris."

"Jonathan?"

"I have eight retired Legionnaires covering east and south central Paris. We have five vehicles, including the two vans you requested. We also have two snipers."

"Okay, it sounds like we're as good as we can get at this point. Make sure all your communication gear is working. We'll use sat phones until the action starts, then we'll go to the assigned frequencies on the radio."

All the men nodded.

"Remember, all action is to be covert if possible. If you have bodies to move, dead or alive, call for a van. If action does attract attention, all requests for official assistance go through Al. Okay?" Robin looked around at everyone. "One last thing. You're all experienced and you know this can get sporty in a flash. I trust you and assume you made good choices in picking your teams. Tell your men they all have authority to make necessary decisions, if contacting one of us is impractical. Any questions?"

Al spoke up. "Robin, do you think it would be wise for an official contact here in Paris?"

"It would definitely be preferable, but I'm not sure how wise it would be given the intelligence we have."

"I know a captain in the Judicial Police I trust with my life. He heads up a counterterrorism team."

"But the minute you contact him about something like this, he has to alert his superiors."

A twinkle flashed in Al's eyes. "Robin, my friend, what makes you think I haven't been in this predicament before?"

"With this inspector?"

Al nodded.

Robin felt a smile form on his face. "Al, you just made my day. Anybody have any objections to Al making contact with the Judicial Police captain?"

No one spoke up.

"All right. Let's get on with it."

CHAPTER THIRTY-FIVE

July 2, 1992

The Chateau

2100 hours

Robin received a call from Bill.

"Robin, the meeting location is 25 Rue de Leroux at two o'clock in the afternoon the day after tomorrow. I'll be going through a side entrance with a red metal door. I'm supposed to knock twice." Bill hung up.

"Damn!"

"What's the matter, Rob?" asked Jamie

"Bill is really scared."

"How can you tell?"

"His voice and he called me Robin. He always calls me Rob. Jamie, find 25 Rue de Leroux."

"Here it is. It's near the Arc de Triomphe...about five blocks to the southeast."

"Is there anything else there of interest besides the Arc de Triomphe?"

"Yep. There are some embassies and foreign travel offices."

"Like who?"

"Like how about China. They have a foreign travel office nearby, and a service consulate is right in the neighborhood."

"Well, isn't that just ducky? And we have a Chinese restaurant. We're not getting it, gentlemen."

"Damn, none of this makes any sense," Rocky said. "Why the hell would the Chinese be involved?"

"It makes sense to somebody and that's the problem," Robin answered.

"Rob, we're starting to get some activity," Burke announced.

"Where?"

"The eastern central watch is reporting scouts or counter-surveillance in the area of the Arc de Triomphe."

"Are they Asian?"

"Nope. Just plain ol' white guys."

"Okay, Burke, you and Rocky scout out the restaurant and make a plan on how to handle it."

"You got it."

"Jamie, you and I have to do some more research. We have to figure this out."

Jamie rubbed his face. "It's going to be a long night."

July 3, 1992
The Chateau
0810 hours

R obin was jerked out of a catnap by the ring of his sat phone. It was Chucky.

"What's up?"

"Nothing much. I moved over near the Arc de Triomphe after last night's activity. I noticed the local gendarme at the Hotel Medallion. There are several police cars here, so I wandered into the restaurant for some breakfast. According to the waiter, the cops are preparing for a meeting of ministers from several countries who are against the proposed European Union. They expect some protestors, but he said I shouldn't worry because they don't expect things to get out of hand."

"That's just great. All we need is a bunch of people milling around the area. Okay, Chucky, stay loose there and keep me posted."

"Will do, Rob."

"And Chucky…"

"Yeah?"

"Good work."

"Thanks, Rob."

Jamie handed Robin a cup of coffee.

"Jamie, find out what you can about this proposed European Union. I know what the general idea is, but get us some more detail."

"I already did some research." Jamie handed Robin some papers. "There's the history of the current organization and an outline of the new proposal."

"Thanks." Robin sat with his coffee and started reading. The more he read, the faster his mind started to work. He put the papers down and called Harry Meridan. Harry didn't answer and the phone went to message.

"Harry, this is Robin. Call me as soon as you can."

Robin leaned back in his chair, closed his eyes and tried to process all the information he learned in the past weeks. The idea of the European Union was to break down artificial borders and make Europe united economically and politically. The proponents believed it would make Europe as powerful as the United States, the Soviet Union and China in terms of bargaining position for trade and defense. Its detractors believed it would destroy the sovereignty of the individual nations and cause the forfeiture of the control over their individual destinies. Robin's main learning point was whoever controlled the economy, controlled a country. If Europe went ahead with this idea, then it would be much easier for groups like the Nazis and their sympathizers to gain control of the entire European economy, and therefore gain control of Europe.

Robin had serious concerns about these thoughts. He didn't want to believe that after World War II anyone would try to repeat Hitler's folly, but what he'd seen in the cave and Harry's information made it clear forces were at work to do just that. The European Union had to be suspect in that regard. It didn't mean the Union was corrupt for sure, but it was something the team had to investigate. Jamie's voice interrupted his thoughts.

"Rob, Harry's on the phone."

"Hello, Harry."

"Hi, Rob."

"Hey, Harry, what do you know about this proposed European Union?"

"The EU! Wow, how did we get to this point?"

"There's a meeting of some ministers against the EU here in Paris. I need to know if this meeting figures into what is going on here."

Harry was silent for a minute.

"Are you there?"

"Yeah, I'm thinking I have to give you a quick history lesson."

"Shoot."

"Okay, the seed of the EU was planted in 1951 by the formation of the European Steel and Coal Community. Different groups had been working up to it long before that, but the ESCC was the first formal organization. All the usual suspects we are concerned about now were involved in setting up the ESCC and they or their affiliations are behind the EU. The whole movement is based on what appear to be laudable goals, but the end result is government control of the European economy, with the government controlled by the bankers and such. There's a lot of support for it and a lot of dissent against it."

"Do you think this meeting is connected to what we're looking at here?"

Harry didn't answer for a moment. "You know, Rob, you got a lot of shit going on in a relatively small area. Do we have any other reason for all this other action to be happening in this part of Paris at this time?"

"Not really."

"Then I say the EU meeting *is* the reason for all this shit."

Robin's gut tightened. "I think you're right, Harry. I think we have a much bigger problem than we originally thought. Keep your phone close by."

He turned to Jamie. "Have each team send a man to the Hotel Medallion and set up a four-corner surveillance. I want regular reports on what's going on."

"You got it, boss."

July 3, 1992

The Chateau 1115

hours

"**R**ob, you have a call from our no-trace line. I'll transfer it to you," Jamie said.

Robin's phone rang. "This is Rob."

"Greetings, Gunari."

"Greetings, my friend. What can I do for you?"

"I have two men delivering a shipment of hunting equipment and necessary accessories to Paris. Are you interested in such a thing?"

"Who ordered the goods?"

"Our mutual acquaintance."

"I'm very interested."

"I will have them contact you when they get near. When you meet, they will call you by your Roma name. You answer with, 'Plal'."

"What does that mean."

"Brother."

"Thank you." Robin hung up.

"What's going on?" Jamie asked.

"Sounds like the bad guys are in motion."

July 3, 1992

The Chateau

1415 hours

Robin got a call from Harry.

"We're picking up traffic from the satellite feed referencing Paris," Harry said. "Somebody called Raven is supposed to arrive tomorrow from London."

"Any info on method of travel?" Robin asked.

"Negative, but the nature of the traffic indicated he is a

leader of some kind."

"Any other info?"

"Nope. That's all we have."

"Okay, thanks."

Robin thought for a moment, and then called Al.

"Hello, Rob."

"Hey, Al, staying awake?"

"Of course."

"Got a question for you."

"Shoot."

"Does the codename Raven mean anything to you?"

Al hesitated for a moment. "Yes and no."

"Give me the yes part."

"Raven is rumored to be an assassin."

"Who is he?"

"That's the 'no' part. We don't have any clue."

"Who are his targets?"

"Over the last decade, we've had several high-profile deaths that our guts tell us were homicides. But in each death investigation we couldn't find evidence that the death was not natural...or not a suicide."

"What's high profile?"

"Politicians, bankers, corporate leaders..."

"Very interesting. Why do you think this Raven is involved in the deaths?"

"Whispers."

Robin chewed on that for a moment. "I see. Well, Al, for your information, Raven is coming to town."

"Hmm, our target is moving toward Paris as we speak and should be there in an hour or so."

"Let me know where he ends up."

"Will do, Rob. Oh, one more thing. When the Raven is on the hunt, he supposedly wears all black...hence the Raven."

"Hmm, it seems the Raven may be a little melodramatic."

"If he is, he is dangerously so."

July 3, 1992
Area of 25 Rue de Leroux
1530 hours

B urke and Rocky were looking over the neighborhood of 25 Rue de Leroux. They operated separately, being careful not to give any indication of coordination. After two hours of thoroughly looking things over, Burke retrieved the car and picked up Rocky a mile away from the target area.

"What do you think, Rock?"

"Grassley is crazy to go through with this meeting."

"I agree with you. It's too easy of a setup."

"If he is going to do this, we need to get snipers on some roofs in the area."

"Roger that. Let's talk to Rob and we'll get busy on it."

"I'm with you, brother."

July 3, 1992
The Chateau
1615 hours

J amie watched Robin pace back and forth in the command room they had set up in the Chateau. He kept studying the situation board. Jamie wanted to tell Rob to sit down, but he knew Rob was frustrated not being in the field and was trying to sort things out in his mind. Then Burke and Rocky came in the room.

"Hi, guys," Burke quipped.

"What did you find out?" Robin asked.

306

"First off, Grassley should reconsider going to this meeting."

"He won't do that."

"Well then, we're going to need a heavy countersniper operation in the area of that door Grassley is supposed to go through." Burke took a deep breath. "Rob, Bill will be a sitting duck."

Robin walked over to the large table in the middle of the room and sat down, letting out a frustrated whoosh of air. "I know, but he thinks we're going to flush someone out."

"Who?"

"He says he doesn't know, but our intercepts have picked up some traffic about a guy called the Raven who is on his way here. Al Worthing says they have intelligence on this guy that ties him to unexplained deaths of prominent bankers and corporate types."

"Really?" Rocky asked. "That is some heavy shit, Rob."

"It seems to be."

Emmett walked into the room.

"Just in time, Emmett," Robin said. "I need you to get with these two and work up a deployment plan for snipers tomorrow. You'll be charge of that operation. Get with the other team leaders to decide who the snipers will be."

"Roger, boss."

Robin's phone buzzed. "This is Rob."

"Robin, it is Farrok."

"Tell me you have news."

"I am supposed to be at 25 Rue de Leroux in Paris at one o'clock in the afternoon the day after tomorrow."

"Any idea what for?"

"To kill Mr. Grassley."

"Why you? You're Iran's chief intelligence operations officer."

Farrok didn't answer right away. "It looks like you were right. Someone is the bait, but it's not me. It's Grassley."

"If Grassley is the bait, who is the target?"

"I don't know."

"Where are you now?"

"Stuttgart."

"Are you alone?"

"No...I have to go. I'll try and contact you later."

"Farrok..." The line went dead.

CHAPTER THIRTY-SIX

July 3, 1992

The Chateau

1945 hours

Robin, Carlos and Lev meet Cato's men one block from the chateau. Robin inwardly smiled when he saw them. Their appearance left no doubt they lived on the rougher side of life. One of the men smiled, held out his hand and said, "Gunari."

"Plal," Robin replied.

The man started to speak in broken English. He handed Robin a piece of paper and a set of keys. "This is place to take shipment." He pointed to their van. "Cato says already paid for."

Robin smiled and handed each man an envelope. "For you."

They looked in their envelopes and their faces broke out

in big grins. They grabbed Robin's hands and shook them vigorously. They left in a car that was parked nearby.

"Well, Rob, you certainly know how to make folks happy," Carlos observed.

"You never know when we might meet them again. Let's get this van to our headquarters so we can see what we're delivering."

Robin followed the van into the four-car garage at their headquarters. He met Carlos at the rear doors and they opened them.

"Holy shit!" Robin blurted. "It looks like someone is planning serious bad business."

The van contained AK-47 rifles, rocket propelled grenades, hand grenades, PKM machine guns and cases of ammunition.

"What are we going to do, Rob?" Carlos asked.

"The first thing we're going to do is call Al Worthing and get his French counterpart here. If something goes wrong, I want law enforcement present."

Carlos had a perplexed look on this face.

"Do you have a question, Carlos?"

"I thought we were operating in the shadows here."

"We are, but I'm getting a funny feeling about this. Having the Surete here will be some insurance."

Carlos simply nodded.

Two hours later, Al arrived at the chateau with his friend.

"Robin, I want you to meet Captain Vadim Laurent."

"Hello, Captain, it's good to meet you."

They shook hands. "Please, call me Vadim."

Robin nodded. "Come with me." Robin took the two police commanders to the van and opened the door.

Al let out a low whistle while Vadim's eyes grew wide.

"Two of my men are going to deliver this load to 15 Avenue Michel Alonze," Robin said as he handed Vadim the paper Cato's men had given him.

Vadim took a deep breath. "Who are you delivering to?"

"We don't know," Robin replied.

"Who ordered the delivery?"

"Nazis."

Vadim's eyes narrowed. "Al told me you are investigating a connection between Nazis and Islamic terrorists. Do you expect a terror attack?"

"At this point, we expect anything. We have extensive surveillance in the city, mainly around the Arc de Triomphe, because activity is building around there."

"Are you sure you can contain any violent activity?"

"We have five teams comprised of five to eight men in the area. They are well trained and experienced operators." Robin pointed at the map of the city on the wall. "At this point we expect a violent confrontation at a Chinese restaurant located here, and possibly at the Hotel Medallion."

"I wouldn't worry about the Medallion. We have a large contingent of officers there."

"Well, I've detailed a four-corner surveillance there also."

Vadim shrugged. "It can't hurt. I would like to be with the team who delivers these weapons. Based on what Al has told me about compromised agencies, that's where I may have some concern."

"Do you want to let us in on your concern?"

"Not at this point, because if my concern is valid, I'll be there to control things. If your undercover men are arrested, what will they do?"

"They won't resist, and they won't say a word...except for a wisecrack or two."

"If it happens, I will get your men released quickly. I need to go now, but I will be back the first thing in the morning."

"Okay. Al, Ernie will be running this part of the op. Hook Vadim up with him in the morning."

"Will do."

An hour later, Robin received a call from Al.
"What's up, Al?"

"My team just followed our Moroccan target to a destination. The address is 15 Avenue Michel Alonze, where the weapons are going."

A lightning bolt hit Robin's brain. "Al, get your team out of the area *now* and come to the chateau." Robin pushed the end button on his phone. "That's it," he said aloud.

"What is, boss?" Jamie asked.

"This is a giant setup. I think they're planning to blame western intelligence agencies for something that's going to happen at the Medallion."

July 4, 1992
The Chateau
0020 hours

Al and his crew came into the chateau. Robin waved them into the command center.

"Hello, Al. Sorry to be so abrupt on the phone but we're in the middle of a frame job."

"No offense taken. I had already come to that conclusion and I had pared back my surveillance. I don't think they know we're here, but I should know in a couple of minutes."

"How?" Robin no sooner said that when Al's phone rang.

Al looked at his phone. "Like this," he said as he answered.

"Chief Inspector Worthing. What's that, sir? I see. No, sir, the suspect led us into a very tight area. It was impossible to follow him without burning the surveillance. Yes, sir, we'll get right on it." Al ended the call with a big grin. All of his people were grinning also.

"That was the command officer we suspected was the mole inside of Scotland Yard, Robin. That call just confirmed it. He wants us to go set up on that address."

"That would put you in the area so you can be tied to the bad guys at the location and the gun delivery."

"You're quite right."

"I prefer you stay here for the night and cover the Hotel Medallion in the morning since we have that house location tied up already."

"That is fine with us."

Robin's phone buzzed. It was Vadim.

"Robin, our inside man from the rogue unit says the house where the delivery is to take place is where a group of men designated as a quick reaction force is located."

"That makes sense, but that also means we need more men for that area."

"That's why I'm calling. I have a special operations team preparing for tomorrow. Because of the potential for violence there, I request your permission to use them."

"I appreciate the heads up, but you don't need my permission, Vadim. This is your city."

"Thank you, Robin. I very much appreciate that. I assure you, I will follow Ernie's instructions."

"I'm not worried, Vadim. I'm just glad Al suggested we bring you in to our little problem. See you tomorrow."

July 4, 1992
Area of the Chinese Restaurant
1230 hours

Robin drove to the area of the Chinese restaurant and parked. Before he left the chateau, he used theater makeup to darken his complexion and added a fake beard made to blend with his hair and fit his face. He walked down the street and sat on a bench next to Burke, who was also wearing a disguise. Burke, without looking at Robin, said, "Rocky and Marv are separately on foot in the area north of the restaurant as you ordered."

"Okay, then we'll start checking out this area. Have any of Grassley's men been around?"

"No, not that I've noticed."

"Good. I told him to stay out of the area until ten to two."

"Plan still the same?" Burke asked.

Robin smiled to himself. "Yes, the plan is still the same, Burke. Rocky and Marv will neutralize the restaurant staff. You and I will enter the meeting room first, followed by Bill and his security team. Does it still meet with your approval?" Robin could see a twinkle in Burke's eyes.

"Yes, it does, boss."

"Good. You realize, of course, that the plan will go to shit the minute we get to the restaurant, don't you?"

"Of course." Burke was grinning now.

"Good. Glad to see we're on the same wavelength." Robin stood. "See you in a little bit."

July 4, 1992
15 Avenue Michel Alonze
1245 hours

E rnie nervously watched as Carlos and Lev pulled up in front of the suspect address with the van full of weapons. Vadim confirmed the rogue inspector and his team were in the area. Ernie didn't know what to expect.

Carlos got out of the van and walked up to the door and knocked. The door opened and Carlos went in.

"All units, our man has entered the building," Ernie said over the radio.

Several minutes later, Carlos came out with another man and they got back in the van and pulled away. Ernie hit his steering wheel. "Damn!" He pushed the transmit button on this radio. "All units, we're moving, but hang back. I don't want to get burned by the rogue team." Ernie cautiously started rolling, barely keeping the van in sight.

Vadim tapped him on his arm. "Look, the rogue team is moving also."

"Okay, I think we'll just follow them." They went just a few blocks and then stopped. Ernie could see the van parked two blocks up. His phone rang.

"Ernie."

"Hey, Ernie, are you guys moving?" Emmett asked.

"We've gone about five blocks from the other location."

"Yeah, we see our guys at the house where the quick reaction force is located."

"So it's confirmed that a QRF is there?"

"Yes, sir."

"We're going to hang back. I'm relying on you to tell me what's going on."

"Hang up. I'll have Jonathan call you. He's there. I'm just relaying his info."

Ernie hung up. Then his phone rang. "Jonathan?"

"Roger, we have the eye."

"What's going on?"

"They've met the people inside and now the van is moving…wait…it's backing up into a garage."

"Look, the rogue team is leaving," Vadim observed.

"Jonathan, do you have all doors and the garage under observation?"

"We do."

"I don't want any person or any vehicle leaving. Sing out if that starts to happen and we'll jump the place."

"Roger."

July 4, 1992
15 Avenue Michel Alonze
1315 hours

E rnie's phone buzzed. It was Jonathan.

"Ernie, Carlos came out of the house, opened the door to the van and looked around. Then he pointed to the house and then hit his palm with the fist. I think he's telling us to hit the house."

"I believe you're right, Jonathan."

"Vadim, get your tactical team to the jump-off position."

Vadim got on his police radio and gave the orders. Several minutes later, the tactical team reported they were in position.

Ernie took a deep breath. "All teams, prepare to execute the assault on the target location as planned. Report when ready."

Twenty seconds later, all teams were ready. Ernie's gut tightened. "Vadim, tell the tactical to go to the assault position."

Vadim gave the order. Ten seconds later, the tactical team reported ready.

Ernie cleared his throat and put the microphone to his mouth. "All teams, on the three count...three...two...one, ASSAULT, ASSAULT, ASSAULT."

July 4, 1992
Area of 25 Rue de Laroux
1345 hours

E mmett watched as the suspect snipers got into position. He keyed his mic, "Everyone set?"

All of the countersnipers checked in as ready.

Emmett checked his watch and called Robin. "We're set."

Robin's reply was terse. "Take 'em out."

Emmett spoke into his radio. "All units, you're cleared to engage. SAS, take your man."

Seconds later the snipers called in, saying, "Target down"...except for the SAS team.

Emmett called them several times with no answer. He then broadcasted, "We need someone to check on the SAS team."

"SpearTip Six, I'll handle it," Mike Collins said.

"Roger, Six."

Mike was a block away and he trotted to the building. He took the stairs up the eight flights. He leaned against the door to the roof and slowly forced it open, surveying the area. The stairs were part of an enclosed area that was probably part of the top suite of the building. He looked behind the door—clear. He moved down the side of the wall until he came to the end and scoped out an area with three small buildings. Between two of the buildings he saw a foot.

Mike drew his pistol, took a deep breath and moved toward the foot, constantly looking around him. He got to the corner where the foot was and looked around it. He saw three bodies. He pushed his radio button. "This is Six. Our men and the suspect are down...."

Mike's instincts screamed for him to move. He ducked and took one step to go around the corner when a heavy blow hit the right side of his back. Mike went down face first. He was stunned for a moment, but his training fought it. He knew he'd been shot and his ragged breath told him his right lung was punctured.

When he fell, his left hand was slightly underneath him, just under the scabbard for his karambit knife. He heard footsteps coming toward him and they stopped next to him. He rose up on his right arm and drew his knife in one flash of movement, slashing the leg next to him behind the knee.

His assailant dropped to his knee with a growl. He had a Sig Sauer P 226 in his hand. Mike rolled on his right shoulder and grabbed the gun with his right hand, putting the web of his hand between the hammer and firing pin. Pain and anger wracked his body. With his remaining strength, he pulled on the gun and slashed the man across the right side of his waist. The assailant pulled the gun out of Mike's hand. Mike heard a British voice say, "You bloody son of a bitch." He struggled to get on his knees...then cold steel on the back of his head....

CHAPTER THIRTY-SEVEN

July 4, 1992

25 Rue de Laroux
1350 hours

R obin and Burke were approaching the Chinese restaurant. People—men women, families—were strolling, laughing and talking with no idea of the death occurring on the rooftops of the surrounding buildings. Robin's phone buzzed.

"Robin."

"Robin, this is Ben. *You* are the target. Repeat, you are the target."

At the same time Robin saw Grassley and his men, along with Rocky and Marv, were coming in from the right. "Burke, I'm the target. This is going to be a gunfight. Get ready." Then Robin keyed his radio. "Rocky, get them out of here!" He looked at this watch.

Robin led Burke to the door, where they posted on either side, with Robin on the left, and drew their Glocks, which already had suppressors on them. Each of them also had a stun grenade. Robin's heart was racing...not with fear, but with fury. Robin held up three fingers. He looked at Burke. "I got Farrok—no prisoners."

Burke nodded and pulled the pin on his grenade, gripping the spoon, as did Robin.

Robin lowered one...two...then the third finger. He moved in front of the door and kicked it in, causing a loud *crack* and splintered wood to fly into the room. Both men tossed their grenades into opposite sides of the room. They rushed in as the grenades exploded.

Through the thick smoke, Robin saw six men in the room, including Farrok. Robin went to the right and saw Farrok struggling to get up from behind a table to Robin's front. He shot him high up on the right chest and Farrok went down. In an instant, Robin rotated right and shot two rounds into an Asian man who was reaching into his coat, but in a drunken sort of way. Two bullet holes opened up on the man's white shirt at his sternum. Robin put a third round into the man's forehead. He could hear the thump of Burke's pistol.

A white man, who was standing behind Farrok and wiping his eyes, had a gun in his hand coming out of his coat. Robin flipped the table onto the man, knocking him backward. The man tried to bring his gun up, but Robin shot him twice in the face. Then he was still. Robin turned to the left and saw Burke sweeping the left side of the room. He looked at Robin and with a hoarse voice said, "Clear." Robin repeated the word.

He moved to Farrok. Burke started to get one man's ID, but Robin said, "Leave everything."

"You...you shot me!" Farrok stammered.

"For your own good. They won't suspect you." Robin

gently held Farrok's head, took his cell phone and replaced it with another. "Call me when you wake up."

"Whaa…?"

Robin slammed Farrok's head against the edge of the overturned table, knocking him unconscious.

"Man, that was cold, Rob," Burke said.

"Yeah, but he'll be alive in the morning. Let's get out of here."

"What about the bodies?"

"They're a warning." He looked at his watch. Nineteen seconds had elapsed.

"We need to head for my car," Robin said. His radio spoke into his ear.

"SpearTip, get to the Medallion—*now*." Chucky's voice was tense…frightened. Robin looked around for a taxi and at the same time saw a man dressed in black exit a building across the street and start walking toward the river. He was holding his right side and dragging his right leg.

Robin waved down a taxi and they jumped in. Robin handed the man a fifty- dollar bill and said, "The Medallion and fast." Then he keyed his radio. "Someone check out the guy dressed in black, walking toward the river from the restaurant." The drive took under a minute.

July 4, 1992
Hotel Medallion
1409 hours

R obin and Burke jumped out of the cab. Al Worthing was running from the hotel pointing at a city delivery truck parked in the hotel driveway and yelling. "The truck, the truck!"

Robin ran to the truck, which was marked with a television

news logo, and immediately smelled diesel and fertilizer. The driver jumped out and started running, but Burke tackled him. Robin looked in the cab, and saw a timer counting down from two minutes and nineteen seconds, and no key. "Burke, the keys," he yelled. Burke pulled the keys out of the driver's pocket and tossed them to Robin. Robin jumped in the truck and started the engine.

Al Worthing jumped into the passenger seat and said, "That way to the Arc de Triomphe," and pointed west.

Robin cranked the wheel, turned the truck around and headed for Place Charles de Gaulle around the Arc de Triomphe, going through gears as fast he could to get some speed. They entered the circle and were stopped by a traffic jam. Robin leaned on the horn. "Goddammit, MOVE people!"

"We want to get on Avenue Marceau over there," Al pointed to the right.

Robin cranked the wheel to the right, downshifted and started nudging a small car out of the way. The driver jumped out and started yelling at him. Robin looked at the timer. *One minute and fifty-one seconds.* He pushed the gas pedal down and began pushing more cars out of the way. He rolled up onto the curb, got around the vehicles and turned on Avenue Marceau.

The avenue was a one-way street going towards the river. Robin leaned on the horn and pushed the gas pedal while mentally urging the truck forward. He maneuvered around several cars and then ran into a knot in the traffic. He tried to go to the far left and squeeze by a van, but he sideswiped it, sending the van into the car on its right. Robin sped up. His body jerked as he hit a car, knocking it out of the way...then another. *One minute and four seconds.* "Where the fuck is the river?" he yelled at Al.

"One more block," he yelled back.

The left wheel was scraping on metal from the crashes and

then went flat. Robin shifted to a lower gear to keep the truck moving while his arms and body shook and strained as he fought the steering wheel. He saw a bridge, but the truck was slowing down. *Thirty-three seconds.*

Robin dropped to a lower gear and pushed his foot so it slammed down on the floorboard. The engine roared as they approached the river.

"Angle to the left to that small driveway." Al pointed.

Robin entered Port de la Conférence. The cab of the truck was filling with acrid smoke from the left tire and the engine, almost blinding Robin.

"Get out!" Robin screamed and Al jumped out. People looked at him with wild eyes and scattered as he came at them with his smoke-billowing, horn- howling monster. *Ten seconds.* He spotted a ramp used to load passengers on tour boats. He drove the truck onto the ramp and smashed through the metal pipe rails lining the walkway, sending pieces of metal flying. The smoking truck lurched sideways and rolled into the Seine.

Robin pushed the door open and tried to roll out, but his left foot hung up on the seatbelt twisting from the action of the water. He pulled a knife from his boot and tried to reach the belt but couldn't. His lungs were bursting. He willed himself not to breathe tried to cut the seatbelt again. Then a hand grabbed his knife and his foot was free. He struggled for the surface and then strong arms pulled him up. When he surfaced, Al was next to him, grinning.

"You certainly know how to show a guy a good time, mate."

Robin, gasping for air, started to laugh but sucked in water and started coughing.

The two men swam to the bank of the river and climbed out. A van pulled up and Colin and two SAS men jumped out and ran to Robin and Al—along with several Paris police officers.

As Robin walked toward them, there was a rush of air and he was lifted off the ground. He could see Al in the air a few feet away. Then he was slammed back onto the ground and water mixed with junk, carp and eels flooded over him. He lay there trying to catch his breath and figure out what happened.

"The bloody truck exploded!" Colin yelled.

Robin pushed himself up and looked at the river. The water was still roiling from the explosion. People were down and Robin started to run to the closest person when one of the SAS men grabbed him and said, "We gotta go, mate."

Robin then fully realized what was happening and ran to the van. The police officers yelled at him and one grabbed his arm. Another police car skidded to a stop and Vadim jumped out. He yelled something to the officers and they let Robin go. He ran to the van and jumped in. Thankful to be alive, Robin leaned back in the seat. Colin hit the gas and drove the van out of the area.

Al put his hand on Robin's shoulder. "The water must have delayed the explosion. Thank God it was contained by the river, Rob. I do believe you averted a major tragedy."

"*We* averted the tragedy, Al—and thanks for saving my life."

"You're welcome."

Colin interrupted. "I hate to darken the celebration, but we do have some bad news."

Robin leaned forward. "What's that, Colin?"

"We lost three men on one of the rooftops. Two of ours and one of yours, Robin."

"Who?

"You're man, Mike."

"What happened?"

"After the snipers were taken out, we didn't hear from my team that captured one the bad guys. The men at the chateau saw the take down on the video feed and saw my men drag the suspect out of view. They assumed all went well, but they weren't answering the radio and the video feed went dead. Your man, Mike, volunteered to check it out. He radioed that he had found the bodies of my men and the suspect. Then nothing more from him. We sent a five-man team up and they found everyone...dead. Mike had a knife in his hand and there was a blood trail out of the building...."

"And headed towards the river," Robin said.

"How did you know?"

"I saw him, dressed in black, holding his side and dragging his right leg."

Colin slammed his hand against the steering wheel. "My God, you saw the Raven."

"Apparently." Then it hit him. *The Raven killed Mike.* Anguish and rage surged through Robin, as he fought tears.

CHAPTER THIRTY-EIGHT

July 4, 1992
The Chateau
1545 hours

W hen the men arrived at the Chateau, they were met by Ernie and Bill Grassley.

"Rob, I'm sorry about Mike," Bill said.

Robin just nodded. "I'm glad you're okay, Bill."

"What happened back there?"

"You weren't the target. You were the bait."

"Who was the target?"

"Me."

"The Russians...the Chinese?"

"I don't know. I haven't talked to Ben from Mossad yet. The fact that the Raven was here raises all kinds of possibilities." Robin stopped for a minute and took a deep breath. "Where are our guys' bodies?"

"We have them here, Rob," Ernie said. Vadim put me in touch with French Intelligence and they arranged for Fatboy to land at Paris Air Base. I ordered Fatboy to go there so we can load the bodies."

"Excuse me," Bill interrupted. "Rob, you want to tell me about this Raven?"

"In a minute, Bill. I want to see Mike's body."

"This way, Rob," Ernie said.

Ernie led Robin, Bill Grassley and Al Worthing to an empty room. Three body bags lay on the floor. "This is Mike," Ernie said pointing, to one of the bags.

Robin walked over to the bag and knelt down. He unzipped it and peeled back the flap. He could see Mike had been shot in the back of the head, with the trajectory of the bullet going from the back of the skull to the forehead, where the bullet exited.

"There's another bullet wound, Rob. Mike was also shot in the back."

Ernie knelt down and helped Robin half-roll the body, so Robin could see the other bullet wound.

"What hand was his knife in?"

"Left, which is interesting because Mike was right-handed."

Robin shook his head. "Mike kept his knife in a sheath set for a left-handed draw for a close quarters fight. See?" Robin pointed to the knife sheath on Mike's belt. "That way he could shoot with his right hand and cut and slice with his left." Robin looked at Mike's hands and then he pulled Mike's pant legs up and looked at his knees. The hands and knees all had scrapes and bruises. "Mike was shot in the back and then the Raven moved up on him. Despite his wound, he chose to fight the Raven. He probably played dead until the Raven got close and then attacked Raven's legs with his knife and tried to get up. See that mark on the side of his right hand?"

Ernie nodded and said, "Yes."

"Mike blocked the hammer of Raven's pistol with his hand and they fought over the pistol...but Mike lost that fight."

"Mike must have been bent over when Raven shot him," Ernie surmised.

"That seems to be the case. Where were the other three shot?"

"All head shots."

"Damn, Mike must have realized somebody was there and started moving—just not fast enough."

"Fuck," Ernie spat.

"Bill, can you authorize autopsies on all of these bodies?"

"Get them to Ramstein Air Force Base and I'll take care of the rest."

"Thanks." Robin took a deep, sad breath. "About the Raven..."

"I'm listening."

"Al, can you tell Bill your info?"

Al recapped the information he'd previously given Robin.

"That's all we have?" Bill asked.

"No," Robin replied.

"He just killed three Tier One operators. We now know he is extremely dangerous. In addition, I saw him. He was wearing a black suit coat and black pants. The suit coat was long, down to his thighs...and he now walks with a limp." Robin bent down and put his hand on Mike's chest. Tears started rolling down his cheeks. "Sorry, Mike. One of us should've been with you. But you know we'll get this guy and we *will* kill him."

"Rob, you may not be able to keep that promise," Bill cautioned.

Robin fought his seething anger. "I never make promises I can't keep."

CHAPTER THIRTY-NINE

July 4, 1992
Paris Main Jail
1810 hours

C arlos was happy the handcuffs had finally been removed. They had been on for almost three hours. He looked over at Lev, who was pacing back and forth in the holding cell. He spoke to him in Russian. "Lev, sit down and relax."

Lev smiled. "I have never been able to do that."

"I'm sure, but in this work, it is a talent you must learn."

Lev stopped pacing and thought for a moment. He then sat down next to Carlos. "I'm surprised they put us in the same cell."

"Too many prisoners. They have run out of room."

Three men came to their cell. One ordered the cell door be opened. Carlos recognized the man from photographs from the briefing this morning. He was the leader of the rogue French police squad. Lev nudged him. Carlos simply nodded. The leader and one other man came into the cell. They pulled out handcuffs and ordered Carlos and Lev to stand. Carlos could see killing in their eyes. As the two started to get up, Carlos told Lev in Russian, "These guys have come to execute us. Time to fight."

V adim and Al Worthing, along with four uniformed and armed gendarmes, were walking down the hallway leading to the holding cells when they heard men shouting and cursing. As they approached the cell where the trouble was, they saw bodies on the ground in various stages of pain and consciousness, with Carlos and Lev standing over them.

The rogue squad leader got to his knees and saw the uniformed officers. "Get them!" he said, pointing to Carlos and Lev.

"I do not think so, Bruno," Vadim said, stepping forward. "In fact, you and your men are under arrest."

Al Worthing motioned for Carlos and Lev to come with him and they left.

"What are you talking about, Vadim? They were the men who delivered the arms."

"What arms, Bruno? How do you know what those men did? What were you doing in their cell? They are my prisoners."

Blood started leaving Bruno's face.

"You are a traitor, Bruno. We have been investigating you for over a year and now we have more than enough evidence to put you and your entire organization away for life."

"Vadim…"

"I do not want to talk to you, Bruno. You disgust me." Vadim turned to the officers. "You know where to take him."

"Where…where are you taking me?"

"To the counterintelligence people at the SDECE, Bruno. They know how to deal with traitors like you."

The officers escorted Bruno out of the cell and down the hall. He kept on yelling, "Vadim…wait…Vadim, I'll tell you everything. Wait, Vadim."

July 4, 1992
The Chateau
2130 hours

All of the men involved in the operation met in the large conference room in the chateau. The pearl white walls were framed by Baroque carvings and lined with original paintings by different artists. A massive maple table lit by three large chandeliers filled the center of the room. Robin stood at the head of it, flanked by Al, Vadim, Jonathan and Colin. He cleared his throat. "Gentlemen, I'm Robin Marlette. I command the lead group in this operation. I want to thank you all for the hard work you've done over the past week. Our goal of disrupting a major terrorist attack was achieved. Unfortunately, our success cost us three comrades and good friends and has left us with heavy hearts. Before you is a glass of the finest French cognac, provided by our French partners. Please stand so we can toast those who are gone."

The men stood with glasses in hand.

"Here's to Reggie Handley, SAS, Nigel Wharpler, SAS and Mike Collins, Delta. May their journey to that place all warriors go, be a pleasant one."

The men raised their glasses and took a drink in silence.

Robin surveyed the gathered group for a moment. "Thank

you, and please be seated." After all were seated, Robin began his debriefing. "Despite our victory here, we have to understand this is just the beginning and we need every one of you to continue your service here. You've all been briefed on why you were chosen and why conventional units can't be brought in...at least not yet. Jonathan's group and the Scotland Yard team have volunteered to monitor our major suspects in Austria and Switzerland while our SAS friends and my team go home to bury our dead.

"Besides foiling an attack, we also contributed to the arrest of several high- ranking law enforcement and intelligence officials, who were connected to the leaders of this conspiracy. Hopefully we can gain valuable intelligence from the people who were arrested. And lastly, I understand you have all been given compensation packages and have agreed to those terms. Are there any questions about the packages?"

No one responded.

"Are there questions for me about anything?"

Again, there were no questions.

"Thank you, gentlemen. It's a pleasure to work with true professionals."

CHAPTER FORTY

July 5, 1992
Fatboy
0210 hours

R obin sat on Fatboy waiting for Ben to answer the
phone. A few seconds later Ben came on.
"Hello, Robin."

"Hi, Ben, I just wanted to thank you for the warning
earlier today. It came just in time."

"You are welcome. I suppose you would like to know who
wants you killed."

"That would probably be useful information."

Ben chuckled. "I suppose it would. Your nemesis is the
Chairman of the Russian Communist Party. He provided
Schinner with all of your identifying information and a
briefing of your exploits the Russians know about. Strangely
enough, he doesn't know your location."

"It won't take them long to get a good idea."

"I assume you have taken precautions. I've become fond of you and your men."

"Yes, Ben, they will pay dearly for any attempt on any member of our team."

"Good. We'll talk later."

July 5, 1992
Fatboy

Fatboy arrived at Ramstein Air Force Base in Germany early in the morning. After landing, the plane was pulled into a large hangar and the doors closed. A security team was posted in the area. The bodies of the two SAS men and Mike were delivered to the morgue for autopsies. The pathologists said they would have Mike's autopsy done in two hours.

Robin, Ernie and Colin met in Robin's cabin.

Robin shook Colin's hand. "Colin, I can't tell you how much we appreciate everything you've done for us and how much I regret the loss of your men."

Colin looked down and then raised his head to look at Robin. "I never thought I'd get back into this business again for the reason we're here tonight. It just hurts too much when we lose good men."

"We know, my friend," Ernie said. "Mike wasn't our first loss."

"For whatever it's worth, I'm in this until we get that Raven son-of-a-bitch."

"I'm counting on that, Colin. You're a valuable resource and member of this team," Robin said.

"Well, mate, it certainly is nice to still be needed somewhere."

"Are you all set?"

"Right, I have a room at the officers' lodging and RAF will send a plane for me and my two mates in the morning."

"Good. We'll contact you in about two weeks, so relax until then."

"I bloody will. I'm going to see my friend in Cornwall. We've been friends for years and she has always waited for me to show up at her doorstep. She has a house overlooking the sea, a big fireplace, a warm bed and an unending supply of scotch."

Robin gave Colin a warm handshake. "Safe travels, my friend."

"Adios, Colin," Ernie said.

After Colin left, Robin called for a meeting of the Guardians in the team briefing section of the plane. When all the men were seated, Robin addressed them.

"I know we're all tired, but I don't want us to get where we were after Gary died. I want to start off by saying I'm proud of our actions this last week. We helped avert a major terrorist attack and have learned more about the adversaries we are up against...and learned they are well organized, pervasive and extremely dangerous."

Emmett raised his hand.

"Yes, Emmett."

"Rob, why are we doing this ourselves? I know we have help from our friends, but is that enough?"

"I'm going by what our own intelligence is coming up with and what Bill Grassley has told me. It's Bill's opinion we are it for the time being."

"What about Major John and the Unit?"

"I asked Bill about that, but he's worried about the required dissemination of their after-action reports."

"Aren't ours sent directly to Delta by Bill?"

"Yes, to the Commanding General of Delta—his and Major John's eyes only."

Emmett shook his head. "Boss, we need more people."

"I know. We will be picking up some new operators when we get back. They will come from the group of folks at the sheriff's office we pay for."

"How many?"

"How many do we need?"

"Well, we've lost Gary and Mike, plus Jamie can't operate anymore. As busy as we are, even with the addition of Carlos, Lev and Chucky, I say we could use four...hell, we need a squad."

"Precisely my thought, Emmett...and you're now a squad leader."

Emmett jumped to his feet. "Now, wait a...."

"Along with Burke and Rocky."

Emmett looked at the other two men and they all shrugged. Emmett slowly sat down.

Robin continued, "We've reached the point where we have to formalize our chain of command a bit more. Each of the new squad leaders will choose an assistant squad leader after we bring on the new people and adjust the squads. Myself and Ernie will maintain our roles as commander and assistant commander. Chucky will be attached to us. Now, none of the new people are actually new. They are all prior Marine Recon, Special Forces or SEALs and have combat experience in Panama, Grenada or Iraq. They have all gone through the police academy to boot."

"Are we going to send them to finishing school with Major John?"

"Maybe. We'll see how they do." Robin let a minute pass so the men could digest what had just transpired. "Before we talk about Mike, does anybody have anything else to say?"

Rick raised his hand.

"What do you have, Rick?"

"I know we are going to see this latest mission through until we get the Raven, but what about after that? I think at some point we will have paid back our debt."

Robin looked around the room. "To be honest with you, I think we could tell them to pound sand today. But personally, I'm not leaving Bill and Director Yates out there by themselves. When we catch the Raven, and Bill and Yates leave their positions, I say we should reassess our status. Does that work for everyone?"

"Works for me," Rick said.

Everyone voiced their approval.

Robin held up his hand for quiet and the noise subsided. He looked down at the floor and then looked at his team. "We've lost Mike. Coming on top of the loss of Gary, it hurts...really hurts. I tried to call Suzanne to tell her about Mike's death and couldn't get an answer. Then Rick told me Suzanne left Mike about a year ago. Their divorce was final three months ago. He didn't want the rest of us to know. Mike apparently had no other family. He was alone except for us and somehow..." Robin choked back a sob. "...with us all around him, he died alone."

Hard men sat silent, working through their own painful thoughts.

"We were in a chaotic situation. A call came out for help and Mike got on it. I don't know if there is a policy, rule or tactic we can put in place that would work every time to lessen the chance of this happening again, but from now on we will always work in pairs unless it's just not feasible to do so. Does anyone have other suggestions?"

"Why wasn't Mike wearing body armor?" Doug asked. "It would've stopped the bullet in the back."

"Except for Carlos and Lev, who didn't wear armor for this op?"

Three men raised their hands.

"That stops right here and now. When we're doing any activity that has a good chance of ending in gunfight, I want everyone in armor. That is an order."

"I hate those things. They're so damn uncomfortable," Willie complained.

"A coffin is more uncomfortable," Robin retorted. "Wear the armor." His voice was stern.

Willie squirmed a little. "Yes, sir."

"Any other suggestions?"

No one spoke.

"Mike never complained. He always did what was asked of him, usually with a wisecrack and a smile, and whatever he did, he did well. There is a hole in our hearts and in the team that will be hard to fill. We will surely miss him."

CHAPTER FORTY-ONE

July 9, 1992
London
1810 hours

The Raven winced to a bolt of pain shooting through the back of his knee where the tendon was severed. Every time it hurt, he cursed the man who'd cut him. He had not been wounded since he fought in Vietnam with the New Zealand SAS. He looked down at the bandages on his hands and ran his right hand along his side where the karambit had sliced into his stomach. It had taken two surgeries totaling eight hours to repair the damage to his body. Still, he would walk with a limp for the rest of this life and he would not be able to eat real food for another month. *If that man had not been so badly wounded, he might have killed me.* That reoccurring thought irritated him and he interrupted Schinner's droning on about "real Nazis."

"Gentlemen, we don't want to spend more time on this conference call than necessary. I will conclude by saying that we have some new and dangerous adversaries. Because of them, we failed to blow up the conference against the EU and blame it on western intelligence agencies.

"We failed to kill or capture Robin Marlette so badly, we lost nine men killed, twenty captured and almost lost our Iranian member. The Russian failed to apprise us of just how dangerous Marlette is. It is unbelievable to me that our organization, the Chinese, the Russians, and Iranians could not accomplish this mission. We know Marlette will protect William Grassley, and he will never let Grassley get into the same position again. We must quickly formulate new plans to flush Marlette out once more. It is clear to me he is our most dangerous enemy.

"Five of our important contacts have been compromised and arrested. This has been a serious setback for us. I want new surveillance assets in place on Chief Inspector Worthing and Captain Laurent...AND FIND THAT GODDAMN FBI AGENT!"

The Raven laid his head back on his pillows. *Bollocks, I'm still so bloody weak. I'm going to have to concentrate on building my strength and stamina back. I'm so afraid the security apparatus will crumble without my leadership—and enforcement.* He took a deep breath. *I must sleep.*

July 9, 1992
Blue Marble Headquarters, Seattle
1032 hours

Jamie leaned back in his chair and grinned at Stephan and his group. "My friends you are spectacular. Intercepting that phone call is a major step forward for our investigation. We now have established an international conspiracy between the Raven, Schinner, Felsa and their contact in the Bank for International Settlements. Even though we don't know who the Raven really is, we now know he is in London and we know they are all connected. With you guys and more surveillance, we'll get them identified and located."

"Then you'll arrest them?" Squeaky asked.

"That could be one outcome. No matter what, they'll be neutralized."

"Oh." Squeaky appeared to be taken aback.

Jamie leaned forward and clasped his hands on the table. "Look folks, we told you in the beginning, this is dangerous business. The people we're after finance, plan and execute terrorist attacks and just plain murder people. You already know they had no compunction about killing hundreds in Paris. You helped us stop that. They want to take over the world and are extremely dangerous. Sometimes we must be more dangerous than they are. Do you understand?"

Stephan looked at his friends. They nodded to him. Then he turned to Jamie. "We understand, Jamie."

July 9, 1992
Mukilteo/Clinton Ferry, Washington State
1820 hours

R obin sat in his pickup on the ferry headed to Whidbey Island. His mind wouldn't stop sorting through the last week, searching for what mistakes he may have made that led to the death of Mike and the other men. Their autopsies produced no surprises and supported Robin's theory of what happened. They were able to identify the suspect killed with the operators. Robin gave the information to Jamie for a workup on the man, as well as the others who were killed by the countersnipers. He hadn't heard back yet. It was disquieting to realize their snipers were there to kill him.

Most of the men arrested in Paris refused to talk. The ones that did talk were Paris thugs well known to the police who were recruited for this specific operation and didn't have much information of value. Robin received word from Vadim that Bruno was talking, but that was all he knew at this point. Robin didn't know the laws in France, but apparently French Intelligence could keep all of these suspects out of the public eye, at least for now.

The ferry landed at the Clinton dock and Robin drove his truck off the ramp. His thoughts focused on Karen. Their phone conversations had been strained lately and Robin tried to plan what he would say when he got home, but then gave that up. He learned early in their marriage he was never any good at planned conversations with his wife. When it came to her, his heart ruled, not his brain.

He pulled into his driveway and turned the truck off. He sat there for a couple of minutes. He hated it when he and Karen were not in sync and he dreaded this reunion because Karen had a right to be upset. He had been gone for almost two months with little time for long conversations on the phone. She had every reason not to understand why he couldn't call often or talk for longer than a few minutes. He thought about Colin and how confident he was about his friend. Robin knew his guilt tempered his confidence about Karen.

He got out of the truck and breathed in deeply, savoring

the sweet fragrance of the island and sea. The sky had turned into black velvet generously sprinkled with sparkling diamonds of all sizes. Robin fished out his key and went to the door. As started to insert his key, the door opened. Karen's emerald eyes met his. His heart jumped. She took two steps, put her arms around his neck and pulled his mouth to hers. The kiss was long and wonderful. When it finished Robin looked at his beautiful wife and said, "Karen, I...."

"Stop, Robin. You don't have to explain anything because Ernie told me everything. Just come into our home and let me heal your wounds."

July 17, 1992
KGB Headquarters, Moscow
1015 hours

Anotoli Maravonovitch rose from his office chair. "Comrade Lana, it is good to see you. Congratulations are in order for neutralizing the French operative."

"Thank you, sir."

"Please, sit down," Anotoli offered.

Lana took a seat. "Sir, may I have some time to see my parents?"

Anatoli felt a pang of guilt. "Ah, I'm afraid that is not possible right now. The Chairman has an urgent mission for you." He handed a target package to Lana.

She opened the file and her face turned the color of porcelain.

"Is there something wrong, Comrade?"

Lana raised her eyes. Anatoli could not determine the emotion in them. "This is the man who saved my life in the Philippines."

Now Anatoli understood the Chairman's words when he

said, *There are lessons to be taught here.* Anatoli did not approve of the lesson, but he wasn't going to commit suicide by objecting to it. "I'm sorry, Lana. The Chairman was adamant that you do this mission. You know what he will do if you fail."

Lana slowly closed the file. "Yes, sir. I will take care of it."

BOOKS BY MIKE MCNEFF

GOT-U

Necessary Retribution

Blood Wealth

Other Titles

Hard Justice: The Legend of Jasper Lee

BOOKS BY WHIDBEY WRITER'S GROUP

Beneath the Rain Shadow (1994)

Beneath the Rain Shadow II (1996)

Beneath the Rain Shadow III (1999)

Take Our Words for Whidbey (2002)

Whispers in the Mist (2004)

Whidbey Connections (2007)

Whidbey Writes Again (2010)

Write Around Whidbey (2015)

ABOUT THE AUTHOR

Mike McNeff a retired police officer and lawyer who always wanted to write novels. So when he retired that's just what he started doing. His novels draw from his law enforcement experiences which included working on SWAT and training with special forces. They also reflect his obsession with history and current events.

Mike has worked as a state trooper, a deputy sheriff and a city police officer. He's been a prosecutor, police legal advisor, defense lawyer and a civil trial lawyer, using each experience to learn great lessons about life.

Mike is married with four children and seven grandchildren. In addition to writing, he does volunteer work and spends time teaching folks about firearms and shooting. He enjoys hiking, biking, fishing and playing guitar. Mike lives on an island off the coast of Washington State.

ACKNOWLEDGMENTS

This is my fourth novel and like all the others I had the help of many people to bring it to publication. My writing groups, Whidbey Writers Group and the Sequels Group gave me valuable critiques and advice as I wrote the book. My beta readers provided valuable insight, suggestions, and corrections to the story. Many thanks to Barb Bland, Miko Johnston, Mare Chapman, Pat Brunjes, Ron Hollar, and Mitch Hardin. My editors, Cathy Shaw (my sister) and Audrey Mackaman, did the final technical edits that made the book what is today. Thank you, ladies. Derrick Sutton produced the cover and formatted the work for print and ebook. Thank you, my friend. As always most heartfelt thanks to my wife and best friend of forty-two years, Linda, who puts up with the time I spend at the computer writing and researching. She often asks me, "Where are you?" when I'm sitting next to her. Sorry, Babe, I'm busy dealing with terrorists in Beirut.